# MAN KILLER

A NOVEL
WRITTEN BY:

DENISE CAMPBELL

This book is a work of fiction. Any resemblance to names, individuals, events, establishments, business, locales or incidents is entirely coincidental and products of the author's imagination. All references are used fictitiously.

Copyright © 2005 by Denise Campbell
ISBN 0-9742269-4-7

All rights reserved. No Part of this book may be reproduced or transmitted electronically or mechanical, including photocopying and recording without written permission except in the case newspapers, magazines, and websites using quotations embodied in critical articles, essays and reviews.

Cover Design By: Candace Cattrell www.ccwebdev.com
Book Edited By: Clem Richardson

For information contact:

Universal Write Publications LLC
PO Box 1432
Valley Stream, N.Y. 11582
www.DeniseCampbell.com

Distributed by:
Black Books Plus
PO Box 030064
Elmont NY 11003
1-877-227-6977

# MAN

# KILLER

# A WORD FROM THE AUTHOR

WARNING:

Man Killer is Rated R.
It is graphic with sexual and physical violence. The women depicted within these pages are symbols or real life, of a system that created the need for the imagination to take authority into its own hands.

Look beyond the entertainment and read between the lines for the true reasons that rage and pain would be manifested through the whim of a "Man Killer." Women have been abused and violated for centuries. Some women, loosing self worth and respect for themselves become "turned out" sexually and are promiscuous and even express bi-sexuality (though this is not to say is the case all the time) as we see in the book and in our society. Others become reclusive, hiding away in the shame and taking blame for something that was not their fault.

Being a victim of gang rape myself, I have experienced being afraid and embarrassed, uncertain of who I am and once faced the confusion as to my body, not wanting to share myself sexually and dealt with major insecurity, I felt this book has forced its way into existence beyond my will. I did not realize I was still dealing with the effects of this experience, didn't plan on writing about it , but once I started, I found I was still very resentful that I did not have the honored opportunity of "giving away" my virginity that most young women take for granted. It was stolen from me by a gang of thieves. You would be surprised how many sisters and brothers have told me the stories of their rape, and usually it leaves me in tears, not just because of their hurts, but because of mine. The most heartbreaking thing is when many refuse to talk about it publicly because they are still afraid. That's the power of abuse.

Even more recently in our world, we see headlines that crush us with the reality of this type of victimization: "Pedophiles Prey on Tsunami Orphans: Boy missing? Predators threat to orphans by Cindy Wockner and Jamie Walker 06jan 05. <The boy's father fears his 12-year-old son was taken by pedophiles. Indonesia has imposed restrictions on children leaving the country. Police are ordered to be on the lookout for trafficking, and special guards have been posted in refugee camps. Child traffickers already are well established in Indonesia, and UNICEF fears that orphaned children will be sold into forced labor or even sexual slavery. The child protection chief at UNICEF said the recent chaos provides a "perfect opportunity" for people who prey on children. The last time anyone saw 12-year-old Kristian Walker, the Swedish boy was apparently leaving a hospital in Thailand with a man nobody knows.> http://www.nbc5.com/news/4045556/detail.html??z=dp&dpswid=1167317&dppid+65193

Rape and Incest have become so common that it seems we are desensitized to the true horror of it. That's why stories like this can be in the news and no one is shocked or appalled or even talk about it anymore: THE NEW WORLD DISORDER U.N. accused of rape, pedophilia, and prostitution. Civilians, staff in Congo under internal investigation. Here is a small except from that story <The United Nations claims it is investigating about 150 allegations of sexual abuse by U.N. civilian staff and soldiers in the Congo, some of them recorded on videotape. The

charges include accusations of pedophilia, rape and prostitution, said Jane Holl Lute, an assistant secretary-general in the peacekeeping department. Lute, an American, said there was photographic and video evidence for some of the allegations and most of the charges came to light since the spring.>
http://www.worldnetdaily.com/news/article.asp?ARTICLE_ID=41627
It seems no one pay attention to the dramatic and traumatizing affects of rape, abuse and incest until a disaster strikes and sometimes not even then. The big question would be why? Problem is, much like you I don't know. I am only another victim, an author, someone who knows that pain intimately and would like it to all to STOP.

In writing "Man Killer" I wanted this to be more than just another book. I wanted it to have some tangible information, something to let other victims know they are not alone. There is a glossary of terms, links and definitions that might help to lead you in the right direction to understanding the pain and shame manifested through different individuals. Yes, this piece of work is meant to be entertaining as well, but personally, I found it therapeutic in the ways that predators are repaid for their injustices. So instead of us all going out and becoming vigilantes (which is wrong and there are consequences), I hope that women and men everywhere who share this tragic experience will delve into this book and enjoy vicariously the demise of the evil that have so drastically affected our lives, our children's lives and the lives of our loved ones.

## Dedication

For my daughter Cheyanne. Hoping that you will always have a choice, that you will never know the pain of abuse and the trauma of being victimized. Dreaming for what I visualized since your conception...that you will always be a alpha female; strong, intelligent, powerful so that you can stand alone in your faith and values, yet gentle and feminine so you can choose when to compromise.

# AKNOWLEDGEMENT:

First as always, I would like to count my blessings and humble myself before my God. Walking by faith gave me the strength to press forward. I will always get on my knees in awesome reminder of God's Glory and thank him for counting me among his greatest creations.

I would like to thank God for giving me my beautiful daughter Cheyanne, helping me to bring such divine beauty into the world. Her life has been my metamorphosis and for that I know I am truly blessed. Thanks to my sister Duon Minto my best friend who believes in me and always have my back and her daughter my only niece Jadaine Fraser, the second apple of my eyes. To Kerry-Ann Minto, you are always away but never forgotten, you are always missed and we wish you will finally come home. To my mother and friend Mrs. Beverley Peart, now more than ever I understand your sacrifices and your pain, because I am now a mother too. If I never told you before, I am telling you now, thank you and I love you. Brenda Wezoncroft thanks for being another "mom" in my life. To Vivian Tyme her son thanks for believing in me. To Dwayne Campbell (D.O.C) thanks for being my "baby brother" and adding a big beautiful family into my life. To Hugo Campuzano, you probably won't read this all the way in China, but I want you to know that your friendship and guidance helped.

To Sam Chekwas, the newest Angel in my life. Thanks for coming along just when I was starting to lose faith.

Charles Perkins, more fondly known as Chaz; I was a new mother of only a month with hopes and quickly sinking dreams, but you told me to "just do it" and have been backing me ever since with a beautiful website. Thank you from the bottom of my heart. Calvin Grace, I don't know if there is ever such a thing as a brother/publicist/friend, but you are all those things to me. I cannot wait to see you blow up! Tee C. Royal, a real "royal" lady, thanks for your promoting, support and friendship. Clem Richardson from the New York City Daily News; it's the story you did on me that made me face my victimization to break the silence publicly. Thanks for being apart of my journey. Candace Cottrell, thanks for contributing your book designing talents to my covers, you are truly a blessing. Heather Covington of DisilGold Magazine, thanks for calling me sister and know that I call you the same. Hope C. Clarke I admire your business savvy and literary talent. Thanks for pointing me into the right direction.

To all the Angels that God placed in my life, people who have helped me to grow into the person I am today, have literally saved my life from homelessness and devastation dating back to my early teens. Angels like Prospect Heights High School teachers such as John Senatore a high school English teacher who died of AIDS in 1991, sent me sheets and food so I wouldn't starve my freshman year of college. Julia Resoncroft a high school tutor, who took me to the doctor and had me checked out so I would stop having nightmares about dying. Angels like high school teacher Michael Rozza who still comes to my book signings and Jon Sterngass who told me "to whom much is given much is required." I took that to heart. To Ms. Goldburg, Ms. Turnbull, Ms. Brown. Thank you all.

My High School teachers and mentors passed the baton and entrusted me into the hands of my college professors. Dr. Warren Crichlow in the Grad School of the University of Rochester thanks for helping me pay for books. To My State University College at Buffalo professor Aimable Twagilimana who took my writing seriously and taught me the phrase "Non Omnis Moriar" by the French Poet Horace. Thanks for being there way after I graduated. Thank you to BSC Wendall Wickland and Joanne Pease in the NASE program and the Dean of the English Dept. then Dr. Warner and his secretary Amy Klein. Some of you are still in my life applauding and demanding more, some I don't know if you will ever know that you helped to save my life, but who you were helped me to survive and I will never ever forget you.

Thanks to my online literary groups and my reading writing brothers and sisters: RAW4ALL, Fiction Folks, Authors Supporting Authors Positively, James Lisbon of Awareness Magazine, Trust at Nubian Heritage, Carla Oliver at Barnes and Nobles, Sharon Gray for keeping me smiling, Mama Brenda and Auntie Carol from C&B Books Distribution- The book ladies of New York, Michelle McGriff, Cynthia Hunter, C.F. Hawthorn, TL Gardner, LA Banks thanks so much for pointing me into the right direction. For those are not listed, blame it on my mind and not my heart, you are all loved and thanks so much for your sisterly and brotherly support.

# NO MEANS NO

**BREAK THE SILENCE**

## Prologue

"Don't touch my child you bastard," Carissa screamed, pleading with her husband. She pulled at his pants, which were already coming down his thighs as he released the poisonous snake intent on violating their seven-year-old daughter. The bewildered little girl stared at the only father she had ever known and blinked back the tears, her fear keeping her small body petrified and mute.

"Leave her alone please?" Carissa begged in a whimper that grew into a scream. "Let her be, you son-of-a bitch!" Her pleas fell on deaf ears. He swatted at her hands like they were more of an annoyance than a hindrance. Instead his fist caught her dead in the face, causing her nose to spout a steady stream of blood that ran down into her mouth.

"Bitch, you'll get some of big daddy next," he said in a drunken slur. He chuckled at his attempt at humor. He was sure Carissa would give up, but the fear in Serena's eyes made her mother keep fighting. Serena, backed into the far corner of her small bedroom, shivered with fear. Her mother watched as a stream of piss ran from between the frail child's legs to the floor.

"Its okay baby, mama is not gonna let nothin' happen to you." She promised, knowing in her heart that there might be very little she could do.

She saw him force Serena's legs apart. Carissa began to cry frantically. She held on to his legs but was not strong enough to stop him. He dragged her across the floor, baptizing her clothes and skin in Serena's pee, the pee that also soaked his clutching hands. Carissa began to give up, feeling sorry for herself and helpless to save her baby Serena. Almost blinded by her pain and tears, she could barely look at her daughter. When she did, she saw something in Serena's eyes; a silent determination locked their eyes together.

Tears poured down the child's cheeks but her gaze was steadfast and unforgiving. Willing her mother to continue the fight, she refocused her eyes on her father. Carissa wanted to fight, but instead found herself watching every move her husband made. She watched as he pulled his underwear aside, took out his dick and pulled Serena towards him. Carissa's heart broke into a million pieces.
She didn't fight.

"Please, please John I beg of you. Leave her be." She fell to her knees as if in a prayer, her arms wrapped around his legs and her eyes looking up into the heavens for mercy.

"Nawww," he grunted. "Let me taste some of this sweet young pussy before she turn into a ho like her mother and start giving it away."

He snickered and tried to kick his foot free of Carissa, but she held on for dear life, hitting and punching at his thighs. Her punches fell off him like flies. He kicked her in the face, breaking her nose. She heard her bones crack with a cartoon like explosion in her head as a bloody flood streamed down her face.

"I can't let you hurt my baby John," she cried to his deaf ears. "I gave you everything."
Suddenly something awakened inside of her, a resolve from the core of her womanhood called on when a woman must become supernatural. She released John's leg and dragged herself from the room. In the hallway, she got up and sprinted

to the kitchen.

She had killed before, and she would do it again to save her daughter. Sure, the first time was an accident and, because she was only thirteen, the courts had only slapped her wrists where she only served three years in juvenile detention. This time it would be different. What good is she, her life, if she could not protect her baby? She just couldn't allow what happened to her, what drove her into this, a life of putting up with men like John and all the other Johns who had had her, consume her child as well.

Carissa rummaged though the kitchen drawers but found nothing that could help her. She had to move quickly. It was quiet in Serena's room.

Carissa ran though the house like a wild woman; her thick curly locks flying behind her like a black cloud. Her eyes were wide and crazed the blood from her broken nose made her shirt stick to her breasts. She stood still for a second as a feeling of defeat came over her. She had no idea what was going on in the child's room. All she could hear were muffled grunts that could only be coming from John.

Then she remembered.

John kept a gun under the sofa, a sawed-off shotgun that he kept for protection as he pimped his wife, watching as men took her anyway they wanted.

He'd married her years ago, claiming he was going to take her out of that life. But eventually he began bringing in his own johns, jerking off as she screamed, sometimes in pain, sometimes as part of her entertaining. His unexpected acts of kindness - a new dress here, a night on the town for the entire family - went from occasional to rare. Mostly now he just made sure she took her antibiotics to ward off any sexually transmitted diseases she might have contracted.

Carissa was sure of one thing. He could not have Serena.

She had done everything to keep her child when she became pregnant. John said she could have been his or anyone of the men who shared their bed. He wanted her to get rid of the baby, but she begged and pleaded and he allowed her to keep the child, even promised that he would love and nurture her. But now he posed the biggest threat.

With all the strength she could muster from her five foot, five inch, one hundred and ten pound frame, she pushed the sofa aside. She stuck her hand in the hole John put in the floor there, gasping with relief when her hand touched it. She ran back to the girl's room, dashing through the door to find John's penis stretching Serena's mouth. Tears streaked her face. His hard on was prominent and threatened to choke Serena as he grabbed the back of her head and rammed his penis into the back of the child's throat, causing her to gag. Spit drooled from her mouth and her coughs were muffled.

Carissa's heart sank. Bitter tears and pain worse than childbirth consumed her. Her knees buckled as she stood there, watching the ecstasy on John's face and hearing his moans of pleasure as her Serena suffered. Leaving his manhood in her mouth, he gripped a handful of the child's lustrous auburn reddish hair. Reaching down, he inserted his index finger into the girl's vagina.

Serena cringed. Her eyes squeezed shut for a moment and then reopened.

The child was the only real family she had. Having moved more times than she could count to escape the law; she had eventually lost touch with any blood relatives. Like her, her few friends prostitutes, runaways, jailbirds, and thieves. It seemed her entire life had become a ritual of running, trying to escape something.

She was 16 years old when she met John, the man who promised to protect her and take care of her. Then he had been her savior, taking her out of the darkness of teen prostitution and having to set rattraps for food. John had been her everything, and here he was, taking everything from her. He was jabbing his finger in and out of Serena's vagina now so hard that blood began to run down the little girl's legs. Yet Carissa saw no submission in the child's eyes; only a pain and shame that no child this age should know. It was almost as though she knew it was coming and though she didn't like it, it was just something she had to do. But Carissa didn't see it that way. She would die before allowing him to do what her father and so many men before had done to her, stole her pride and her womanhood. Left her no choice but to accept abuse, sell her body, and then do it all over again to please her husband.

She found the strength to lift the gun.

"I won't let you do this John!" she screamed. He looked at her and laughed, the sound changing to a moan as his body jerked into orgasm.

"I am so sorry baby," Carissa said to Serena as she pulled the trigger.

The kick of the gun was a shock. Her eyes widened in dumbfounded panic as pellets ripped at John's body. She watched as Serena fell, blood splattered all over her face. The six foot, six inch man fell with a heavy thud to the floor, his two hundred fifty pounds barely missing the child's body.

The thud echoed throughout the house. She could see the disbelief in his eyes as he reached for Carissa, who stood back and watched as he struggled to breathe.

"Serena?" Carissa whispered. She inched forward, fearful of what she would find. That he might grab her. Gently she pulled Serena away from John's body. "Baby, please say something to mommy," she begged, but the girl had lost consciousness, her face covered with cum and blood.

The odor mingled with gunpowder nauseated Carissa and she fell to the ground, she was sure she had shot Serena that the daughter she tried to save had instead died at her hands. She had sworn to protect Carissa, but she couldn't. She had failed again.

Her tears fell like a powerful waterfall. She knew what she had to do. She raised the gun to her temple.

"I am sorry baby, mommy failed you," she groaned, and pulled the trigger one last time.

DENISE CAMPBELL

## And Then...

It was about a week before the neighbors smelled the stench of death.

No one saw anyone coming or going out of the normally busy house, not even the girl the woman put on the school bus at 7 a.m everyday.

The neighbors, who were always complaining about the loud music and raucous noise that came from the big house that sat on one and one half acre of land, eventually became concerned. Everyone feared "Big John" as he was called. He would threaten anyone who called the police to complain about the almost nightly freak parties at the house. Some feared for the child, who seemed full of life but ventured outside only for school.

"We can't just sit around and say nothing," said one neighbor, an old man with a mustache that made him look like a character out of Charles Dickens' Pickwick Papers. "I can understand him being upset about us reporting him about his business or whatever he has going on in that house. But a child is involved and there is no one around."

The smell that seemed to thicken daily had brought several of them to the property line

"He has most of the cops on his payroll anyway. He ain't gonna get but a slap on the wrist for our benefit and we gone be left with hell to pay," snickered another man who was always in everyone's business but pretended he didn't care.

# MAN KILLER

"I think you right," chimed a woman who looked to weigh more than three hundred pounds. "But we haven't seen Big John or the little wifey in days. And we all smell dat," she said, pinching her nose between her thumb and index fingers.

"I don't care what you people say. Something is going on in that house," said the fat lady's nineteen-year-old son. "I say we break in and check it out."

"Hush your mouth boy. You ain't got no sense," said his mother, swatting at him playfully.

"So what we gonna do?" asked a quirky looking mustached man, "we gonna check it out for ourselves or should we call the cops?"

By now a small crowd had gathered. Everyone wanted to know what the foul smell was and where it was coming from. There were whispers and hushed chatter among the neighbors, all speculating on what was happening. The blazing Florida sun mixed with the July humidity wafted the foul smell over the entire neighborhood.

"Enough!" the mustached man said. "We can't sit around wondering what is going on. If Big John got a problem with the police coming to his house then maybe its time for him to clean up his damn house and leave."

"Amen." The crowd agreed.

"I say we go in." This came from the scrawny white lady from across the street. Everyone looked at her in shock. She was the type that never wanted to get involved. She could see someone beating you to death and go in her house, lock the doors, turn up the radio and tell the cops she didn't know a thing.

"What, cat catch y'all tongue? I say lets call the goddamn police. There's that pretty half white baby ova there that need help. I love that pretty lil' half nigga," she said before she remembered she was addressing a mostly black liberal

crowd. Her eyes flew open and she slammed her hands over her mouth
"You ol' bitch!" the fat lady yelled. "Who you calling nigga?" Everyone turned to look at the old lady.
"Whoa, hold up. She is not our concern right now. Like it or not she is right," said the young, light skinned teacher. She knew Serena and took pride in the child's brilliance. She desperately wanted to check on the child, and knew the crowd stomping the old white woman would put them in more trouble than they would already be in for entering John's house uninvited.
"The teacher is right man," said the fat lady's son.
"We can't pay attention to this ol' biddy right now. We have to help the little girl."
Everyone murmured their agreement.
"Okay, I will call the police," mustache man said.
"Some of you grab a bat or a stick or something. We're going in."
"YEAH!" The crowd chanted as everyone scrambled to find something to protect themselves with just in case Big John was not in the mood for company.
Even the trees seemed to sway menacingly as they advanced toward the house. The ripe sun made their clothes cling to their sweat drenched bodies.

"Are you sure you called the cops man?" asked the teacher's husband. "I don't want this knucklehead John to start with me because I might have to flatten his ass." The comment made a few people chuckle.
"Don't worry, I explained what was going on and they said they were on the way," said the man who lived directly next door to the Kowtows. He was privy to a lot of the beatings and often heard Carissa bawling. He feared the worst.

He and his wife had listened through their open window to all of the yelling and screaming a week ago. The house had been dead quiet since then.

The group pushed the gates opened and crept in as quietly as they could, up the steps and to the large wooden door with the skull doorknocker facing them as if to say, beware. They touched the door tentatively and it swung open. The stench shot up their noses, and pinching them shut didn't help.

They walked into a house alive with flies and rodents. The teacher screamed when a rat climbed up her thigh and on her back. She was jumping around frantically when her husband sent it flying across the room.

"This is just plain ass nasty," said the fat lady, a neighborhood cook known for her cleanliness and immaculate kitchen. The others nodded, not wanting to say anything or remove their fingers from their noses.

"Oh my gosh! What the devil is that?" asked a lady no one had noticed before. They walked closer. It looked like a cat that had either starved to death or ate something it shouldn't.

The old white lady started to cry.

"That poor chile', oh Lord that poor Nig…" Everyone turned to look as she stopped in mid sentence and blew her nose. Her face became contorted from the stink and she quickly replaced her fingers on her nose.

"Let's just hurry up and get this over with," said the mustache man. "I don't think we are going to like what's upstairs, but we came this far so let's just go." He led the way up the spiral staircase in a home that was obviously a showcase. They all felt a little envy toward the Kowtow family, who seemed to have everything. Big John was well to do, the kind of white man that they all respected more out of fear than anything else. For years they thought he was a Klan member, and everyone was shocked when he brought home Carissa. Mahogany colored, well built and voluptuous with perky full breasts and wide curvy hips, she was only a teenager when John brought her home and claimed her as his wife. Though there was talk in the town and gossip about what Big John really wanted with Carissa, nobody dared say anything.

The fat lady was the first person to notice Carissa's body. She gasped and fainted, and everyone moved out of the way so she could fall except for her teenage son. He tried to catch her while being careful not to get caught under her weight. She hit the floor hard, causing short snickers and laughter among the rescuers. Then they saw what she saw. Worms crawled about the walls, floor and furniture. Flies buzzed happily around the room. Tiptoeing like the dead could hear them the group peeked into what was Serena's bedroom.

The teacher started to cry. There they were Big John and Carissa on the floor. Carissa lay dead, half of her skull missing, what they could see of her brain congested with maggots and flies. Same for Big John. What chilled them was Serena. The little girl sat in deathly silence, her knees pulled into her chin and her arms wrapped about them. There was feces and piss everywhere. Rats, roaches and files seemed to have found enough food among the grisly scene for second, third and forth generations of their kind.

Nobody moved. Everyone wanted to turn and run. The nineteen year old vomited all over his mother, who was still passed out on the floor. The guy with the mustache covered his mouth to try and prevent himself from doing the same.

No one noticed when the old lady left. The next door neighbor and his wife held each other in fear. Then they heard a slew of sirens, and then listened as the cops ran into the house through the already opened door and up the stairs.

"Move!" said the cop in charge as he pushed through the crowd. The fat lady had come to and her son was apologizing profusely for vomiting on her. Paramedics ran around the fat lady to the little girl, who said nothing. Her eyes looked wild and bewildered and she made no move. She seemed alive and dead, staring at them through unblinking eyes. They checked her for a heartbeat, which was faint and fading. She was half staved and beginning to look malnourished. When she realized that there were no other live bodies in the house she passed out from shock and hunger, her eyes still open.

"What they lookin' fo mama? Ain't it obvious that they dead," the teen whispered. No one answered him, spellbound by the gruesome scene. After a quick examination, the child was rushed to the hospital. She had caught some shotgun pellets in her left shoulder, hip, side and thigh.

At the hospital they could not get her to wake up. She seemed to have fallen into a coma. They feared that she would not survive.

## MAN KILLER

"Let me go, please." The woman whimpered, begging the man she had been so attracted to only hours before. Her pleas fell on deaf ears. His powerful hands reached up and grabbed her shoulders, squeezing out a scream so eerie that Serena's heart sank.

"NOOOO!!!"

The first screams from the dark, secluded streets of downtown Miami had startled her. Serena knew what she had to do but she wasn't prepared for the heart thumping anxiety that rushed through her body.

"Bitch!" he said.

Hearing that word moved her to act. She knew she had to move fast, had to be quick and deliberate. In downtown Miami, with the fast nightlife and excited tourists, no one would look twice at a woman being manhandled by her man. But it made Serena cringe and she walked into the alley with the determination of a lioness stalking her prey.

"Well, hi there! Looks like I'm interrupting something," she cooed with enough eroticism to make the tall, gorgeous Latino pause in his attack. He held the woman's hands behind her head on the cold concrete pavement and had been ramming himself into her.

Her whimpering made Serena's blood boil.

"What the fuck do you want?" he spat at her.

Unnerved by the sudden presence he pulled his suddenly limp

dick out of his victim. As Serena drew closer she could see that blood running down the woman's thighs. Her attacker was disarmed momentarily by the beauty of the woman approaching him. Her alluring eyes and sensual vibe aroused him, and his manhood rose again in appreciation.

"You see that's just it."

"What do you mean, that's just it?" he yelled, annoyed that his voice came out as a squeak instead of the manly growl that he wanted.

"Well, you see baby, you told me to get the fuck out of here, and I am telling you that I would, as long as I get to get out of here and fuck you," she said with a smile.

Shocked, he stared at the tall, slender, caramel beauty that was obviously stacked in all the right places. Her bosom rose and fell with each breath, straining to break from her bustier.

She watched as the man dropped the frail woman's arm, she scurried to a corner of the alley as if he would no longer notice her. Her eyes were black and blue and her clothes were ripped, and she was pulling at the panties that hung around her ankles. Maybe she was a prostitute, Serena thought, but that does not justify any man taking her against her will.

Serena boldly walked to him, fueled by the hatred and anger that she knew would be quenched once she had him where she wanted him. She was no longer afraid, the venom she felt was now her protector.

Serena's tongue was in his throat before he knew what was happening. She wrapped herself around him, feverishly making promises with her mouth and body. Pangs of desire surged through her and captivated him.

"Let's go," she said with enough yearning that he could only follow her lead. The lady who was being victimized only moments earlier stared after them in shock. She had known him for a month; he had courted her for two weeks before she agreed to go out with him. But watching him daily at the office could not have prepared her for this night.

She stared off at them, traumatized, as they got black Cadillac sedan that with dark tinted windows that waited for them and then they vanished.

He looked around inside the car sheepishly, in awe of the technological wizardry and lavish comfort, like something from a James Bond movie.

"Wow" he exclaimed as he climbed in. As he got comfortable, Serena took her cue and began kissing him fervently. She was the new recruit and only a distraction.

"You are my type of woman; you know exactly what you want," he moaned. Serena moaned back, then pulled her skirt up to her waist and slipped her leg over his thigh, straddling him.

"Yes daddy, I can be any woman you want me to be."

He yanked her curly red dangling locks, forcing a surprised shriek from her lips. The sound of pain sent his manhood on overload and he tried to ram himself inside her, but he was met with the barrier of her panties. She grabbed his crotch and massaged the tip of his erect penis; the whimpers from his lips didn't sound like the animal that he was.

"You want me to fuck you right. That's what you said back there chica," he reminded her. He pressed his hand and cupped between her legs to find her underwear wet with heat emanating into his hands. She squirmed and gyrated against his body until she felt as though his dick would burst right through his pants.

"Yes I want to fuck your brains out daddy, but not here," she said, looking behind her to see the back of the head of the female driver as the car raced on I-95 from downtown Miami and into Dixie State Highway 1 that would lead into the ritzy neighborhood of Coral Gables.

"We have company, and I don't want any witnesses to the naughty things I am about to do to you," she panted, losing herself in the sexual abyss that she had worked herself into. Yes, she could tell he had a big cock and from the way he was moving between her legs she wished she were going to feel how he would be inside of her. But he was not the one. So she closed her eyes and focused on the matter at hand.

"Fuck that bitch! I don't give a shit that she sees. Matter o' fact, the more the better," he snickered, giving her a flashback that caused her to shake her head in disgust. She wanted to jump off of his crotch and snap his neck on the spot. But she knew she had to follow the process. She would enjoy it so much more to see him suffer like the vicious dog he was.

"She will join us when we get to our destination. You can have as many of us as you like," she moaned in his ear before flicking her tongue across his temple then sticking it in his ear.

"I like that! I got lucky with you bitches tonight!" he growled. Removing his hands from between her thighs, she forced them to his side and stuck her tongue down his throat. Pulling on his tongue and lips with heated passion, she reached for the metal rings that sat inconspicuously on the back seat next to him. Before he could do anything else he was handcuffed.

"What the fuck is this?" he demanded.

"Easy daddy, you are going like this," she consoled him, stroking his ego and the tip of his shaft simultaneously. She stuck her tongue in his mouth again and ripped the buttons from his shirt so she could play with his nipples. He groaned softly, louder when she lowered her mouth to his love stick moistening the crotch of his pants with her saliva. What she wanted to do with him was not make love; Serena wanted him to sample the Black Widow's ambrosia in the most horrific sense, and smiled when she thought of Elizabeth's gifts and the Black Widow Spider's mark that showed she embraced the killer's most dangerous characteristics. She would make him pay.

"Oh you feel so good," she muttered as her tongue tantalized his shaft and her fingers pulled his zipper open. With his hands cuffed there was not much he could do but surrender to her expert skills.

She unzipped his pants releasing his erect penis. Moving her heated mouth over his cock caused him to shift his hips so he could push his swollen member into her oral orifice. She allowed him to plunge deep into her throat until he could almost feel her tonsils and to his surprise, she didn't gag. She took it as if her mouth was her pussy and he couldn't help the thrill that made him tremble. She flattened her tongue and massaged the sides of his shaft.

"Holy shit!" He grunted. "Holy shit!"

She swayed her body and moved her ass, squeezing her thighs as the overwhelming urge to mount him consumed her.

"How much time Cath?" She stopped briefly to ask.

"We are on Sunset Drive love, two minutes. Just hold down the fort."

Serena was glad the trip was almost over. Moving swiftly, she pulled a silk scarf from her cleavage and tied it over his face. She could feel the car pause briefly waiting for the gates to open. The car doors open and they got out and moved inside the house, guiding their masked victim between them. Jason had wasted no time. He had everything they needed laid out in the underground lair and watched silently as this victim enjoyed his last taste of pussy.

"This is it Daddy, you ready to experience the time of your life?" cooed the voice in his ear. The sensuality and excitement that oozed from her caused his manhood to rise again, making him rock hard. He was scared, enthusiastic and impatient. He couldn't tell who it was, but he could hear hushed whispers all around him.

"Hell yeah! I'm gonna give it to you good, bitch! Real good!" He spat out the words, trying to sound in control. But it was slowly dawning on him that he had no control. He felt hands all over him, pulling his pants down and cutting off his shirt without removing his handcuffs. Suddenly, there were mouths all over him, sucking, and licking, fondling and massaging every part of his body.

"Hey what the..." he started to say when he felt the clear cool liquid squirt over his backside and the soft delicate hands that began to knead it into the crack of his ass. He felt the sensual press against his back before the hair on her mound pressed into him, making him sigh.

Cathalina gyrated against his backside and massaged the spine of his back as she prepared him for a very special treat. The heated lips that devoured his cock and slobbered on his balls relaxed him. His senses tried to decipher what was going on, who was in front of him and who was behind, but soon none of it mattered. His body and the desire for passion took over and he yielded to the pleasure of it.

He felt smooth fingers slip into anus, and this time he didn't object. He leaned his body over as strong yet delicate hands pressed his head towards his knees. He groaned, and the whispers of female voices heightened his arousal. He could feel breasts on him; smell the aroma of excited woman.

"Oh put it on me. Give it to me," he begged. "Oh Gosh, how many of you bitches are here?"

The hands that finger popped his anus and rubbed down the

crack of his posterior began to spread his cheeks apart, squirting oil to make sure it was fully lubricated. Before he realized what was happening he felt his ass being mounted. Soft feminine fingers kept his butt cheeks wide apart but it was a very masculine dick that was sliding in and out of his anus.
He was in shock; he couldn't breathe. His head was being forced into his knees from the butt thrusting pressure behind him. He squeezed his eyes shut to refuse the tears from escaping his eyes. Pain saturated his body, his head seemed about to explode with excruciating pain. He wanted to moan and scream at the same time, but his pride wouldn't let him.

Soon the sound and feel of Elizabeth's dick slipping in and out of his now slick anus turned him on. The butt fucking began to feel good.

But fear took hold of him. Feeling it, Elizabeth lifted his head and bit his tongue to prevent himself from making sounds of pleasure. She pulled the strap on out of his ass and slapped his reddened butt cheeks. "That's it baby," Elizabeth laughed. "You took it like the bitch you really are."

"You like that, don't you?" Cathalina teased.

"You fucking bitches are crazy. I didn't agree to this, let me go."

The laughter that echoed around the room startled him. It sounded like hundreds of them but he knew it couldn't be more than then four. Their voices were heavy with desire and sensuality. Even the cynical laughter excited him.

Before he could get another insult in he felt his legs being pulled wide apart and another penis, one that felt twelve inches long and at least two and half inches wide rammed into his asshole to the hilt. His screeched like a banshee and knew he was bleeding from his ripped flesh.

"Is that what you wanted you little man slut?"

Elizabeth hissed. "I was trying to be nice, but since you can take it like a man and talk shit, I am going to give it to you like a man." She hurled herself into him again. They have decided that the pleasure they usually gave their victims would be denied him. He was about to feel a bitch do her thing.

Hands, once soft and delicate, became as strong as gorillas, pulling his body in all kinds of angles.
Tears streamed down his face.

"You didn't ask for this?" asked a voice; soft and low in his ears.

"Did she ask for what you did back there in the streets?"

"Oh God no, please help me," he whimpered. "This is crazy."

"Crazy?" the voice spat at him as laughter shot around the room.

"I wasn't doing this to her. I didn't do anything," he said as the penis four times the size of his own stroked him deep and hard, surrendering nothing and showing no mercy. He tried to talk a few times but his voice caught in his throat. Underneath the fear he could feel himself getting aroused.

"Fucker, what do you mean you didn't do this? Didn't you just rape a lady only moments before we picked you up?"

He snickered a weird type of laugh that they couldn't understand.

He could feel the momentum building and the thrusting into him get deeper still, as though his ravisher was about to climax in his butt.

"You turnin' me into a faggot? Is that it?" he asked. He was rewarded with a lash across the back so deep and quick it jolted him into trying to throw the women from him. He knew they drew blood, because he felt the slow slid of a wet drop down his spine.

"Oh, yeah...this ass it good. Fuck." He heard the voice simmered behind him. And as she exploded inside of him they removed the blindfold, so he could see who had been all up in his ass.

"So this is what a chick with a dick looks like," he laughed sarcastically in an attempt maintain his manhood.

"How about what a chick with a dick tastes like?" she asked. They put him on his knees and she stuffed the limp cock in his mouth.

"Bite me motherfucker, and you are gonna wish you were dead." She seethed.

He could see that he was outnumbered. One lady as beautiful as he could imagine stood in the corner dressed in nothing holster with two guns straddling her hips. Another hung from what looked like a bees nest made of chains that hung from the ceiling.

Even the woman whose cock he was sucking - woman, man, he didn't know which - was beautiful. Her cinnamon colored combination Black Asian skin was flawless. Lustrous, long straight black hair hung to her shoulders. But her eyes glowed red. Were those contacts?

"Okay, so you had your fun, let me go," he croaked.

"What did he say?" Cathalina smirked. "The fun is just getting started."

He watched as the girl who had just fucked him like he was a piece of pussy pulled her dick from his mouth and walked away. Suddenly he felt something crawling on him. Spiders!

Running over him were dozens of spiders. Though he would never know it, he was being attacked by two of the most deadly spiders alive, the Black Widow and the Brown Recluse. The venom felt like acid under his skin. He could feel it paralyzing him.

Cathalina and Elizabeth moved away.

His eyes widened with fear as a glass cage was quickly lowered over him. He was locked in. He could hear the women's laughter mocking him.

"You did good Serena. Next time though, you get to fuck him."

It was the last thing he heard as his frozen body fell to the floor.

## MAN KILLER 2

"Your honor, your honor." The bailiff knocked persistently on her door. "The attorneys are ready for you to hear their petitions," he said through the closed door.

Inside, Serena was lost in thought.. She looked at the folder on the desk in front of her again and shook her head. She couldn't stop the violent headaches and anger she felt every time a case like this came before her.

It never ceased to amaze her. The women, their fear, how reluctant they were to testify against their predators, their abusers. Many of them died and left their families to find justice.

She slammed the folder shut and pulled herself together. She picked up her judges' robe and stared at it, momentarily detached. All this time, all her hard work to try and make a difference. It all just seemed to have been a waste, the late night studying to be the top of her class. After graduation she had been a black female lawyer on the move, rising quickly from an assistant district attorney in the Dade county prosecutors' office to District Attorney and finally, winning a seat as a State Supreme Court Judge in Florida. Serena wished she didn't feel like her hands were bounded by the law and as though her seat was worth nothing. Her anger flared as she carefully pulled the robe around her, transforming herself as if she believed the false ideals and image that the black cloth carried.

The weight of it hung heavily on her shoulders, and she felt it had become more of a burden than a blessing.

She moved with the graceful stride of a runway model, collecting her full auburn curly locks from her shoulders and tying them in a bun. She thought of how all the attorney's drooled when they appeared before her. She would soon celebrate her thirty-second birthday, but she still felt empty, alone and unsatisfied with her accomplishments.

The despair had begun to consume her.
Serena snapped her hair into its place, collected the folder and walked out the door. She stood in the hallway between the courtroom and her chambers and waited for the bailiff.

"The honorable Judge Serena Kowtow presiding," he announced. She glided into the courtroom and behind the bench. The sternness of her face and her locked rigid cheekbones made her appear even more stunning. She sat slowly, and her gray eyes glowed with the angry fire she struggled to contain.

"We have some notes I presume?" she asked. Both attorneys nodded.

"Good!" Judge Kowtow said. "Let's start with the defense. Be quick and precise about it, gentlemen."
Both attorneys felt a chill go through them, as well as a stirring in their loins. Serena zoned out like she normally did during cases like these. She could imagine the slime bag defendant raping and murdering his wife even as his attorney now claimed he was now a new man. She knew the prosecutor would tell how the dead woman had left kids and family behind.

"This is a waste of my time and the taxpayer's time," she mumbled under her breath. This is the part that really disgusted her. Sitting there in a place where she should be able

to help, a place that should give her the power to wipe away the heart wrenching pain she felt as prosecutors told how a husband raped his children and allowed them to watch as he murdered their mother in cold blood with his bare hands. Convicted and now about to use some flimsy legal technicality to launch an appeal that would set him free.
She knew she would have to let him go. She forced back her own tears, maintaining a stoical expression.

Serena's day wore on until it was time for her to drive home to Coral Gables home, one of the most historic and beautiful districts in Miami. She relished the spacious homes in that area, the way they marked the streets with gold colored rocks on the ground the bore the street names. If you didn't pay attention, you could get lost in the sheer beauty of the neighborhood.

The street were lined with hundred year old, giant oak and Weeping Willow trees that grew tall and majestic, their upper branches entangling high over the street like a leafy bridge.

Serena let the convertible top of her Porsche midsize SUV vehicle collapse into its secret place as she sped home. She had had the one of a kind sports car made to her specifications. Leaving the top down allowed the sunlight to sprinkle across her olive skin and radiate through her curly auburn hair that now flowed pass her shoulders. Her Calvin Klein sunglasses hid the anger in her eyes; the ruby rouge she wore on her lips gave her the face of a seductress.

Her mind was racing a thousand miles a minute. She could feel her hatred for men and the system burning inside her; both were demanding and confining.
She was on the brink of losing it when the cell phone rang.
"Yes," she said
"Looks like I called right on time. Sounds like you

were about to go into one of your rage sessions." It was her therapist and friend Cathalina. She had noticed the anger growing in Serena over the past year, usually working into a rage on her way home.

"No, I am fine Cathalina dear; you underestimate the power of self control and an active imagination," Serena said amicably.

"I don't believe you Serena. You say the same thing every time, yet there's no smile in your eyes and no glee in your voice."

"How do you know? You're on the phone."

"I don't need to see you to know that you're not smiling," Cathalina said. "And I know this, because I know you. You're my friend and I love you."

To Cathalina, Serena was like a shy plant she had seen in the islands. Reach out to touch it, it closes its petals. Leave it alone and it re-opens.

"Okay Cath. How about telling me about your day?" Serena asked, changing the subject.

"Well, I'm sure it wasn't as exciting as yours. I had a couple patients today suffering from schizophrenia." She hesitated, waiting for Serena's response. But she said nothing. Serena listened for what she knew would come, the story behind the story, that some man, maybe even a parent or relative, had brutally raped or abused Cath's patients. This was routine. She had studied enough cases and overseen enough of her own to know the rhetoric.

"But you know the story Hun, its always one thing or another," Cathalina said, avoiding the details. She knew Serena understood what had not been said.

"So who are they?" Serena asked as she pulled to the gate blocking her quarter mile long driveway. She stopped and pressed the button on the visor of her car. The wrought iron gates retracted to allow entry. Serena removed her glasses and placed them on the dashboard where, activated by a motion detector, a compartment opened to receive them.

"Cath sweetheart, I'm home. Are you stopping by for drinks tonight?"

"I thought about it. Let me call you. It's only three in the afternoon and I have a few more patients. Sounds like you need me. I'll try and rush over," Cathalina said with a chuckle.

"Do you feel like having some fun tonight Serena?" Cathalina asked after a brief silence. There was mirth in her voice.

"Whatever you like Cath, whatever is on your mind," Serena smiled and hung up the phone. She really liked Cathalina. She was the only person she trusted. Serena grabbed her sweater that shielded her thin frame from the early chill of the Florida spring. The state was usually warm, but at five in the morning when she is out and about, the cool crisp scent that she loved from the trees and the chirping of small birds was not the only things that greeted her. The iciness in the air always surprised her.

She walked to the door, swaying effortlessly in her mid-thigh length black dress that rode her curves. The nude stockings she wore with her imported Stiletto heels made her legs rival those of any runway model.

Serena shed pieces of clothing from the moment she entered the house. It was immaculately kept. Her manservant would soon greet her with her customary champagne, caviar and crackers to munch on before dinner. By the time he entered from the servants' quarters, which were set up like a home within her home, she would be completely naked, heading to her the staircase that led to her bedroom.

"Hello Serena. How was your day today?" Jason

asked in his sexy baritone voice. He smiled at her seductively.

"Hello Jason. My day was the same. And yours?"

"My day has just started madam', now that you are home." He winked at her and she blushed. She loved Jason in a way she could not describe. He was different to her.

"May I help you with these Serena?" He asked, looking from the door where the first article of clothing landed, following the trail to the stairway and then casting his eyes to her feet, then up her now naked legs to her bare ass..

She turned around, exposing her cleanly shaven mound and he smiled, revealing deep dimples that enhanced the dark richness of his mahogany complexion and exposed beautiful even teeth that had a small space in the front.

"I would have nothing less," she said, giving him permission to clean up after her. Jason was about six feet tall, about the same height as she was, slender and powerfully packed. His six-pack abs glowed from the oiling down he performed before approaching his mistress, which is the way she liked him. His only clothing was a loincloth covering his groin that was attached to an elastic thong that was laced between the cracks of his buttocks.

Serena watched as he bent over to pick up her garments. He was posing for her - the daily ritual was their dance. He would gyrate his waist in seductive circular motion and flex his pectoral muscles as well as his ass cheeks to entice her as he bent to retrieve each piece. Serena became wet with anticipation.

Piece by piece he retrieved her clothing until he was on the staircase. Finally, clothes in hand, he knelt in front of her, his mouth opened like Pavlov's dog, ready to do the licking.

He waited for the signal that she was ready for him, and when the deep sigh came with the throw back of her head, he put the clothes aside and launched at her in slow motion, holding her gently and laying her back on the staircase as he licked and caressed her midsize perky breast with his tongue. She relaxed in his arms and allowed herself to be carried away. He tantalized her areola until she moaned with pleasure. He watched her movements, which were specific instructions for him as to where he was allowed to touch her and when. Serena's hands grabbed at the neatly twisted dread locks that hung in the middle of his back. The crimson colored dye that he used to highlight his locks added to their beauty. Her hands traced his back, feeling the hard muscles.

Jason's strong hands led the way below her breasts and lingered on her torso, gently kissing and moving always southward, tonguing her belly button while his right hand requested permission to enter the wetness that screamed for him to plunge something deep within her. They both moaned deeply when his index finger teased her swollen clit.

"I love you Serena," Jason whispered, staring deep into her eyes. His eyes looked like those of a lovesick child. He looked upon her face passionately, still, waiting for the response that never came.

He returned to the task at hand, pressing his body into her. She sighing sweetly, arching her back and writhing her waist to meet the thrusts of his finger as he moved quickly, down the trail pass her navel and then falling into the triangle of her womanhood.

He replaced his fingers with his tongue, working the tip in the secret places that released her love juice.

"Ahhhhh your pussy is so wet!" he exclaimed, tossing his head back in pure ecstasy. He shook his hair loose, then again to get it away from his face, so then buried his face back in her groin.

"Come on lover, eat my pussy you piece of shit!" she

cooed. The start of her verbal assault sent shivers through him. This was her way and he knew it, so he moved, allowing his hands to cup the curve of her ass, pulling her cheeks apart and fingering her asshole. With her chestnut legs wrapped so tightly around his neck that they threatened to suffocate him, he plunged his tongue deeper into her, listening as her sighs became more fervent.

"Mother fucker, that's right! You want this pussy don't you?" she asked, lifting her ass from the stair and fucking his face, forcing his head, lips and tongue against her wetness and the urgency that was building in her abdomen. Jason used his teeth to nip at the outer lips of her pussy. He loved the smell of her when she was on the verge of coming. Nestling his nose into her hairless mound and breathing hard he pressed on, avoiding the thought that always hung between them, that he could never truly have her.. Never truly satisfy her.

Her finger nails raked his back with crazed scratches that he endured each time they had this intimate interchange. Jason braced himself for the orgasm that he knew would come any second and the pain he would have to endure for the pleasure he had bestowed upon her.

Serena grabbed his hair and pulled at it as though she was riding a horse, pressing her hips into his face and throwing her head back in anticipation of her volcanic eruption.

"Yes, yes, yes!" she sighed softly, prodding him to keep the pace. Jason's fingers pushed into her anus as if he was digging for gold and his tongue did the same to her pussy, licking low on the pussy, then hoisting her ass above his eyes so his tongue could taste the dew on the sweat drenched finger that her butt hole once housed.

"I want it. Now you bastard, put it in," she demanded. But he kept licking her. It drove her crazy when he tossed her salad right when she was about to come. The way he pulled her ass cheeks apart caused a deep chill to shoot through her body until she was caught in the whirlwind of uncontrollable spasms.

"Now mother fucking asshole, I want you to fuck me!" her voice was soft and quivering as she begged. She grabbed at his loincloth, the place that once boasted a proud ten inches in length and almost six inches in circumference. He heard her, he wanted to, he could feel the desire to enjoy the excitement of their exchange build inside him, but there was nothing he could do about that.

"Fuck." she yelled in anguish, remembering what she always forgot as her orgasm overtook her. "You don't have a damn dick. You are no where the man you used to be. A fucking Eunuch!"

She spat the words at him vehemently.

The torture was sometimes unbearable but this is the price he paid for his life, the price to love her. He choked back the anger that was raging inside of him, a battle that he fought daily.

Jason licked softly, soothing her clit as if asking it to relax, releasing her ass cheeks and using his hands to caress her legs as he kissed her inner thigh. Her legs relaxed and she moaned lightly in the after glow of her orgasm. Tears began to stream down Jason's face.

He pulled away from her and put his head on the floor, prepared to be devoured like the black widow devours the male spider after mating. Then when no assaults came, he stood up, walked to the center of the grand living room. The Cathedral ceiling concealed the laced chains that would descend and uncoil at the press of a button. She stood, her skin glowing with sprinkles of sweat that twinkled on her body like stardust. She waved her hand in a circular motion and a panel in the stairway wall opened, exposing a cat of nine tails and the spiked dog collar she would tightly squeeze on Jason's neck.

"So you like to eat pussy?" she asked, touching the button to release the chains as she descended the stairs. She approached Jason, who stood as the chains descended around him. There were seven of them, some with spikes and others with cuffs.

"Only your pussy, Mistress, and I would die for it," he told her unemotionally. His back was turned to her and Serena could see the lash marks, raised scars that had healed and reopened and healed again. This was her way of loving him. It was the only way she could, and he accepted that.

"Is my hot pussy worth dying for Jason?" she asked seductively, weaving a web of hatred that had built itself inside of her for years.

"I live and die to fuck you Mistress, if licking the shit out of your ass gives you pleasure then that's my fate."

With those words Jason stretched his out his arms, legs apart. She latched the chains on his wrist and his ankles. Stepping back and still naked, Serena drew the whip back and swung it. She wanted to hurt him, to hear his cries. Jason knew this too, so he succumbed to her will. She poured her revulsion into every lash.

"I am so sorry Serena. I didn't mean to do it," he said, teeth clenched against the pain.

"Then why, why you worthless piece of turd?" she asked, her tears drenching her face. Each snap of the whip reminded her that Jason was just a man and not worthy of her love. But she loved him in her way for the sacrifice he had made to her, bearing the burden of those who caused her pain, a memory that had festered and grown more infected as the years went by. Serena fell to the floor, curled into a fetal position, and wailed uncontrollably.

Jason unlatched himself. Timidly he knelt and lifted her in his arms. He looked at her as she whimpered, frail and vulnerable, and released a tear for what they had both lost. Without words, Jason proceeded with the ritual. He glided up the stairs, taking her to the master bedroom, which was designed as two small apartments in one. The crystal chandelier hung low in the center of the room, illuminating a canopy bed draped with white linen. Red silk sheets adorned her king sized bed that was covered with pillows and all sorts of stuffed animals.

Her room was a cross between a woman and child who never truly grew up. Jason walked across the tan Italian marble floor to the bathroom, itself the size of a large bedroom.

The large, claw-foot tub was marble tiled with Michelangelo's "The Creation" drawn into it just as it appeared on the ceiling of the Sistine Chapel.

The tub had four legs, curved into the floor. The shower had sliding, opaque glass doors. Jason, placed her in the tub, allowing warm water tainted with cinnamon and mirth, to wash over her. He washed her as gently as a baby while holding her head gently on his chest.

After a half hour he lifted her from the tub, walked back into the bedroom, and placed her in the bed. Walking briskly back to the bathroom, he retrieved her towel and patted her dry before pulling the covers over her.
Bowing, he paid homage to her. He was her submissive, her slave. He pulled the covers from her sleeping frame. Taking one more breath of her he turned her over and kissed her beautifully rounded posterior, then crawling on hands and knees, exited her bedroom and quietly pulling the heavy doors shut.

## MAN KILLER 3

    Cathalina walked slowly from her desk and sat next to her patient, who had tears streaking down her face. She glanced briefly at her clock and realized it was already quarter to six. She had hoped that she would have gotten out of the office and headed home to shower and change into more comfortable clothes before going to see Serena, but it seemed as though she might have to cancel. She hated making plans with Serena and canceling.
    Cathalina believed that Serena suffered from some Malignant Eroticized Counter Transference, caused by the paternal rape suffered in her childhood.
    The patient across from her reminded her of Serena when she had first, reluctantly, sat in that very chair. The arrogance she displayed was not out of conceit but came from knowing what she endured to still be alive.
    "Lara, I am so sorry about what you have suffered. It's a form of Childism; a term developed by an African American psychiatrist Chester Pierce in 1975. You were weak and vulnerable and the trauma you suffered has lingered, bringing the anger you feel," Cathalina explained to her distraught patient. "You see it's really not your fault, this rage." But her words didn't seem to cause much comfort. Both of them knew Lara had overstayed her visit and needed to get going.
    "I'm so sorry Dr. Shekhar, I know that I have been

here close to four hours now, but I just really need your help. I don't understand why people who were supposed to have loved me more than anything else in the world, violated me the way they did. I've become a bitch because of them, just a slut," she said, staggering through her words. Cathalina felt sorry for her, it was the same empathy she usually developed for her patients. She could only imagine the rage Serena would feel if she were to hear this woman's story.

"I'll tell you what; I'll give you a prescription for a mild antidepressant. Whenever you feel overwhelmed, just take it and it will give you some peace."

"I just feel like killing him, you know? I feel like killing them all. I wish all men would die. Anyone who rapes and abuses a child does not deserve to live, and the men who take advantage of vulnerable woman is just as bad," Lara said as she walked towards the open window. The serenity of the city below her did not touch her heart. Her mannerisms seemed under control, but the look in her eyes and the tone of her voice told an entirely different story. She was ready to kill, and Cathalina recognized it. Serena had the same look in her eyes whenever she speaks of men.

"I do understand. That's why I want to see you back here next Monday. Today is Friday, but if there is anything you need before your appointment, please don't hesitate to call. If you call my office line and say it's an emergency, they will page me, okay?" she asked, hoping that would quell Lara Lopez enough to get her out of her office so Cathalina could be on her way. "You know I'm here for you, Lara," Cathalina said, resting a hand on Lara's shoulder.

"Okay," Lara said, her tears drying as quickly as they had come. Cath noticed that her pleasant disposition returned at the same time, a classic symptom of her illness.

Laura had been her patient for almost six months. It took

about as long to make Serena not just a patient but also a friend. A degree in psychiatry and behavioral sciences, all the studies she conducted, the treatments she was taught, her hospital internship, nothing prepared her for the psychological damage she found in her patients. That was one of the reasons she wanted to specialize in working with women.

Though she tried not to become friendly with her patients, there were a few that she gave special privy to. Lara would be one, but no one was more important than Serena. As Lara got up and walked gracefully out of her office, she couldn't help admiring how gorgeous she was. Her hair, cropped short on her head, sported blonde highlights that brought out the yellow hue in her skin. Her light gray eyes flickered when she was angry. Her body was well developed with full breasts, a small waist and wide, childbearing hips. She sported slightly bowed legs that showed off the roundness of her ass and accentuated her walk. It's a shame that this thirty five year old woman could not find love, Cath thought. The only drawback to her beauty was the facial hair under her chin. Lara had confided that she spent years and much money shaving, plucking, and for electrolysis, the hair just keep returning and coming back thicker each time.

The little beard hurt her self-esteem and was another reason she avoided men. Sitting in the chair that Lara just left, Cathalina breathed a sigh of relief and looked at the clock that hung over her mahogany desk with a high back leather chair behind it. She loved the serenity of the painting that hung next to it, a landscape of a waterfall gushing through a peaceful forest. The oil painting was a graduation present from an old boyfriend who had decided to have a sex change and was no longer Brian, but Brianna. Cathalina chuckled. Her mind went back to the day when she had severe burnings in her vagina along with abdominal pains. She noticed a foul odor whenever she used the bathroom and sores appeared all over her. She remembered the panicked rush to the hospital, where she found out she had gonorrhea, syphilis, and herpes. Her devastation was complete when she was told that she had the disease so long that her reproductive organs had been permanently damaged. She would never be able to have children. She really should have trashed the painting when he broke their engagement and embarrassed her with his nonsense. But she kept it, as a reminder why she was doing what she did. As reminder of her pain so she would never forget, in a way that fueled her anger and pushed her to help the women who came to her office everyday.

It was seven o'clock, and Cathalina wondered if they could still get the girls from the agency to come over and entertain Serena. She picked up the phone and dialed "Sex Cell." the most popular underground group of sex slaves, submissive and fetish hunters around.

"Sex Cell," a seductive voice answered on the second ring.

"Madam Cleopatra please?"

"Please hold."

While Cathalina waited the phone gave out screams and moans. Madam thought of everything.

"This is the Madam, can I help you?" came a soft voice. If Cathalina had held on any longer she would have started to masturbate to the screams. Her breath caught in her throat - Cleopatra had caught her off guard.

"Hey Cleo, it's me."

"Cathalina darling," Cleo said, her voice changing to normal. "I was wondering if you were going to call. When you called earlier I had everything arranged and you know my clients get upset when they cannot get their usual."

"I am sorry Cleo; it was Lara that I was meeting with

again."
   "Oh that poor dear. How is she?"
   "She is getting stronger. I can feel the anger festering inside of her, but she needs to feel that first before she can grow. She needs to feel the power of being in control before she can heal."
   "But is she ready?" Cleopatra asked the anxiety and impatience obvious in her voice.
   "I told you Cleo, I'll let you know when she's ready. Now is not the time," Cathalina said. Wanting to get on with the matter at hand she smiled and exhaled softly.
   "How about we follow through with that night of fun and passion? I'm sure Serena is still waiting for me, and I've never broken my word to her without calling first."
   "Yes, I know Cath," Cleo teased using the nickname Serena used for Dr. Cathalina Shekhar. Cleo knew she was treading on dangerous ground but she wanted to drive her point home.
   "Why don't you send the package on over, and meet me at Serena's," Cathalina said, putting her plan in motion. There was no need for Cleo to respond.
   "Sounds good to me. I'll see you in twenty minutes," Cleo said and hung up the phone. She hated being put on the backburner by Cathalina for Serena. She hated that Cathalina would jump through hoops for one woman and one woman only and because of her blinders, could never see how much Cleo loved her.
   There was nothing she wouldn't do for her. Yet Cathalina was the only person who had her on a string. In her world, she was the feared Madam Cleopatra. Cathalina hung up the phone and felt that usual uneasy feeling that swept through her body every time she got off the phone with Cleo. She knew what the problem was, but this was no time for her

to be concerned with it. It was Friday, and they had been waiting for this day since meeting Serena more than a year ago now. They had groomed her, molded her and taught her the art, the passion of what to do with her anger, pain and hatred so she could function in her daytime job.

Tonight, she would be initiated and crowned. Cathalina was proud that she found her. Serena was her protégé. Cathalina walked to her window s and gazed down on Biscayne Bay and the most beautiful parts of downtown Miami. The ocean seemed to stand still, so still it could have been a mirage.

Cathalina closed the blinds and walked to her office door. She looked around her office with appreciation. She had done a nice job with the decoration. Nothing was overdone. If anything, there was an undertone of humility. She didn't want to make her patients to feel uncomfortable. Most of them were middle class women who worked hard for what they had. She didn't want her office to look like she was brandishing her money in their faces.

She walked back into the now darkened office over to the 27 inch plasma television that was hooked on the wall above a mahogany DVD stand. Most of the DVD titles bore medical seminars. She glanced at the seven-foot snake plant that spread over the centerpiece, giving the office an outdoors indoor feel.

All the colors were earth toned, except for the carpet. It was at least four inches thick, white and plush. No one was allowed to enter Cathalina's office without first taking off their shoes. Taking off their shoes was the first step to bearing their souls, and the 20 x 15 office floor helped. It was underlined with a massaging vibrator tucked neatly beneath the carpet. Walking to the chair in front of her desk was pure ecstasy to their feet. Cathalina closed her doors, walked out into the warm Florida evening and got into her car. As the doors closed, Cathalina couldn't contain the excited flutter of her heart. A black woman like her has come a long way. She breathed the scent of her customized Cadillac. She liked the way she felt whenever she got into the car. On the outside it looked normal, but on the inside it was all about status. To Cathalina the car symbolized her ability to live a white upper class lifestyle and still be a black professional to help her sisters. She smiled and sped off to Coral Gables where her friend awaited her.

Serena was still lying in her bedroom when Jason knocked on her door. He was not allowed to enter without permission. Serena usually went into a comatose sleep after a session with Jason. Somewhere deep within her, it hurt to think of Jason and what she did to him. She still, sometimes, in the recesses of her mind, felt regrets that he could not have been the one; she could not have allowed him to seep into her heart.

The moment that she heard the rehearsed knock on her door, she knew that Cleo and Cath had arrived. Suddenly she began to tremble and her heart raced at the idea of what was about to occur. She had prepared for this and she was ready. She was excited and she was not turning back. This was something she had to do.

Rising, she walked to her huge walk in closet that was the size of a small room and pulled out her Vincentia Secrets black velvet see through gown, with flower patches that covered only her nipples and her snatch. Serena glanced at the gold embossed grandfather clock over by the fireplace and realized that it was a little past eight at night. She couldn't believe that she had slept that long but that was not a concern right now.

Jason stood next to her, wearing his Zulu leopard print

loin cloth. He was holding a shotgun, the same kind of sawed-off shotgun that her mother used so long ago to protect her and to die by. She kept all the reports of that day locked in her safe with all her valuables, the newspaper clippings, and the videos, even of the snickers, sneers and information that the psychologist's used to explain her past to her. She kept them like treasures.

She moved next to the picturesque window looking out into her front yard and pressed the release lock for the gate and watched as four cars pulled into her driveway, fitting neatly into the spacious parking area in front of her house. She recognized Cleo and Cath's cars, but she didn't know whom the Ferrari and Rolls Royce belonged to. Not that it mattered. They were with the two people who she had come to trust more than anyone in her life. She watched silently as the doors of the other two cars opened, and didn't stay to watch anymore. Instead she went down the stairs and stood by her front door and waited to hear their approaching steps.

She opened the huge door and allowed her visitors to enter. First it was Cathalina, who kissed her lightly on both cheeks and stood next to her. Serena blushed, and felt Jason look at her. She knew he wasn't happy, but that was not her concern. She felt safe with Cathalina's hand snuggled tightly in hers. Cleopatra, whom Serena had never met, followed her. Serena was shocked. Cleo was a big woman. She wore black leather that covered nearly her entire body except Serena could see that her ass cheeks were exposed as she walked by. She had to be just below two hundred pounds. But she was the sexiest most beautiful big woman Serena had ever seen. Cleopatra was heavy on top, with a waist that curved into her torso and thighs. One's eyes would naturally follow the curve of her perfectly rounded ass into long cream-colored caramel legs.

Her skin was as smooth as milk and the deep dimples of her smile made her hazel eyes glow and dance. The black leather against her body was like a second skin gripping and holding everything in its place.

"Cleopatra." Serena sighed under her breath. This woman was a legend among the women in their circle, those who favored the night and the things that illicit fear and fascination in most, but are treasured partners to them. Cleopatra was not considered a "true" spider; she was the gatekeeper, the protector of them. She had the information, the cover for their toys and exotic taste in prey. She bore the mark of the Crocodile. It was tattooed on her back and looked as if it were alive. The rough stubble skin of the crock dinosaur was tattooed as brown as the muddy waters of its natural habit.

Cleo was as fast and as dangerous as any crocodile. She paused briefly in front of Serena and then waited for the others to enter. When the door closed behind them, there were six women headed to the secret basement room. Serena waited as Jason put in the codes and watched as the wall moved, opening into a hidden secret passage that led to a world of sexual delight. Cleopatra was proud of this space, even more so than her own palace of pleasure because she had a hand in creating it. She delighted in how she gave Cathalina all the instructions for the construction workers. She gave them all of her secret thoughts to implement in the underground development plan. This was a manifestation of her mind.

"Come," Cathalina, urged them all, "let us begin." A sneaky, evil smile crept across her face. Her look at Serena bid her to not be afraid. She was prepared for this.
Cleopatra took a whip off the wall and snapped it once. The package walked in behind Cathalina. They were to be the entertainment for the rest of the night.

The two women that came out of the Roles Royce

took off their clothes and lay on two stone tables the size of hospital beds. One girl was Russian with pale white skin, brown eyes and long stringy hair. She didn't speak much English, but her sighs and her body spoke the language they needed to know. She was about five nine, medium built and her body was covered with hair. From the top of her head down to her arms, the center of her stomach and into the mound of joy that she now offered them. The other was an African beauty. Her skin was as smooth as silk and as dark as a black stallion. Her legs were thick and powerful, her arms muscular and strong.

She was about six feet tall and as cleanly shaven as a brand new baby. She had no hair on her, not on her head, not under her arms, not on the entry way to her love hole, and not in the crack of her curvaceous ass cheeks. She too had not been in this country very long, but her threshold for pain and pleasure was immense and she was willing to do anything to feel passion that would send her mind into overload.

Tonight she would get just that.
Cleopatra went about the room, gathering their tools like a surgeon about to perform surgery. She squirted scented baby oil over the women's bodies As if on cue, they began to massage the silky liquid into themselves.

"Get the pets." Cleopatra coaxed, and Elizabeth slowly marched to the center wall of the hidden room, and knocked twice. They could hear the scratching. The pets were preparing to be released.

Elizabeth walked over to another table off to the side that held a large urn displaying condoms of all flavors and colors and a tray of biscuits. Picking them up along with a whip of her own, she returned to the door and used the huge ring in front to open it.

Two beautiful wolves walked in. Elizabeth greeted

them with the biscuits in one hand and the whip in the other. But this was no ordinary whip. The tip was the head of a cobra snake, the teeth still in place. They walked to Liz, cowered, ate the biscuits and waited for directions.

"Ready." Liz announced, and brought a beautiful smile to Cleopatra's face. Her dimples sank within her cheeks and she stuck her tongue between the small space in the middle of her front teeth.

The two submissive began to moan and gyrated feverishly in anticipation of what was to come. They plunged their fingers in and out of their vaginas hungrily, willing their bodies into excitement. The two wolfhounds, as white as snow with eyes that glowed silver, began to sniff as they had been trained. Cleopatra stood over them and spoke softly, almost soothingly.

"Ready to be satiated my pets?" she asked of the bald African whose juices flowed eagerly onto the table.

"Madam, I have waited for this. Grant me this pleasure," she said in her strong foreign accent. Cleo seemed to have been the only one to understand this beautiful sacrifice. Cleopatra reached on the table next to her and grab what looked like a pair of circular rings. The rings were about a half-inch thick, and sported inverted needles on the inside surface. Cleo opened each one like a handcuff, and locked one onto each breast of the African. As Cleo closed each ring, the needles dug into the woman's flesh, causing her to wail in pain.

Serena watched her even as the screech assaulted their ears. No fear or concern crossed face. Only her eyes danced wild with curiosity. Her love for causing pain in others rushed through her. She had watched videos of them in action during her preparation, and has seen Cleo and Cathalina ripped the dicks off of many a man. Many were taken from the list of violators who stood before her in court; cases she couldn't solve were delicately handled by her Spider friends. But this was the first time she would see them torture someone together right in front of her.

Once she is initiated she would become used to these techniques, but for now she could only watch, becoming familiar with bondage and other tools of their trade. She felt herself shudder, and her juices began to flow as she watched the women build themselves into a sexual rhythm.

Elizabeth stood and Cleo now stood beside the Russian woman and took hooks from the table that stood next to her. Clamping them between her index fingers as she made a fist, she approached the woman's opened legs and slipped apart the lips of her pussy. The slave jumped, but her hands kept massaging her breast. The scars around her clitoris and bottom told that she was not a stranger to this, she was still waiting.

"Oh you are a fucking bitch. I knew you would like that," Elizabeth moaned, enjoying the pain being inflicted. Her male tool flexed, rising in anxious need to plunge into the meaty pink flesh of this toy.

The woman looked at her with wild aroused eyes and licked her lips at the visual excitement of her tormentor.

"Not today pet, not today." Liz responded as if reading her mind. "Today and for no more todays after this, you belong to them, my faithful pets," she whispered. Grabbing a tray of acupuncture needles, she began masterfully slipping them into the woman's body. Again, the slave clenched her teeth but a smile as eerie as it was evil plastered itself on her thin lips. Her head swung from side to side in an attempt to bear the pain for she wanted more, all that was to come.

Cleo gave the signal and the women were on their knees, dog collars placed around their necks and chained to the stone beds. Liz snapped her fingers and almost as suddenly the dogs became excited, sexually aroused, their pink dicks hung from beneath their bellies and their panting became heavy and excited. The pinkish red and bloodied pussy of the Russian girl sent the first dog into carnal frenzy. He stood on the table and began licking the flow from the Russian girls' ass and legs. She and the African woman turned onto their hands and knees. Animal instincts taking over, he climbed on the table and mounted her. The other dog followed suit and soon there were feverish cries of pain and pleasure blended into one.

The whip from Elizabeth's snake head lashed their backs, faces, legs and ankles, where ever there was a space of human flesh. They screamed for mercy they did not want, their orgasms sending the dog's senses on overload and causing them howl as their paws scratched into the stone beds trying to maintain their balance.

Cathalina gently massaged the tattoo on her right shoulder, below her collarbone. It was a Brown Recluse Spider, one she could handle and pet. It was a symbol of the spider each woman became bounded as each surrendered to the same ritual that Serena must now endure. The smells of sex excited her and her pussy was becoming wet.

She stood close to Serena, whose black transparent garment clung to her shapely body. Catalina's hand found its way to her spine and like a spider's spindly legs dancing across its web, her fingers began tingling the sensory nerves of Serena's raw flesh.

This is to be a very delicate process, because if not done correctly, the poison of the Brazilian Wandering, the spider they would use tonight, could kill their queen. They needed to be quick; they had already prepared her anti-venom serum.

"Come now Serena, its time to be baptized," Cathalina

whispered, taking her hand and leading her into their midst. Behind glass cages in the four corners of the room were four of the most venomous insects in the world. Each cage was outfitted as that creature's natural habitat.

To the east of the room was the Black Widow, who spun her chaotic web without design. Hundreds hung upside down on their webs. The males, smaller and without adornment, hid under leaves, waiting their time to attempt to mate. In doing so, most would be killed by their mate.

To the west and north of the room were cages of the Brown Recluse and the Brazilian Wandering Spider. These two spin no web, they liked to hunt, feed and breed in the dark. Loners, they hid from wandering eyes on the forest floor.

To the south were the scorpions. They had no master yet and were restless to be apart of the festivities. But their anti-venom serum was being prepared for the one who would be marked with the sign of the scorpion. Cathalina began aggressively and passionately kissing Serena. That drew deadly stares from Cleopatra, but there was nothing she could do. She wasn't even a true spider and in a few moments, all going well, Serena would be anointed spider queen. Cleo thought she best remain respectful. There was no loyalty against thieves, Cleo thought, "or in this case, spiders," she whispered under her breath.

"Don't be afraid Serena; I won't let anything to happen to you. I would die first," Cathalina vowed. Serena was taken between the stone beds and chained between the women. Her legs were pulled apart for oral tantalization during the baptism. Elizabeth nervously toyed with a nest of black widows, rubbing their legs to calm them.

Cleo walked to a small refrigerator and pulled a small jar from it. In the clear bottle were white liquid, sticky and gooey, and a large hypodermic needle. The painful looking thing was the only thing to inject enough of the serum in their queen, and act fast enough to counter act the poison about to be injected into her.

Jason was called in. Glancing around, he mourned for the woman who had destroyed him as a man, lamented without sound that his only crime was to love her too much. He was too pushy, should have left her alone when she refused to date him the first time. But six months of arrogant courting got him exactly what he wanted in a way he never imagined.

He was made to kneel between her thighs and touch her in that familiar way that quelled her trembling legs. Silent tears ran down her face and she channeled her negative thoughts and the hate in her body as she was taught to help repel the spider's poison.

"I am right here Serena," Cathalina moaned in her ear, her warm breath causing Serena's nipples to stiffen. Cleo handed the anti-serum to Cathalina and a jar containing a Brazilian Wandering to Elizabeth, then stood on opposite sides of Serena, in between the two women who lay on the stoned beds. They too would face the pain that Serena took. She must not scream alone.

Jason was afraid for her, and did his bidding as best he could under the circumstances. He gently kissed her inner thigh, allowing his tongue to soothe her. Cathalina removed Serena's scanty robe and allowed it to hang on her arms clearing away any barriers so that Jason can perform his task of ecstasy. She kissed her bare shoulders softly, allowing the warmth of her lips to send shudders of desires through Serena's body while she carefully blindfolded her.
One snap of Elizabeth's fingers and the wolf dogs dismounted their willing lovers. Before they were able to gather their thoughts, Cleo and Elizabeth opened the jars of spiders and

dumped the onto the sweaty women's bodies. They squirmed in astonishment and excitement as the spiders plunged their fangs into their flesh.

Their screams were beyond description, their pain echoing around the room. The spiders seemed to be melting into them.

As the screams burned their ears and Jason's tongue melted between Serena's thighs, Cathalina careful not to get bitten herself released the Brazilian Wandering Spider onto Serena's shoulder. Serena was on the verge of orgasm and Jason held her fast as her legs began to vibrate and her body shuddered from the convulsive eruptions of pleasure.

The spider wasted no timeand just as her sighs and moans of pleasure peaked in orgasm and she screamed Jason's name, the spider's fangs found the sweet taste of her flesh, stinging her for as long as she shook.

Serena's eyes rolled back in her head. It was hard for Cathalina to snatch the spider from Serena's shoulder because she was shaking so hard, both from the orgasm and the pain of the bite, and she didn't want to yank it and leave fangs in Serena's flesh. If the spider was left on even a fraction of a second too long the bite could be deadly.
Cathalina carefully reached for the spider's back, urging it to return to its jar with a gentle push. Jason held onto Serena's weak body as Cleo, Liz and Cathalina hustled to release the restraints from her hands and legs. Women on the tables had passed out. They were carelessly shoved to the side and Jason was told to throw them into the spiders' lair. The spiders clung to the comatose bodies of the women, who had succumbed to the spiders' attack. There would be no serum for them.

Jason opened the cages and threw their bodies in.
"Quickly," Cathalina said. "Give me the anti-serum."

Her voice cracked with fear, her eyes were wide open with terror and hope. Cleopatra picked up the needle after it fell from Cathalina's hands. All were afraid they might not save Serena.
"Cleo move faster for crying out loud!" Cathalina's eyes were huge with fear.
"Here," Cleo said, taking the sheath off the needle and squirting a small amount from the tip to test it.
"Elizabeth, hold her hands. You're stronger than us both," Cathalina demanded. Jason looked at the all in disbelief.
"These bitches are crazy," he thought. But all he could do was to stand by helplessly.
Serena began foaming at the mouth and puking almost as soon as the serum was administered. She passed out soon after.
"Take her up to her room and clean her up. Make sure she is comfortable and stay with her until I return," Cathalina told Jason, and he wasted no time. Again, he effortlessly scooped Serena into his arms and rushed out of their underground lair. The place was now foul with the smell of sex, bodily aromas, urine and feces and he wanted to take Serena away from it all.
Cathalina, Cleopatra and Elizabeth worked fast, cleaning the room until it sparkled, as if nothing had happened there. It was now the wee hours of Saturday and dawn was upon them. It was time to be transformed back into harmless women of everyday society and put the Man Killers they had become behind them for this night.

## MAN KILLER 4

"How is she?" Cathalina asked Jason, who left Serena's side only to go to the bathroom and wet the warm wash cloth he used to wipe away her sweat.

"She had a fever all night," he growled.

"Leave us," Cathalina told him.

Jason stood slowly, not really wanting to go but knowing the wraith Serena would visit upon him if he didn't obey Cathalina. His hesitation angered her and she began to fume, her eyes narrowing to a slit and her hands balled into fists. She had no idea why Serena tolerated this useless man, though it was Cathalina who saved his life when in a fit of rage Serena grabbed a butcher knife and sliced his penis off like it was Swiss cheese.

He was connected to her somehow, Cath though.

"I must find a way to be rid of him," she thought.

"I said, get out!" Cathalina yelled. This time, Jason did not hesitate. He placed the wash cloth on the nightstand next to Serena and backed out of the room, not only because that's the way Serena preferred it, but he knew to turn his back on a spider like Cathalina could be deadly.

Once he was gone, Cathalina took off her clothes and got in bed beside Serena. She had to survive. She was running a high fever and tossed and turned. Taking some home made herb concoction that she solicited from a doctor friend; she opened Serena's mouth and gently put a spoonful of the sweet liquid on her tongue. She continued this routine until midnight, when Serena's fever broke.

As Serena snored lightly in peaceful slumber, Cathalina left, content that their mission was successful and the Spider Queen, Serena Kowtow will reign with such horror and vengeance that it would leave heads spinning. Serena was greeted with breakfast in bed. Jason had gotten up and prepared it a little earlier than usual. He knew she should be starved as she had been sleeping since their Friday night ritual.

"Good morning madam," Jason smiled brightly, happy to see Serena awake. She was so beautiful. She was standing naked at the window that gave her a panoramic view of her estate. He basked in the almost orange glow of her complexion and fell silent as he was reminded that he could never make love to her the way a man and woman was meant to. He felt the tingle in his groin that he had become familiar with, a tingle that would have sent his once proud manhood on the rise.

He allowed his eyes to drink in how exquisitely created she was and permitted his eyes to linger on the sight that was not there before; her spider mark. He could see the scar on her left shoulder, or what seemed like a scar, a webbed design created from her flesh leading above her shoulder blade and disappearing below.

He walked slowly to her, cautiously, so he could get a closer look. His breath caught in his throat as he neared her and stood by her side. The mark of the spider was more than a web; it was raised as though a spider lived beneath her skin. Five inches in length, it was as real as if he was looking at one crawling across the floor. Serena turned to look at him and smiled.

"Hey there," she said warmly, "guess I had a close call eh?" She said it unemotionally, as though her life hanging in the balance was as routine as night turning into day.

"Yes my love, I was concerned," he told her honestly and let his gaze drop to the floor.

"Well now you see that your worries were unwarranted," she said matter of factly. "I am as fit as a fiddle and feeling better than I have in years." She grinned, her smile warming him as she took his chin within her hands and lifted it to her eyes. Before he realized what was happening, she kissed him softly, lovingly on his lips.

This was the reason he fell in love with her.

Serena ate and took a long bath, aided by Jason as she relished in his re-count of the weekend. She mused as she took the soapy sponge and lovingly caressed the image of what she had now become. To her surprise the skin pulsated on her shoulder. It seemed impossible, but she could swear that the thing was inside of her. She could feel its life and its soul surging through her.

"Hello?" Serena jumped to answer the phone. She caught it on the fifth ring and was glad that she did.

"Darling!" said the voice.

"Cathalina," she shrieked with excitement. "Where are you? I thought you would be here."

Cathalina began to laugh.

"I am actually treating myself to a late brunch on the beach," Cath said.

Serena sighed disappointedly.

"I wanted to make sure you got your rest," Cathalina continued.

"But you know that I would have loved to join you," Serena pouted.

"But you were ill and no doubt only got out of bed a few hours ago. Besides, I know Jason has told you that I was there. You know I would never leave you."

Serena relaxed. She took a seat on the bed, still naked.

"When will I see you?" Serena asked. "I'm sure there is much work to be done."

"Yes, we need to do a little cleaning in your spare room. There're things there we need to dispose of." Serena knew what, better yet, whom she was taking about.

"Yes I understand. When do you think?" She asked again, still unsure of the way of the spiders and their routine.

"Take today and rest my queen, tomorrow is Monday and there is much to be done. The team will meet on Wednesday. Do you work tomorrow?"

"I just told Jason to check my schedule; I think I only appear twice this week for some routine hearings," Serena said. "But I can confirm that later today."

"Sounds wonderful. So we will meet on Wednesday again. Get some rest and let the spider acquaint herself to you," Cathalina said. Just the mention caused Serena's tattoo to pulsate. Her mind already swimming with thoughts of anger and anxiety, and an uncontrollable thought lingering like a whisper: "Attack!"

"Okay," Serena said, barely audibly. "I will rest and wait. Somehow I feel a little out of place, like my body is no longer mine and I'm a guest in my own skin." Serena shook off the brief fear that she might indeed be in for more than she bargained for. "I think your idea to relax is a good one."

"Well then, my lady, I bid you good day! I am excited about our new destiny," Cathalina said. She couldn't believe they had done it. They all had a close encounter with death when they were injected with the deadly poison of their chosen specimen. They were chosen to join the group because of their anger, fear and bloodline. All the ingredients had to be present, like they were in Lara Lopez. Now she only had to agree.

"I'll talk to you soon Cath," Serena's said, cutting through her thoughts. "Bye now."

Cathalina hung up the phone.

## MAN KILLER 5

"You need to stop shutting down. This is only going to hinder your progress," Cathalina said. "You need to let it out, let yourself feel the anger and distress you feel, allow the torment to consume you. It's the only way you will be able to let go. The only way you will know the power within you." But Lara was afraid. Whenever she felt herself on the verge of boiling over she would stop and collect herself. The calm that she had exacted over the past fifteen years of her life would overpower the hatred. Her passive aggressive behavior had become her way to deal with the pain, giving her a moment, a small space where she could seek peace.

But this was not good in Cathalina's eyes. She wanted Lara to grow angry, to let the hatred that seethed within her soul to guide her. But most importantly, Cathalina wanted her to discover the power of control and when to unleash the wrath of her pain.

"I am a slut, doctor. That's what everyone calls me just because I like to express myself, just because I take advantage of the opportunity, the only time I am not afraid to have someone look at me, at my body. Why is it that a man can do this? Screw around with ten women at the same time; claim to love each for what they bring, and its okay. But then a woman does it and she is a whore?" Lara asked.

"It's hypocrisy," Cathalina responded with the same serenity. "Just because they have a dick between their legs does not give them divine right to pussy. Women like you even the field, and that scares them. The whole proper image, the whole philosophy that they teach baby girls about keeping our legs closed for that one man. That's for them, not us."

"In all honestly Dr. Shekhar, is there a way to fix this? To fix me? I don't want to be like this anymore. I cannot help but want sex. The very thought of a man sticking his tongue or cock up into my pussy is all it takes to make me excited. I love the feel of every opening in my body filled; I love two, three or even four dicks in men at the same time. Does this make me a nymphomaniac like they say?"

"You have got to stop beating yourself up. Embrace who you are!" Cathalina was excited. Lara was almost ready to join the team.

"It is not your fault that you were raised by two women who loved each other and who fucked each other. Not your fault that you met your gay father on his deathbed as he was being sucked dry from AIDS. It's not your fault that you love men."

She paused to let the words to sink into Lara's head. She wanted her to find a loophole. It was obvious that the patient did not want to stop, she wanted permission to be who she was, to continue to do as she wanted, and Cathalina wanted to give her that freedom, give her that space and free her sexuality, rid her of her one and only inhibition, the restraints of society, the box that the world tries to paint women in to. Fuck conformity, Cathalina thought.

"In my heart, I know you're right," Lara said. The tears flowed slowly down Lara's face, and she took her hands and ran them through her closely chopped head of hair.

"But..."

"But nothing." Cathalina reached for her hand. The touch sent a shiver through Lara. She sensed a power about

Cath she could not describe.

"But," she continued, placing her other hand on top of Cathalina's, "I cannot get over this dirty feeling I get every time I have sex with these men. I know they are only using me. They look at me with disgust until they need to get laid again. Then I am their first choice. If only I could change that."

"Snap out of it woman." Cathalina barked, pulling her hands away. Her voice was stern but her face remained soft. "Don't you know the power within yourself? You should snap a man's neck who dares to disrespect you." She saw the look of confusion on Lara's face and tried to rephrase her statement.

"They wanted to be intimate with you as much as you wanted it right? Did you force them?"

"Of course not," Lara replied.

"Then why should you feel scorn? You are not asking for payment for your services. You deserve respect. They empty themselves inside you and then you are suddenly not good enough?" Cathalina stood now, pacing. She moved to her desk and touched a door to reveal several buttons. Cathalina pressed one and could hear the light hum of the massager beneath the carpet purring, rippling under their feet, pulling the tension from their bodies.

She could tell the session was taking a lot out of Lara. She needed to move fast while she was still angry.

"This is nice Doctor Shekhar," Lara complimented, getting up and walking to the huge widow. With the plush white carpet pulsating under her feet and the calm, greenish-blue water out yonder, Lara was starting to make sense of it all.

Looking at her watch, Cathalina realized that their hour was up. She wanted to keep going, but she didn't want to scare the woman off. They had been meeting for more than six months and she felt she knew her pretty well, Lara came to Florida illegally like many of the Cubans and Puerto Ricans in South Miami. Like others she was able to blend in because of the huge population that made their home there. She had quickly got involved in orgies, group sex she thought she wanted. She liked the sex where one man would move from partner to partner, she would spread her legs wide invitingly like all the other women in the room.

She remembered this as she walked to the waiting area of Doctor Shekhar's office, crossing her legs primly as she sat to slide her open heel and toe slippers. She shook her head and squeezed her eyes shut at the memory of hanging out with a guy she thought she liked, a guy that she had planned to have sex with because she actually liked him. But before she knew it, he had friends over, all guys and one by one; they took turns plunging their dicks inside of her. Did one of them ask her permission? Did even one refused to fuck the creamy moisture that she felt compelled to make available? Did they care? No they didn't

All the guys she really wanted, the ones she really liked, just used and took advantage of her. It had happened two nights ago, when she was the guest piece in a threesome.

Cathalina watched as Lara left her office. She knew she had pushed it but she hoped that she had gotten her point across. Lara was needed to complete their circle, and to do that she had to accept the blessings of the scorpion.. She will take the will and respect from those who took it from her. She will avenge her sisters and brothers who had their voice and choice taken from them. She was the one.

Lara tried to contain her anger as she walked to her beat up 1988 Mazda 626. She hated the way her rage would just come on her as easily as the rising moon and consume her like the sun at high noon.

# MAN KILLER

She opened the car door hard and slammed it shut behind her. She sat at the wheel starring at Dr. Shekhar's office building.

"I hate this shit. I wish she could help me already," she murmured through clenched teeth. "Two more weeks and I am out of here. If she can't help me, then I will help myself." Even as she put the key in the ignition she couldn't stop the memories from invading her mind. She thought back to that gang rape, the day that guy and his friends ran a train on her. Even to say his name shot her temperature up.

Her drive home was reckless and unfocused. She sped down the Palmetto Expressway to Hialeah Gardens like a racetrack driver or someone in a video game. She turned the radio on to see if she could drown out the dangerous thoughts in her mind.

"No, if I killed him then I would be locked up. That's not practical," she said. "But then again, maybe I need to be locked out. That fucking Mariposa! Maybe I need to get people like him off the streets."

Lara snickered uncontrollably as she sped down the highway. Her beat up car with the loud muffler and old engine that was always over heating surprised her this day. Her car took on the challenge, like it was fueled by the hatred in her heart, and sped steadily home.

The twenty minutes it took for her to drive home was not enough to quell her seething rage. Lara tried to use the techniques that Cathalina had taught her, to breathe, relax, and think of a time and place that brought her serenity. But today that would not work. Today she needed something more and she did not know what that was.

"Hey Lara," a man in his late twenties called to her. She had seen him around plenty and he had made it obvious that he was interested and admired her beautifully sculpted physique. At first Lara tried to pretend she didn't see him, lowering her eyes as she placed her car into her parking spot in the apartment complex where she lived.

She could see the pool. She was fortunate that her apartment balcony gave a good view of the pool and recreation area. Looking at the still water always offered her some peace. But today it failed.

Buried in her thoughts, she forgot her greeter. Turning to open her door she stood face to face with the six-foot tall, muscular, gorgeous man.

"Are you okay?" He asked as she stepped out of the car.

"Yes of course. Why do you ask?" she stuttered slightly and maneuvered her way past his hard flesh. She felt her nipples hardened involuntarily and she silently cursed the natural reactions of her body.

"I know we have only seen each other in passing, but I was hoping to change that by asking you out to dinner," he said. Lara just looked at him, studying the movements of his mouth, the way his wavy black hair curled into his face, the mellow spell that allowed his eyes to soften as his greenish blue pupils hypnotized her. His even white teeth seemed to casually bite and tuck at his lower lip. His tawny complexion blended into his body as he made subtle movements to flex his muscles as he spoke.

She listened with more than her ears. She had become accustomed to do this with men, listening to what they are really saying, which is lets just drop the formalities and get to fucking.

She smiled. She knew her over active imagination was getting the better of her, but more often than not she was right about what men wanted from her.

"I don't think that's a good idea, huh…" She didn't

know his name, and at that moment she realized that he had called her by her name before he came over. How did he know it? She wondered before the sound of his voice broke through her thoughts.

"Leslie," he finished for her, "Leslie Thomason at your service." He took her hand as he said it, and without his eyes leaving hers he kissed the back of her hand.

"I am really not in a going out mood."

"It doesn't have to be today," he said. He was quick to offer a way out but to leave the backdoor open. "It could be tomorrow, next week or even next month. There really isn't a rush."

He flashed her a devilishly handsome smile, watching her weaken.

"I'm sure there will be a day when you wouldn't mind some company."
He meant to drive his play home, but his insistence just added speed to Lara's legs. She squirmed around him and entered the apartment as fast as she could.

Leslie looked after her helplessly. He was about to feel rejected, but his ego kicked in. Never had he been denied the sweet juices of a woman he craved. So he let her go, knowing that she would not be the first to break his record.

Lara opened her door quickly and just as she closed it felt the deadly rage sweep over her. She felt in control again, blocking out the evils of the outside world. She leaned her petite frame against the door to her apartment and looked around.

She could feel her palms becoming sweaty even though she maintained her outward composure, her eyes were glowing with pure rage. She looked around her one bedroom apartment. Her eyes searched the kitchen. She looked from the bar table to the kitchen cabinets. Walking through the dimly lit living room and feeling the rigid gray carpet below her feet, she clenched and unclenched her hands and fists. Tears ran down her face as she made it to the bedroom door, walked to the bed and laid across it on her stomach.

She closed her eyes then, and suddenly felt the loving snuggle of her cat Peter nestled against her cheek, his tail swooning over her head and his gentle purr urging her to wake and pet him. Her eyes shot open like bullets and her mind vaguely remembered or recognized her pet. She knew he belonged to her, she felt that she cared for this animal, but the inner urges to hurt and to destroy overwhelmed her. She took the creamy gray color cat into her arms. The more she touched him the more he purred.

His excitement irked her.

Rolling onto her back then sitting up, she looked as he relished in her touch. She struggled to find the sensibility she knew was in her, the reason. But as her hands stroked the animal's head and landed on his neck, all she remembered was that he was male, and like all males he was interrupting her peace, her time. Demanding attention to have their needs met.

A smile crept across her face as she snapped the cat's neck in one quick motion.

She held him up and looked into his eyes as they went blank. She felt a thrill that she had never known. It was as though she was starving and was given her favorite food. Her elation transcended all the orgasms and pleasure she had ever experienced.

Lara allowed herself to lie back on the bed, taking her treasured pussy with her. She stroked the body as it lay on her chest. Though this time, it didn't purr, she felt her body come alive in the most unlikely of places. She felt the tingle in her toes rising up her calves and into her thighs. She felt her body shudder and tremble and she grabbed a hold of the bed as though there was an earthquake beneath her.

    She felt the moisture between her legs and her wetness seemed to flush out of her. She could not control the explosion that followed, grabbing her and throwing her legs open. A breeze hit her clit and she moaned a loud. Her nipples hardened and she grabbed them, kneaded and massaged them. She felt her groin thrust and gyrate as the swelling within her vaginal muscles exploded. She became possessed, aching and gyrating as she never did in a man's arms.
Her anger had given birth to a sexual satisfaction she had never known.

**********

    Leslie Thomason had a date. He watched Lara to run off to her apartment, but he was not concerned. Not only was he convinced that she liked him and was playing hard to get, but he lived in her apartment complex. How difficult could that possibly be and how much longer could she possibly resist? Not much by his calculations. So he continued, admiring himself in the mirror of his Indigo blue convertible PT Cruiser. He had been thinking of Lara a lot lately. Her body called out to him.

    Speeding out of the parking lot, Leslie glanced at Lara's second floor apartment window and imagined what he could do with that woman before jumping on I-95 to North Miami Beach where he was meeting the girl he had danced with all night the night before. He planned to take her to the café outside of the mall so she couldn't get distracted and then return home with her.

## MAN KILLER 6

As soon as Lara was gone, Cathalina picked up the phone and dialed Cleo's number. She wanted to tell her that she thought that Lara was almost ready. She knew Cleo would be happy to hear that. But there was another reason why she didn't want to see Cleo right now. Being with her would bring back stuff she didn't want to dig up, but them spending time together was something she could not ignore or avoid.

Cleo sat in the Empress room in the Dungeon in a miserable mood. She couldn't get over how this whole situation made her feel. She couldn't help the feeling of wanting to kill Serena, to get rid of her. Adding her to their team was supposed to make them stronger. Adding someone of Serena's status was a blessing; after all, she had just kind of fallen in their laps.

But all Serena had done so far was disrupt the relationship Cleo knew she would have had with Cathalina had Serena not come into the picture. Cleopatra, Madame, Empress of Sex Cell, was the center of everything first.

Now her anger grew and boiled not only for torturing men, but also for Serena Kowtow. Cleo sat back into her leopard print recliner and looked about her special recluse. The hammock that hung from the ceiling brought back many memories. She shook her head at the many broken handcuffs hung as memorabilia around the room.

Cleo closed her eyes as she thought back to the many murders that she and Cathalina had pulled off without a hitch, all the disappearances and half eaten victims found in the everglades, the work of her beloved crocodiles. That's how she knew she wanted to be branded with the image of the dinosaur.

She smiled as she remembered how the brutal deaths that were plastered across the Miami newspapers. She smiled at how the rush of the moment would consume her and the way she and Cathalina would release each other's tension, violently sucking the juice out of each other's pussies. She remembered wrapping her body around Cathalina, who sucked and licked her breasts until Cleo had a full orgasm.

Now she felt lucky if she could get Cathalina to smile at her.

A knock on the door jolted her from her thoughts. Her caramel brown skin burnt bright red from the in rage for the disruption. The girls knew not to interrupt her when she was in her private quarters.

"What is it?" she demanded.

"It's me, Madame. Natalia."

Natalia was her favorite girl. She brought in the most customers, all usually high profile clients. Besides, she had a talent for using her body that most women never master. Cleo herself had fallen for Natalia's juicy fruit.

"What is it Natalia?" Cleo asked, softening her voice some but no less angry.

"Cathalina is on the phone." Natalia said. She and everyone knew how Cleo felt about Cathalina even if she had never said a word about it.

"What line?"

"Ten."

"Thanks Natalia. You have customers?"

"Yes I do. I'm on my way to get into costume for Trump Dupree." She giggled openly and Cleo couldn't help but laugh too. Everyone knew the tycoon who would fly down from New York and visit with Natalia. They enjoyed his tips even more, so they accommodated him even if he was not scheduled.

"Go do our thing Natalia." Cleo urged happily as she picked up the phone. She wished all her girls were like Natalia. She enjoyed what she did, would even occasionally take a good dick as payment over dollars. There was only one other who was better than Natalia. But she was not all female. Cleo took a deep breath before picking up the line. She wondered why Cathalina didn't call her private line directly. Maybe she was hoping to get the voicemail instead of me, she thought.

"Hello Cathalina. Did you miss me already?" She joked half heartedly, really wanting to know the answer but not willing to push Cathalina.

"Hello sweetheart. How is business today?"

"Awesome, just sitting here waiting for our next move," Cleo chuckled and wondered what Cathalina was getting at. "Cathalina, why didn't you call my private line?" she asked before she could stop herself.

"Didn't I?" Cathalina smirked, trying not to let her mirth drift through the phone lines. "I didn't realize that I didn't call your personal line. I was just in a hurry to talk to you."

"So, here I am. What's the great news?"

"I think it's almost time to make our move on Lara," Cath said almost in a whisper. "Her anger is at peak levels and I think she would be receptive to the mark."

"Are you sure?"

"A few more weeks and she will complete the circle."

"So we must prepare then. We must meet and decide on our initiation process for the one who must bear the mark of the Scorpion."

Cleo knew that this had to be done. She loved the sisterhood they shared in their hatred and vengeance, though in a way they held no other loyalty for each other than to protect their secrets. She wouldn't trade those secrets for anything. The taste of blood, pain and anguish pleased her most. She wished she could please and make her her own.

"That's an excellent idea. Have you spoken to Elizabeth? I think she was supposed to be out of town. She's starring in that play A Woman's Wrath in Atlanta. Being an actress keeps her busy." There was something special about Liz that Cathalina liked, special beyond her physical attributes and unique contributions to their team. Not only was Liz a hermaphrodite with a fully functioning penis, unlike most hermaphrodites her vagina was also fully developed.

Elizabeth was a woman true and through. She was sexy and curvaceous. She was slender with silky olive skin and a mixture of jet black hair that was intermittently curly and straight that hung down her back, tapering off into the crack of her ass. She was stunning, with high cheekbones and slanted eyes with pupils as black as her hair.

"No I haven't heard from her, but you know how Liz can be. She is an artist. She likes her space and her privacy. She will come to us when she needs us I suppose."
Or when we need her. Cleo thought.

"Yes, I guess you are right." Cathalina said. Elizabeth had always been the quieter of the threesome. She was their first recruit and her methods and daring bordered on crazy. It was getting late and Cathalina didn't really want to, but decided to spend some quiet time with Cleo anyway. Still she cringed when she heard herself make the offer.

"So what are you up to for the rest of the evening here in Miami where the possibilities are endless?" she said, willing her voice to sound flirtatious.

Cleo thought for a second, holding her breath. It had been more than six months since she and Cathalina spent some time alone. Most of their recent time had been spent planning and punishing those who deserved punishment. She was afraid to dare to hope for alone time.

"I am as free as free can be, Cathalina. Why? Did you have something in mind?" Cathalina chuckled.

"Well, actually I was hoping that maybe we could go and grab a bite. I haven't eaten, and maybe we can do some catching up," she said.

"Sounds inviting," Cleo said, not entirely taking the sarcasm out of her voice. "Name the time and place."

Cathalina thought for a moment about the most public place she could find and where they could probably find some action. But she couldn't think of anything.

"You pick. I can't think right now for the life of me."

"I know just the place," Cathalina said. "Meet me here and I'll take it from there."

"Okay, I'll see you in a few minutes then."

Cathalina exhaled and hung up the phone. No use in prolonging the inevitable. She knew that Cleo would not let it just drop there. Something had to give in their relationship. If she wanted to pacify Cleo she was going to have to present her with a peace offering.

Cathalina tried to keep the conversation to a minimum as they sped to the Aventura Mall in North Miami, even as she blasted the latest Matchbox Twenty CD and sang along.

"I'm not crazy, I'm just a little impaired I know, right now you don't care."

⊕

Cleopatra looked at her weirdly but appreciatively. Music was one thing they had always had in common. Cleo had picked up the CD on Saturday, the day after Serena's initiation. She had not known til now that Cathalina had also bought it. She loved the way Cathalina drove, speeding down I-95 in a car that was made to go, and allowing the music to seer her soul while enjoying the presence of her secret love. The mall parking lot was huge and gorgeous, the plants and trees in the surrounding neighborhood adding to the beauty of the place. Cleopatra was glad this is where they were. She was ready for an anything goes kind of moment and if the mood struck and Cathalina decided to give her a taste of that memory she would take it, would enjoy her here. This was Miami, Florida and anything was possible.

    Cathalina cruised into a spot near the front of the lot. There were special parking for handicapped, so Cathalina reached for her medical parking sticker and flipped it on the dashboard. Cleopatra watched the sleekness of her movements and the way Cathalina's skirt hiked up her beautiful long brown thighs. Her mouth watered and she allowed her hand to accidentally slide down the length of Cathalina's leg as she reached for her purse.

    Cathalina looked at her and smiled knowingly. Not wanting to shoot Cleopatra down, she reached for her hand and gently fondled her fingers, allowing her caress to linger and then creep up Cleopatra's forearm. Cleo shuddered and trembled. Just the thought of what it might be like to bury her face between Cathalina's thighs again had her juicy fruit melting into a watery existence.

    "Com'on hot stuff. Let's go eat. I am starving." Cathalina broke the trance, smiling at her reassuringly. Her eyes twinkled with promise that Cleo hoped would be realized that night.

"Hum! Smell the ocean and the feel of the breeze. It's a beautiful night, Cathalina. Thanks for inviting me."

"Now who else would I enjoy a night like this with, if not with my partner in crime?" Cathalina laughed out loud.

"No pun intended." She winked. Giving Cleopatra a playful shove, she took a long stride towards the restaurant.

Cleo bubbled with joy, thinking possibilities and taking quick sidelong glances at Cathalina. Her heart would drum as she accidentally brushed Cath's arm or fondled her fingers as they walked. Cleo sashayed her voluptuous body and felt her thighs rain the sweet juices of an excited woman. Anticipation filled her and held her body captive in a way that she didn't want to end. She sighed as they neared the popular pasta eatery that was nestled in a tunnel of peaceful plants and palm trees. It was directly outside a crowded movie theatre and was the place where kids and adults gathered to get their groove on while they waited for their movie.

Cleo noticed that there was a man hustling a young woman hard. His hands were everywhere, his feet playing footsie. The girl, seemingly shy and timid, tried fruitlessly to fight him off.

Cleo watched as he reached for her shirt and unbuttoned the top with one easy snap of his nimble fingers. His index finger trailed down the center of her chest to her bubbling cleavage. She heard Cathalina rambling on about Lara who Cleo desperately wanted to be ready for the team. But her interest laid elsewhere.

Her sexual desires heightened and she began to breathe hard. She was hot for someone of her own and she felt the young girl's repulsion for the vulture that would not stop touching her.

Their pace slowed when Cathalina realized the source of Cleo's distraction. Both found themselves being led in the direction of the couple. Glancing quickly around the diner, they saw waiters and waitresses flirting shamelessly for tips and women and men engage each other in tireless persuasion for that well sorted after sexual release. The voices mingled into noise and the crocodile plastered on her back began to breathe. Cathalina took Cleo's hand and squeezed it tight, sensing the urges that were building within her.

"It's okay Cleopatra. Let's go eat." She urged and gently pulled her as the waitress led them to their seat. The voices became louder and clustered together in Cleo's ears, a high-pitched frequency that she just couldn't stand. She wanted to go over there and snatch the soul from the boy's body and suffocate it.

"Okay," Cleo said. "But please let's sit somewhere where I can keep my eyes on him."

The crocodile on her back dug the claws of his feet deep into her flesh. The open back tank top she wore was a visible display of her internal anguish. She wanted to hurt this man and the crocodile wanted it too.

"Are you okay?" Cathalina asked, bidding Cleo to sit at the table where the hostess had led them. She noticed the grimace on Cleo's face and became concerned. "Maybe it's a better idea for us to leave, Cleo. I don't think this is a good time to take on anything." But Cleo was already too far gone. Her mind was made up. She wanted to get involved; she was already involved.

"We are already here Cath," she smiled calmly, using Cathalina's nickname reserved only for Serena. "We'll have a nice quiet dinner as planned."

But Cathalina knew the night was on whether she wanted it to be or not. And whatever happened or was about to happen, had to be done right.

"Can we have a couple glasses of Chardonnay to start

please?" Cathalina smiled warmly at the server, a tall white boy with blonde brownish hair. He couldn't be older than twenty-one years old. They watched as he walked away and then simultaneously their eyes went back to the couple.

The guy had gotten up and roughly grabbed the arm of the petite woman he was eating with. His hand moved from her arm to behind her neck and ruffling her neatly pinned hair that fell down to her shoulders. Cleo clenched her fists and held the edges of the table.

She stood tensely and watched as he led the girl out of the restaurant and towards the now dimly lit parking lot. They followed, with Cleo's hairs standing on edge. She checked the cars parked neatly in vertical rows to see if they had company. Cathalina tried to hold her at a distance; even as her spider, sensing d g the thrill of a hunt, writhed under her skin.

"Leslie, this is not at all necessary," they heard the young woman say. "I think you have had too much to drink." Leslie heard her, but the only thing he was thinking with was in his pants. He grunted and pulled her into him so close they seemed as one. She struggled against his body then went limp.

"Now that's better," Leslie said. "It would feel so much better if you relaxed.

Cleo was ready for action, but her companion held her back.

"Lets just walk up on them, he will let her go and this whole episode will be over," Cathalina said.

But at that moment, Leslie threw the woman face down on a Volvo. The space was dark and there were so many lovers in the throes of intimacy that no one bothered to interrupt the couple.

She began to whimper as he hoisted her skirt and pulled her panties to the side. He took his finger and gently rubbed it along side her clit and lips. He stood still for a moment, an electrical charge of anticipation flooding his already gorged penis in preparation for entrance. He took his fingers from between her legs and licked them, closing his eyes in pure ecstasy. He whispered something in her ear.

Cleo cocked her head in an attempt to listen, but he was speaking too low, too softly. Holding the girl down, he took his dick out of his pants and rubbed the tip against her opening. She moaned and he took that as permission. He slipped it in an inch and threw his head back from the pure pleasure of it. Without being able to control himself, he plunged himself deep within her and she screamed, throwing Cleo into action and Cathalina on her heels.

Before he knew what was happening, Cleo's 200 lbs was on him, beating him. For a second he saw a light flash before his eyes and thought that it was the excruciating gratification of what he was sampling between the legs of his unwilling lover.

But when it hit him that he was being attacked, he pushed off of his victim and began to swing wildly. Cleopatra's fist connected with his jaw and he staggered back. The frightened young woman who was being molested grabbed at her clothes and ran. Cleo called after her, but she just kept going and refused to stop.

A crowd gathered to watch as this beautiful faired skin woman twice the man's size pinned him by his neck to the same Volvo he had been using as a bed. Cathalina ran back and pulled Cleo off of the man.

Cathalina managed to get her off of him and through the crowd before the police got involved. She shoved Cleo in her very high profile and noticeably unique car and sped off before things got anymore out of hand.

"What did you do that for bitch?" Cleo shot at

Cathalina. The shock on Cathalina's face rendered her speechless. "I almost had that sonofabitch Cath!" she spewed anger from her very soul and Cathalina realized that this was more about Cleo than the situation.

She tried to contain her urge to respond in the same volatile manner.

"Cleo, you were out of control love. We try not to act in the way of the spider in public. I know that your nature is different. But we have to be careful. Did you see the crowd?" Cathalina asked her as gently as she could without raising her voice. Cleo was wiping her ringed fingers over her face, and her long black nails dug into her temple in frustration.

"This feels like an unfulfilled orgasm," Cleo laughed. She felt like a junkie needing a fix. But she wasn't joking. The thrill of the kill was always exciting. It brought with it a very special kind of satisfaction that could not be measured. If she were lucky to get "lucky" after such adrenaline rush, she would enjoy such bliss that dying at that movement would be worth it. She could only remember such a moment now. The very thought of that brought tears to Cleo's her eyes.

Cathalina, speeding down the I-95, noticed her friends' anguish and pulled over by the Fort Lauderdale airport and parked. That area at night was deserted and quiet, illuminated only by the runway lights on the other side of the fence.

Cathalina pulled onto the deserted grassy area and turned off the lights. Turning slowly, she looked at Cleo and reached for the hands that clutched her face.

"Cleo, you helped that girl. It was enough," she told her softly. Cleo only shook her head in disagreement. "Yes, you did. She got away and he will probably never do such a thing again."

"You are wrong Cathalina. He got away too. By the time I acted it was too late," Cleo mumbled under the hands that was now covering her face but were unable to stop the flow of tears. Cathalina removed her hands and wiped at the tears that had seared Cleo's flawless mascara.

"That was neither the time nor the place; we don't want to become hot again, not now while we are just fortifying our team," Cathalina said and reached to hug Cleo. Cleo grabbed her like a life vest, buried her face in the tattoo of Cathalina's spider and shuddered, crying angry tears.

"It's okay," Cathalina said and stroked Cleo's hair softly. She kissed her temple, then her forehead, her nose and her closed eyelids. She knew this was what Cleo needed, what she wanted most, the comfort of Cathalina's arms, and the softness of her touch. Cathalina thought about where things were obviously leading. She knew it would happen, but she didn't know how. She chuckled softly as Cleo pushed away from her shoulders and pressed her lips into hers. Hindsight was amusing to her.

"What is it?" Cleo asked blushing.

"It's been so long." Cathalina lied.

"I know. I've missed you Cathalina," she said before pressing her lips on Cathalina's again, forcefully leaning forward to touch Cathalina's lean body. She reached for Cathalina's head and pulled it deeper into her kiss, caressing her tongue and licking her teeth and gums. Cathalina moaned softly and deeply, relaxing her mind to what she knew she would not be able to resist tonight.

They shared the covenant of the Man Killer code; they bore the marks of animals that needed to be appeased.

She needed to make that sacrifice tonight for the greater good of her comrade, so she would.

"Cleo," Cathalina moaned, "you drive me crazy."

She allowed Cleo take full control of the moment. Pulling Cathalina across the gearshift and simultaneously releasing the seat so that it reclined back, Cleo had her right where she wanted her. She slipped her hand under Cathalina's skirt and found her panty-less soft cheeks already moist. Cleo's fingers sought out her clitoris, and with agile flickers she brought a soft sigh from Cathalina's lips.

"You missed me too didn't you baby?" Cleo asked. To hide the disgust on her face and in her voice Cathalina moaned. Yes, she was excited, but it was thinking of Serena that turned her on. She felt her abdomen quiver at the thought of Serena's tongue licking the life sources from her thighs and she trembled when Cleo's fingers masterfully and knowingly brought her to full orgasm. She clenched Cleo's back and bit into her shoulders so she wouldn't in her blissful delirium call out Serena's name.

Allowing her mind's eyes to guide her, Cathalina ripped open the tight knitted top that barely concealed Cleo's double 'D' bosom and buried her face between the soft mounds of her cleavage. She inhaled and started to cough but she forced it to come out as a muffled sound of pleasure. She allowed her hands to roam over Cleo's pierced belly button and allowed her face to follow, planting soft butterfly kisses as she went. Cleo was impatient to have her desires quenched. She pulled roughly on Cathalina's hair and pushed her to the triangle of hair that covered her garden of delight.

Forcing herself to continue and feeling an overwhelming sense of betrayal to Serena, Cath opened her mouth wide and attempted to suck the full womanhood of Cleo into her. She guided her tongue in between that delicate area of Cleo's ass and anus and skillfully licked the entrance of her womb. Feeling the shudders that had began as soft tremors though Cleo's body, Cathalina prepared herself for the exuberant wail that Cleo with give out when she came.. She licked and sucked and touched and fondled until she heard satisfaction crooned from Cleo's lips.

    Only Cleo was not faking it when she told Cathalina that she loved her, and that she didn't want to ever forget again the sweet touch of her body against her. Cathalina pressed her face deep into Cleo's belly and wept softly. She knew this was a dangerous connection. She felt a silent alarm warning her of what was to come.

## MAN KILLER 7

Lara awoke just after eleven and wrapped her arms around her body, still feeling the after effects of murdering her cat. She looked next to her on the bed where she lay and saw that the cat was still there. His tongue hung out of one side of his mouth.

The wetness between her legs caused her to squeeze her thighs tightly together and moan deeply, wanting to feel the swellings of a penis inside of her. She rocked herself in an unsuccessful attempt to comfort her body but she knew from past experience that only one thing could give her the comfort she really needed. A man.

Her mind ran wild through her little black book, wondering who she could call at this time of night to come to her aide. Most of the men she was intimate with had wives and girlfriends and were predisposed at that hour without previous planning. The urges sent a pang of sexual hunger through her and it shot her up from the bed.

She searched through her closet and found a red, lacy Fredericks Of Hollywood, feathered boa with crotchless matching underwear. She found a pair of white and red matching stiletto heels. She squealed with delight of the thought of dressing up and ran to the shower to get cleaned up.

"Who can I share all of this lusciousness with? Damn I am horny!" Lara said out loud as she stepped under the piping hot water and allowed it to wash away any guilt or concern for anything or anyone from her mind. She wanted her body to fully focus on the need that was boiling like a untamed volcano between her legs.

"I wonder if Mark is still hanging out with that bitch Pauline, or that slut Patrick for that matter," she mused to herself. "These two way niggahs are starting to get on my nerves." She lathered the soap all over her, lingering over her throbbing pussy.

Out of the shower, she rubbed the water from her body and looked around her small apartment. "Damn, I have more sexy lingerie than food," she said to herself. "You really are a bitch aren't ya?" She swayed towards her mirror, modeling the flimsy pieces of fabrics that she had just put on.

Thinking quickly back to earlier that after noon her mind lingered on the gorgeous creature that introduced himself to her as Leslie. He was scrumptious; she thought, the image of what might be hidden in his pants causing her to squeeze her legs together again.

"So you wanted some of this Mr. Leslie?" she asked the mirror in a seductive voice. She inhaled, trying to recapture the scent of him, trying to visualize the length of him. That brought on a second soaking that dripped from the crotchless panties. She quickly ran to the door and looked up and down the open corridors that overlooked the parking garage, the swimming pool and the main building with the rental office in it.

The complex was unique in its apartment designs, allowing for breath taking views from each apartment. She glanced at the clock on the wall that was now chiming midnight.

The lot was empty so she took the two flights down, still in her sexy lingerie, to where she parked and tried to survey the area where she thought he might be. Then she spotted the PT Cruiser. He had a PT cruiser earlier. Black convertible top and it looked like it could use a new paint job. Couldn't be more than a nineteen ninety-nine. A guy driving such a dump she usually wouldn't consider giving up the punani to, but desperate times called for desperate measures.

She hustled over, timidly at first and then in an urgent dash, stooping on the ground to check out the number underneath the car. It was marked 405 and she stood up, brushed off her knees and sighed a sigh of anticipated satisfaction.

"Apartment 405, I'm coming baby," and she began to laugh. "No pun intended." She sashayed her over heated body back to her apartment and ran to the bathroom, reaching for the washcloth and wiping the drool that was running down her thighs. She grabbed her favorite perfume, Obsession for women, and squirted a tad on all the vitals; her neck, her chest, belly button, inside of her thighs and behind her knees.

Still wearing nothing but boa feathers wrapped around her shoulders and feeling the heat permeating from her body, she was propelled to his door where she stood for a good five minutes before knocking.

Leslie lay in his bed thinking back to his incredible night. Who was that woman? His thoughts pressed into his mind, causing his head to hurt and his jaw to throb. His apartment was definitely a bachelor pad, boasting a black leather sofa and loveseat with getting busy red lights that colored the almost dark room. A big 64inch stand alone television, with all types of sport videos and DVDs to each side, shared space with porno movies stacked in the bottom. His refrigerator was loaded with liquor, beer, chips and dips. A jar of glow in the dark condoms sat on his nightstand.

He looked at the clock and saw that it was 12:30 a.m. and then looked at the door as the knock came for the second time. He looked at the clock again. Could it be that those crazy bitches followed me home? His curiosity got the better of him so he rose to go look through the peephole. As he neared the door he stopped and turned back towards the kitchen. He got a baseball bat that he kept hidden behind the kitchen door, just incase he had to defend himself.

"Holy Shit," Leslie said as he peeped through the peephole before opening the door. He tried to compose himself, willing his erection to subside, and attempted to conceal look of surprise on his face.

"I knew you would come around," smoothing out his wrinkled silk shirt.

"Yes, I came around," was all Lara said, smiling at him. He placed the baseball bat behind the door and opened his arms so that she knew she was welcomed to come inside.

"No."

"What do you mean no? You're the one who came knocking on my door at one in the morning." He was becoming agitated and his libido was rising again at the sight of this practically naked woman at his door. A woman he had fantasized about on more than one occasion.

"I meant, if you want me, take me. Right here," the words came out of her mouth, surprising her. Usually guys came onto her and she would give in. But to solicit a guy was a first for her. She felt this bold new energy consume her, as if she was being pushed by some unknown entity within her.

Leslie laughed and stepped to the doorway, reaching for her waist. As he stepped forward she saw that one of his eyes was partially closed and that his lip looked as though it was bleeding, but she ignored it, she had an urgent need to have the cavern between her legs filled and right now he had what she wanted to fill it with.

She let him pull her into his body and began to kiss

her neck and shoulder. She unbuttoned his pants and sought out what she craved. Grabbing his shaft in her hands she didn't have to do much before he was fully erect and ready for action. She lifted her legs around his waist, and thrusting her hips into his groin. She felt the tip of him pierce her. He groaned and moaned as he felt her guide him inside of her already soaking pussy. He grabbed a hold of her legs and braced himself against the door posts for balance

"Shit, oh fuck. Bitch your pussy is so fucking wet." He was excited and ready. Still, she took him by surprise. She didn't seem like the bold type. This was a pleasant surprise.

"Yes, I knew you would like this," she said. She heard the words coming out of her mouth but couldn't believe they were her words, her thoughts. She wrapped her legs around his thighs and braced her arms between the doorways. He held her tight and hoisted her up so he could thrust himself deeper inside her.

"Yes, that's it daddy. Oh yes!" she screamed at the top of her lungs.

"Shhh," he begged, knowing he had other mistresses in the same building and he didn't want to be caught out in the hallway doing her.

"Don't tell me to shut up you bastard, fuck me if you are going to fuck me and let me enjoy the shit." Realizing what she had just said and seeing the look of a combination of shock and newfound respect for her on his face, she began to giggle and then laugh.

She grabbed his neck and met his stabbing thrust by slamming her buttocks downward and pulling him into her with the back of her calves.

"I'm coming, I'm coming!" she exclaimed louder and louder as her passion rose within her. She creamed all over him. But she wasn't finished. She adjusted her panties and walked into his dimly lit apartment. That was not good enough, she thought to herself. Killing the damn cat was a better orgasm than what she had just had and she needed something more powerful. She felt like a junkie off of the high she had hours earlier.

"Damn, what about me Lara? I didn't come yet." He whined.

"Don't worry; I'll take care of you," she promised, taking him by the hand and leading him to the sofa where he willingly sat down. Pulling his pants down below his knees she spread his legs and fully exposed the meat that she wanted to please her so badly. Slowly taking the tip of his love stick into her mouth, she played with his pee hole until he felt the need to ram himself down her throat.

"More," he grunted. His penis was deep within her throat, the pleasure almost choking him. She moaned as she slowly took him deeper with swallowing motions, at the same time allowed her tongue to bath his shaft, consuming the full length of him. "Ohhh shit," he sighed, enjoying the pure ecstasy of the experience. "I want to cum baby. Oh Gosh I am going to blow right now." He told her, grabbing the short tresses of her hair and pushing her head into his crotch. But she wouldn't allow it. She pulled off of him and straightened herself out. She could feel her pussy throbbing as though it was about to explode.

"Where is the bedroom love?" she asked in a sexy sultry voice. It didn't take a second for Leslie to respond, because before she could complete her request, he was on his feet and heading down the short dark hallway. She could see that he had paintings on the wall but she had only one thing on her mind. They entered the room and he threw himself on the bed.

"Baby, where can I go freshen up a bit?" she asked almost hypnotically. She had dropped the boa and revealed her hourglass curves, rendering him speechless. She watched as he pointed back down the hallway. "It's okay Hun. I will find it," she assured him and swaggered out of the room. As soon as she was out of sight she dashed stealthily to the kitchen and searched for a knife. She couldn't find one. But she found an ice pick, which was better. She needed her fix like an addict and she was going to get it by any means necessary.

Placing the handle in the waistband of her underwear, she glided back into the bedroom and slid into the bed next to him. With his eyes closed he reached for her. She took the pick out from her panty and put it under the pillow. She moved so quickly she didn't feel what was already under the pillow.

"I can't believe you're the same woman I tried to kick it to earlier," he whispered in her ear as she lowered her body on top of his. He grabbed a firm hold of her arms and wanted to hug her tightly. She was like his dream woman, and she felt his manhood rise.

"You feel so good against me. I wish I had followed you here from the first time I saw you wave at me a year ago when I was moving in," she told him genuinely. He fit her so good. She knew she was on a high and that she was feenin. Maybe that was it? She thought to herself, but she just couldn't shake it. It was something powerful.

"Yeah baby, I been trying to get your attention for a good minute, but you always seemed uninterested and on the go."

"Don't make out like I am a saint now," she giggled.

"I would be stupid to do that. I noticed all the brotha's you had creeping up in your crib at nights.

Sometimes I thought it was only you and your girls hanging out but I see that you know how to play the game," he revealed.

"I wish it was as nice a time as you make it seem," she said sadly. "Anyway, I am here now, and there is only one thing on my mind, and there is only one man that can give it to me."

"Now you talking sweetheart. You are my kinda woman." He told her, wrapping her into his arms and burying his tongue down her throat. He flipped her over so he could be on top. He inhaled her scent and licked her nipples, nibbling until they were hard and taunt.

"Just like that baby," she urged him on, encouraging him not to stop until his face was buried between her legs. She squeezed them shut over his head and he gasped for air. She released him and pulled him up to her. She could feel his hard on pressing into her midsection and she arched her back and shoulders, pressing her thighs to meet his thrust.

"Oh girl you've got heaven and hell between your legs," he confessed as he moved gently at first and then faster, meeting her in an erotic that they both surrendered to. They sighed and danced the horizontal mamba until he felt the urge to explode inside of her. "Girl, let me stop and put on a condom." He told her, not really wanting to stop.
She didn't respond. She felt her body tingle all over, her tummy fluttered with a thousand butterflies and her toes curled. She got flashbacks of the after shock waves she experienced with the cat and wanted to know what it would feel like to have that experience with a man. She figured it would be ten times as powerful.

"I hear ya, and I feel ya. You don't need a condom trust me. Just keep moving. I don't want you to stop," she begged. He gave her what she wanted. She could feel the length of him grow longer, the width of him widen, and the gorge of blood strengthening his powerful plunges. Heaven help her. She was about to come.

As she pushed him to bring on explosion, she felt herself reaching under the pillar for the gift she placed under it earlier. She couldn't wait. She felt the insides of her thighs ache with that beautiful pain and she opened them wider, inviting him for a deeper.

Noticing she was up to something he grabbed her hand just as she grabbed the ice pick. He couldn't stop himself from the primal act he was engaged in. She wrestled free, and reached the pick behind his back. She was ready, primed to cream all over herself, and braced herself to experience the orgasm of a lifetime. He saw from the corner of his eyes that she had the pick behind him ready to plunge and he reached for the gun he kept hidden under the pillow. How did she miss that? She was in shock but it only heightened the excitement of her ecstasy.

"What are you doing?" he asked her. But she smiled a grimace so scary and ugly that he thought he was fucking a demon. "Are you possessed or some shit?" He asked her, still moving, still not believing what he saw, and thinking it some sort of sick role-play.

"Now this is one fuck worth dying for," she whispered. He came closer to hear what she was saying. As he pressed his body into her and she heard him say, "Oh shit, oh shit...O." She rammed the pick deep within his shoulder blade, puncturing his heart.

"What the fuck?" he asked, as blood ran out of his mouth. She let go of the pick and grabbed his ass, wrapped her legs around him so he couldn't move, forcing the cum to come before his dick went limp.

"Oh YESsssssssssssss!" she screamed. "Fuck this

pussy baby, isn't this pussy worth dying for?"

"You are a sick bitch." He gargled and placed the gun next to her temple. Her body convulsed so hard she closed her eyes; her legs trembled so hard she released them from around his body. She shook so much she could have suffered a seizure, and with his last breath he pulled the trigger of his gun, splattering her brain on the bed where she laid, her body still feeling the after effects of her orgasm.

"I hope that was an orgasm worth dying for." He whispered. He realized that he couldn't move and that he was badly hurt. He allowed himself to rest on top of her and lay down, trying to gasp for air. He closed his eyes and chuckled to himself. What a fucking way to die! He thought, and his eyes went blank.

## MAN KILLER 8

As Cleopatra and Cathalina drove leisurely back to Miami still reveling in their lovemaking and the toe curling after effects that still riveted their bodies, they heard sirens in the distance.
"Oh boy, looks like something huge happened somewhere close." Cathalina observed. Cleo didn't want to hear about it or even think about another person. She was only concerned with how she felt at that very moment, and that she was with the woman she wanted, the woman who had denied her for so long.
They cruised on I-95 and watched as ambulance and police cars sped past them, sirens blaring and screaming so loud that they could not resist their curiosity.
"I think we should go see what the problem is or where they're going. I am a doctor," Cathalina said, steering the car after the fleeing ambulances. She didn't want for Cleopatra's input. All Cleo cared about was that she is sexed up and satisfied.
"Why can't we just go back to your place and relax Cath? People are in accidents all the time. We should know. We have put quite a few in them." She chuckled at her own humor.
"I just have this really eerie feeling about this one. I don't know what it is but I feel that we should go." Cathalina dove in and out of traffic, staying close behind the police

vehicles.

"What kind of feeling? You're always feeling sorry for these no good low lives that get themselves in trouble. Can't you see by now that you can't save the world? This is why we do what we do, set things right that had gone drastically wrong." Cleo bitched about Cathalina's choice, but Cathalina was used to it. She is a doctor, a psychologist. That's what she did, care about people. It's who she was.

"I'm not going to have this conversation with you again Cleo. You want me to be this unfeeling callous bitch, but that's not who I am. I would much rather not be running around at night fucking and destroying God's perfect creation. Men and women were made to be soul mates, the opposite of each that should be whole, but somewhere along the line we screwed that up. That does not make what we do right. Its just a small way of appeasing what I feel is an injustice. Now if you don't mind, could you shut the fuck up so I can concentrate on driving?" Cathalina told her. Her annoyances were now clear bringing, Cleopatra to attention.

"So is it my fault that things got screwed by assholes who only think of themselves? It's my fault that creation has become undone by nasty, psychotic, freaks who think with what's in their pants, then with their brains?" The venom and revulsion she felt escaped her mouth as easily as breath.

"We are not doing anything by dealing with it the way we do. I personally feel that it's so messed up that what we are doing is the only way. But if we think about it...and notice I said we, what we are doing is adding to the problem, not fix it."

"Well you can WE your own damn self Cath. You talking as if you have regrets, like you want to throw in the towel after all the shit we did, turn us in to 5-0 and just say forget it. But it won't be that easy, trust me! We are going to do what we star..."

"Oh my goodness!" Cathalina exclaimed cutting her off as she pulled into the apartment complex behind the police officers, ambulance and detectives.

"Really Cathalina. Stop with the theatrics already. We already have dramatic Liz, we don't need you acting too," Cleo spat. "Ouch! What did you do that for?" Cleopatra screeched as Cathalina's fist connected with her shoulder.

"Keep your fucking mouth closed for a change and use your damn brains. Sometimes I wonder how I got mixed up with your stupid ass," Cathalina allowed her anger and resent get the best of her. And though she realized what she said, it was too late to take it back. Besides, she didn't want to take it back. It was about time she said what was on her mind.

Cleo just stared at her. She hung her head and silent tears flowed down the side of her face and under her chin. Cathalina's words hurt. She felt the truth in the words and was dumbfounded. Cathalina didn't even look at her. She just parked the car off to a corner and watched the police.

"This is where Lara lives," Cathalina broke the silence; her cadence was soft and soothing, but fear had her almost paralyzed. "When I pulled up behind the cops just now, my stomach did flips and my spider curled up." She almost whispered, as she felt the churning in her abdomen telling her something was deadly wrong. She felt connected with Lara already. She was already groomed, now something was fatally wrong.

"Do you think this is about her?" For a moment Cleo stopped thinking of herself and her own insatiable ego. For a moment, it hit her that the time and energy they had spent seeking out the right person for the forth spot, the months of preparation, might all be lost in a moment.

"I don't know what it is; I just feel that something has happened to Lara," Cathalina said.

"They're coming from the second floor," Cleo observed

"I know she is on the second floor, I just don't know where her apartment is located," Cathalina wrapped her arms around herself and sighed deeply.

"Oh God."

"Don't call God now Cleo. Stay here, I will be right back."

Cleo watched as Cathalina walked briskly toward a group of medics taking instructions from the police. She watched as police explained something to Cathalina that made her shudder.

"I don't understand? What do you mean double suicide?" Cathalina asked with more urgency than she wanted to express.

"The couple was found in a compromising position. They were in the midst of lovemaking and something went wrong. They seemed to have agreed to kill each other simultaneously."

"Excuse me, sir; they would like to bring the bodies out now," said a young uniformed officer. "What would you like to do?"

"Wait officer, I am not sure but I was seeing a woman in this building who was ill. Could you possibly explain to me who the woman was?" Cath grabbed the sleeve of the detective who had began to walk away and make his way toward the coroner who had already separated the bodies and bringing them down to the ambulances.

"Seeing her how?"

"My name is Dr. Cathalina Shekhar. I am a psychiatrist." Cathalina spoke the words slowly, as though she wasn't sure if she should really say them. She hoped she had not compromised herself by identifying who she was. But she knew that sooner or later there would be an investigation anyway, and somehow they would find their way to her office to find out the same thing she was telling them now.

"How did you know that something had happened here tonight?" The detective turned to her suspiciously. "Why are you here?" He turned to her in mid-stride and stopped to look directly into the tall dark skinned woman's face. He could see she was in a lot of pain from the expression she bore. Damn she is stunning! He thought to himself, willing his face not to blush.

"I was on my way in from dinner with a friend. She is waiting for me in the car right now," she told him. She shied away as he reached to touch her shoulder.

"No its okay, you are bleeding on your shoulder." He informed her with gentle concern.

"Oh its nothing, I accidentally hit my arm on the car door in my rush to get out and come speak with you."

"We have medics here; you should let one of them take a look at that before you go. You know, doctor to doctor." His humor was lost on Cathalina.

"I am okay. Really."

"Okay then, come with me and you can take a look for yourself. See if this is your patient or someone else. After all, she had no identification on her, so whatever you could help us with would be greatly appreciated."
He stopped again and looked at Cathalina with deep concern.

"There is one other problem." He paused and waited for her to focus on him.

"What is it?" she asked, impatience bubbling within her.

"The woman was shot in the head. Half of her face

has been blown off. You may not readily recognize her," he warned.

The detective turned on his heels and strutted away quickly, forcing her to keep pace as she approached the two dead bodies on the stretchers ready to be sent to the morgue. Cathalina cringed and braced herself as they reached for the white sheet to roll back over the female victims head. A squeal escaped her mouth. The part of Lara's head that remained made her identity evident.

Cathalina doubled over as the Brown Recluse raked its legs into the wound on her shoulder. She began to vomit up the dinner she had shared with Cleo only hours before. The peppered garlic Alfredo sauce with fettuccini chicken and shrimp did not look as appetizing as it did when she devoured it.

She heaved again as she turned her face away from the blood and gore of the gray mass of brain that had settled in a clustered mass to the side of her head, face and shoulder. Lara seemed happy, a smile on her face in death. There was still a blonde mass of hair left on the right side of her head, as was the butterfly tattoo on the right side of her neck that Cathalina had once admired and made a mental note to complement her on later.

"Are you all right?" The detective asked, extending his white handkerchief from his blazer pocket.

"I'm fine." Cathalina reassured him, thanking him for the offer with a shake of her head and dry heaved as the thought of what she saw again grabbed her insides and forced her to try and bring up what no longer existed inside her body.

"Did you recognize her?"

"She is Lara Lopez. She was my patient. She lived in Apartment 2HC. I am not sure which direction that is in. I have not been here before. But she spoke of it often during

our sessions." Lara's identity confirmed, Cath began walking back toward the car and Cleo.
"Wait. Dr. Shekhar. Here is my business card. Please feel free to contact me if there is anything else you can think of to explain why this happened."
"Okay." She took the card and continued walking.
"Dr. Shekhar, if you are not busy tomorrow, could you please come to the office and make a statement? I will fill you in on the details once the report comes back, which should be sometime tonight." He hoped she would say yes.
"If that's what you need me to do...eh" She paused and stopped to look at the card to get his name. "Detective Jamie Taylor." She finished as she locked eyes with him for a brief moment and smiled. She paused a moment longer as she watched the white drain from his face at her smile. She also knew that the black was draining from Cleopatra's face at the same time, since she was back within range of the car, and she knew that woman well enough to know that she was on pins and needles waiting for her return.
"Thank you," he mumbled bashfully. Cathalina did not turn around again. She just waved her hand goodbye and proceeded toward the car where a litany of questions awaited her.

*********

Serena sat in the judge's chamber wringing her hands and pulling on her hair. She just couldn't stand it. It was almost the end of her work week and only a week since she had received the mark of the Brazilian Wandering Spider. She wasn't sure if it was just her normal repulsion to the situation or if the spider was having an effect on her, but she just wanted to be free.

# Man Killer

She felt trapped every time someone came before her and got off with just a slap on the wrist. In the past few days, she found herself taking notes, writing down names and addresses of every vagabond, every lowlife, every woman beater, and every pedophile let off by a technicality and with a slap on their wrist, while simultaneously silencing the voice of so many innocent children. She made notes of the who's, what's, where's and whys. She would research their location, follow-up with their parole, and everyday she fondled and caressed the words on paper, words that bore information that would make her lethal to those whose names were on her list.

It took everything inside of her to restrain herself from jumping over the bench and strangling the life out of these useless members of society. Predators. She felt renewed, and invigorated with each thought. The spider sense in her was powerful, fresh and new, waiting for the moment to emerge and blend fully with her. She could feel its talons raking at her shoulder where it lived and breathed as surely as she did.

It was hungry. She wanted to hunt. The urges she felt were unreal. Leaving the courtroom for the day, Serena got into her car as though in a trance. She wore a sadistic smile on her face and was propelled to move forward with a will she felt she didn't control. She drove aimlessly north towards Broward County, moving toward Ft. Lauderdale on I-95, and headed in the direction of Coral Springs and the Everglades off Hwy 441. She would study her list of predators who have violated the essence of women who had trusted them, preying on the vulnerability of women like her and children, innocent children.

"Yes, I know," her words drooled off her tongue.
"What? What was that?" She giggled sadistically.
"Yes, those bastards think they are messing with idiots? Nincompoops?" She drove steadily, doing eighty miles

an hour on the highway and gaining speed as her mind locked on to her destination, her goal.

"Marcus. Marcus what? Yes, his last name." She listened as though waiting for the answer from an invisible friend sitting with her and responding as though that person had given her what would be considered viable information.

"Marcus Cummings, yes. That would make sense." She snickered as she associated his name with an orgasm. The thought was intoxicating.

"Don't worry; they will not get away with it." Her mind melted as one with her now closely guarded emotions as the reckless spider insinuated its anger and aggression on her, multiplying her already existing confusion and pain that had festered and grown into hatred.

Almost as a third eye she saw that she neared the home of Marcus and she wondered why he had made his home the town of Sandalfoot Florida so close to the Everglades. As soon as the thought registered she sneered.

As she drove, she became more and more delusional and paranoia gained strength in her fragile mind.

"Duh, of course he made his home near the Everglades; Easy disposal of bodies, willing Alligators to eliminate evidence. Bastards are nuts!" She was almost flabbergasted at Marcus's audacity. "Yeah I know, as if no one would figure that out. I mean, they swear that they have changed, that they didn't do it, that they are now rehabilitated and productive members of society. But it's all a damn lie." She bellowed so loudly she jumped and looked around to see who had said that. She was alarmed that the voice did not come from her.

As she neared Sandalfoot, she could almost smell the moss of the vast piece of land spanning miles deeply planted muddy waters with reefs peaking above the plateau. She could almost see the wide space with all the creatures that has made the Everglades their home.

She saw something else, a man, walking towards a popular tourist resort. He was not quite what she would expect. He was a nerdy looking Caucasian male with frail looking limbs and big ears. She heard herself laugh.

"That's it? That's all you are? Taking lives and destroying what you don't even have the brains to develop in your own self!" the look of him appalled her. She expected some big burly guy with tattoos and scars on his body. But then, what should she expect? It's the ones you thought wouldn't do it.

"Look at the puny little wimp!" She couldn't believe it but her disbelieve soon faded. She no longer saw the frailness of his physique but the image of a man who had hurt and destroyed her, she embodied emotions of those he had killed and violated as she began to hear screams. She drove to the resort parking lot and parked. She became impaled with visions, the spider egging her on, pushing her to move her legs and get into motion. She no longer saw herself as a woman.

She felt as though she was growing extra legs, extending from her back, shoulders and sides, the elongated limbs lifting her from the ground and placing her face down to face to floor. She felt as though she was in a vision, locked in a trance. She felt herself emit a sound that she didn't recognize but she knew she was laughing.

Too fucking cool! She thought she heard her words in her mind. She remained focus on one man, one target that must feel the wrath of a woman scorned, taste the bite of the bitten and face the consequences that only the spider could administer.

She felt her arms grow additional muscles that attached themselves to tendons and ligaments that were not there before, her legs folding into a crevice like a Kangaroos pouch, her back flattening to the ground. She felt huge and strong. She felt herself spring with the wind as she took motion, moving towards the man and she could hear one word emitting from her senses...Cummings!

"What the fuck?" And it ducked, as it positioned itself for an attack, not wanting to be a complete surprise. She needed to taste the sense of fear, for him to be afraid. To feel powerless and overcome by something one would think to be harmless. She lifted a talon and reared her head. Her eight eyes starring at a being that now seems ten times smaller than the image she first registered in her head.

"That's right Mr. Cummings, bet you don't feel that powerful now!" She knew she was thinking this, felt she was saying it, but the words seemed to come from someone else, somewhere else.

"Holy Mother Fucking Christ!" His heart raced at what he had just seen. "Impossible!" He uttered under his breath as he backed away, heading deeper into the path that lead to the pond, stumbling as he tried to run.

"You have no conscience."

"Lady, I don't know you and I have no idea what you are talking about." He snickered at Serena. She was obviously insane and he began to laugh.

Serena was tired of the game, she wanted to hear him screech in pain, she wanted to rip him from limb to limb, and she wanted to get him where it really hurts. She lifted a talon and encircled it around his waist. She pulled him into her and used another of her talons and ripped his pants open so his genitals were exposed.

She sniffed him and her senses exploded. She felt an erotic pulling sensation that made her ache in a sexual way but harbored desires of destruction.

"Oh no, gosh please," came his pleas as tears made their way down the man's pale cheeks. He kicked and screamed once the initial shock wore off and tried with everything in him to loosen the grip of the thing on him.

Serena sniffed again, this time excreting saliva that she slowly drooled on him. The secretion fell from her jaws and dropped below his waist, burning into Marcus's groin and melted away his penis. The hair on his pubic area singed and smelled like fried flesh and dead animals, yet the smell was intoxicatingly sexy to Serena. She felt her vulva swell with longing so she regurgitated again, letting herself slobber this incredible spit upon his arms and legs. Excruciating pain galvanized his body and he shook as shock chronicled his pain. As his brain registered that his body parts were dissolving, his skin melting, he began to shriek.

She coughed, as though trying to bring up cold from her chest. Then in one spitting motion, spat the white yellowish foam on his face. It saturated his mouth and began eating away at his face. He opened his mouth to holler again and the secretion dripped on his tongue and dissolved it as well, his tonsils visible to the world as his flesh was eaten away. His eyeballs began falling out of their sockets.

She laughed, but it was a sound she could not, and did not recognize. She peered over him as she dropped to the grass. He now resembled the scum that he truly is, was the thought that emitted an involuntary reaction for her to rest her body on him. She too was surprised as she webbed the acid eaten body.

Serena woke up in bed, not knowing how she got there. She was still wearing her Donna Karen suit, only it was shredded to pieces. Her ached as though she had worked out for the first time. Jason sat across from her, starring at the woman he had serviced now for almost two years, watching her go through transition after transition since having met this so called doctor Shekhar who was supposed to be helping her. But that was not the case. Day to day she got increasingly worse. He was becoming scared for her.

He watched as she trembled. She was sweating profusely but she was not feverish. Her body would curd like spoilt milk and then become as a mass ball of incomplete webbing. He ached for her; he ached to reach out to her. But he couldn't touch her. He couldn't clean, change or go near her. She dragged herself into the house without her normal routine. He panicked when he noticed that her body seemed elongated and things were extended from her body. She snarled as he neared her and he wisely backed off. He followed her to her bedroom where she curled into a ball and emitted a painful sound that bordered on erotic as she writhed her body into frenzied masturbation. She had finally fallen into a fitful sleep and he watched her till dawn crept though the windows.

**********

Dyania tossed and turned until she suddenly jumped from her bed. It felt so real. She got up from her bed and stumbled over a pile of clothing she had been meaning to take to the laundry for the past two weeks. It was dark and she squinted to adjust her eyes to the darkness. She walked to the bathroom to pee. She sat on the toilet seat and when she got up, her pee had curded to the top of the water in the toilet bowl like French onion soup. She turned to flush and screamed.

"Oh my dear Jesus. What have I done to deserve this?" She flushed the toilet and ran back to her bedroom, knocking over her night lamp and hitting her chin hard on the foot of the bed. "Damn!" she exclaimed, hopping on one leg and falling back under the covers. Then tears began falling down her face.

      Slowly she got up and moved towards her foot looker. She reached under the mattress and took a purse that was locked to the bedspring. She opened the purse and retrieved a key. She opened the locker and pulled out her journal. She began writing.

*Journal:*

*The dreams have started again. I don't know what I did or ate or what to trigger them.* Her body jerked as tears developed, she paused to wipe the tears from her face as renewed fear gripped her. *I haven't had these nightmares since I was twenty. Why would this be happening now nine years later?* She hiccupped and coughed, then placed her face in her hands and had a good cry. She had to keep going; she needed to journal the account of these attacks or whatever the hell they were. The journaling helped before, the doctors used it to chronicle the episodes as they came. *What is happening to me? Why is this happening again? Why am I having dreams of transforming into spiders? Why am I waking up horny and I have never even fucked a man? Why am I soaking my bed with excitement that melts and burns my sheets but not me?* The thoughts ravaged her mind. *The only difference is that they are stronger this time, more powerful. The dreams are manifesting physical evidence. This time I don't have to wonder if something was happening. This time I can see that it really happened.* She didn't understand all the conflicting emotions that riveted her body and her mind.

*What did I do to deserve this? I mean, for crying out loud I am having puncture wounds magically appear on my body as though I am being bitten again and again. But...but that's impossible.* Her mind raced to understand what she was feeling. *But then they disappear almost as immediately as they appear. No sign of blood, no pain, just sexual desires so strong that I feel like I am going to rip myself in two with anything that resembles a dick.* She laughed at her own corky sense of humor as she visualized the act. Maybe I just need to go get fucked! She wrote, and new tears formed in her eyes as she remembered her parent's death.

    They had told her over and over that she imagined it. Back when she was three years old. Imagined that her parents where in Brazil on some government scientific expedition. She wondered why anyone would lie to her. She had no reason to think they did. Yet she felt something happened that they are not admitting.

    She put her journal back carefully at the bottom of the footlocker and reached for one of the only photos she had of her parents holding her proudly. Her thick Afro puffs in what the Jamaicans of her parents' heritage called Chiny bumps. She held the frame close to her heart and heaved as new tears forced their way from her body.

    "Why did this have to happen to you? Why did this happen to me?" She questioned the smiling images of the last memory she had of the people who brought her into this world and held it closely as the remnants of the nightmares passed. Then she drifted back into a peaceful sleep.

**********

    Another day at work and Serena experienced the same passionate sensations. She couldn't control the thoughts and had no memories from the previous day. She left work again, with the same uncontainable desires to wipe clean the face of the earth from the predators that she felt castrated her.

She drove back to her Coral Gables home feeling like a hound, wanting to go dig somewhere. Her pulse raced and she was sweating abnormally. She clutched the steering wheel and crumbled the paper in her hands that held information of newly released serial killers, murderers, pedophiles and other disgusting members of society. She couldn't understand this sudden need to go and do something about it. She thought she was doing something about it all this time through the career path she choose, and quietly she would harbor secret thoughts to annihilate the bastards, but this was different. She felt desires so real she could taste their blood in her mouth. "Why am I going through this?" She asked herself, and felt her body stiffened as she felt the rotation of the spider on her shoulder.

"Don't do this to me," she begged. Memories of the way she liquefied Marcus in the Everglades petrified her. She still didn't know, couldn't tell if she dreamt that or not. She had not heard anything about the incident on the news or any where else.

She absorbed these thoughts and feelings until she noticed that she was instinctively slowing down. It was three o'clock in the afternoon and motorist had begun to show their impatience for her casual driving. Seems with each drop of her speedometer she could feel the ambition of the spider. She was almost spooked when she felt something, a sensation of crawling on her left shoulder where her tattoo was. She shrieked.

She was almost at a full stop in the middle of traffic when she slowly removed a portion of her silk white top to see what had crept under her shirt and froze to her seat as pure horror consumed her. But then something familiar calmed her, a tranquil emotion ran through her and she relaxed. A new sense of pride washed over her as vague memories of her initiation gave her a snapshot of who she was and what she was morphing into.

"Damn this is some really powerful shit. I mean, gosh! This is better than freaking drugs or booze or anything else," she said out loud excitedly. Then she sank back into her seat troubled by the memories of her recent metamorphosis.

"But I don't understand," she said as the invertebrate beneath her skin communicated with her. And then she smiled, as if she was given an acceptable response. It seemed to echo Spider Queen in her ear.

Looking up from where it seemed she sat for hours, she surveyed her surroundings and had a sense that she was in someplace familiar. She looked at the crumpled piece of paper in her hand and opened it up. She noticed that as she opened the paper, it seemed to stick a bit with some mushy white gooey stuff. She chuckled, not really knowing why but was amused and truly fascinated.

"This shit is real?" she asked out loud. But her concentration was immediately changed as her eyes were drawn to one particular address of a Mr. Vincent Ratigan. He just registered as a pedophile with the department of police and community protection, got off practically free for the murder of a little girl that was found beaten to death in Hialeah Gardens. She touched his name, and somehow she was able to see that this man was indeed guilty of a crime and was not punished. She got flashes, glimpses into the reality of what he did, like a movie clip, shooting images into her mind. She saw him take the child from her own back yard. She seemed to go with him as if she knew him, running and smiling, her beautiful thick black bouncing Afro that was almost into her back. Her black trusting eyes lit up like fireworks and her arms swung freely as she ran to him. She blinked back, the honking of motorists behind her bidding her out of their way. She realized she was still in the middle of the street.

"Oh no, it's happening again."

Panic stricken she stepped on the gas and pulled over. The images gave her pangs of hunger for revenge, the tattoo, vibrated and pulsated beneath her skin, and her stomach curled. She parked not too far from the lavish home that this criminal had made for himself.

The images were different this time, more powerful. This time she is seeing the faces of the children, the crime in motion, and the atrocity. Her anger multiplied.

"What is going on with me today?" She asked herself a bit concerned, but distracted by the images that would not let up. *You are the one. Make this right.* She could hear the voice as clear as if someone was whispering in her ear. She looked quickly over her shoulders to see if there was someone sitting beside her or behind her. To see if there was someone playing with her mind, but there was no one. *I have got to shake this feeling.* She thought to herself, *I am an appointed judge for crying out loud. This is insane.* The thoughts lingered in her mind. The flashback continued assaulting her mind like bits of memory.

He took her down by the swampy lake areas of the Hialeah; he played with her clothing until she was almost naked. Serena squeezed her eyes shut as he unzipped his pants. The memories skipped. He punched her to the side of her temple and knocked her down. She couldn't be more than four years old. Tears began welling in Serena's eyes.

"Latoya." She uttered the girls name and something stabbed into her shoulder. She looked again towards her shoulder and there was a small drop of blood seeming through her silk white shirt. Like a needle pricked her but it hurt as badly as the punch that put Latoya's lights out. Something pushed her and her body was thrown into the steering wheel with a thud and she horn started beeping. She regained her composure and looked again through the mirror that her eyes were showing her. He threw her in his trunk, sat in his old Chevy and smoked a cigarette.

"The bastard is evil." She said out loud, silent tears streaming down her face. Latoya was suffocating, after hours of being back there she came to. She coughed. He opened the trunk and unzipped his pants again, unzipping her every time she cried. Punching her in her mouth until a tooth fell out and she spat blood, fear and shock took over her helpless body.

Serena couldn't take it anymore. Her anger was so great it was as though her very life depended on what she did. She wanted him to feel pain in so many ways her own body ached. When she couldn't withstand the pain any longer, she cried.

She must have stayed like that for hours, because it was now almost eight in the evening and a darkened hue had come over the sky. The sun was beginning to set, and she must have blocked out because her phone registered that there were seven missed calls and her Onstar emergency system was blinking alert because Cathalina was concerned about her and had been trying to locate her. She seemed to remember putting her friend's fear at ease and told her she was okay. Somehow she just felt that.

Suddenly Serena had an overwhelming urge to look up. There he was, two hundred and twenty pounds of hard muscles and six feet four inches tall. His baldhead looked as smooth as satin, and he was wearing cotton knit top and Sean John Jeans. His rich dark skin seemed to glisten against the falling night and his eyes, light and agile, seemed to dance as he made eye contact with her. His face was cleanly shaven except for the goatee he sported with an attached moustache. His smiled exposed highlighted full delectable lips and beautiful white even teeth that seemed to dare her to come kiss him. She swallowed hard and took a deep breath. If she didn't feel such repulsion for him, she would find him stunning. She could feel herself getting wet between the knees and she squeezed them shut to stop herself from putting her hands there to soothe the ache he had brought on her with just his attentive stare.

"Do you need any help Miss?"

"No thank you." She said almost choking on her words. Her body was screaming "yes, yes, yes, get in here and take me right now." But she knew better. Her palms were so sweaty and sticky; she couldn't let go of the steering wheel and her mind just kept seeing little Latoya's body through his eyes.

"I think you need help Miss." He insisted. "You are blanking out. Did you just hear what I said?" He moved closer to her car and stood at the window, bending slightly to look in.

"No, I am fine." She tore her eyes away from him; afraid to see more when suddenly her vision got fast-forwarded or re-winded. She couldn't tell which it was, but there were flashes of children, each under fifteen years old. She couldn't tell how many of them, but they were hurt, in pain, crying, dying, and bleeding. She couldn't focus on just one, they just kept coming and coming and she wanted them to stop. She put her hands to her temple and pressed into them hard. She suddenly found some control, some power within her to calm down to stop and focus. Oh gosh did he see that? See me flipping out? Thoughts flooded her mind to find sense in what was happening to her, but she pulled herself together and felt the spider on her shoulder curl up, pacified for the moment.

"How about a drink of water ma'am, I live right here. You could come in if you like. I won't hurt you I promise." She surveyed his disarming smile and the sincerity that danced behind his eyes. Is this the way you lured those poor children? She asked him without words, but looking at his outstretched arms, the strength of them, the gentleness of them, she somehow found the strength and reached up, allowing the power in him to guide her out of her car. As he opened the door to help her out, he almost wet his pants when he saw her shirt rise like a hump on her shoulder, then talons coming out from under her collar. He swallowed hard and shook the image from his head then reach for her again. He must have been hallucinating; there was no hump on her shoulder and definitely nothing with legs to crawl out from under her shirt.

"Are you okay?" Serena looked at him cautiously. The blood seemed to have drained from his already dark skin leaving it looking ashy. It was as if he saw a ghost.

"I am fine. I am sorry. For a moment I thought you might be someone I know." He told her. He shook the disturbing image from his thoughts and helped Serena to her feet and onto the sidewalk.

"Have you been sitting here long? Its late." Serena smiled warmly at him and her knees almost buckled when he smiled back. Thick full lips curled into a curvaceous and flirtatious smile, glistening eyes twinkled with sex appeal. She could feel his thoughts in her most private erogenous zone. She struggled to find her voice and almost chuckled at her own awkwardness. Suddenly she felt a sharp piercing in her shoulder, almost a warning for her not to lose focus.

"Honestly, I don't know. I guess I could really use

that glass of water." She could almost feel a purr from the thing on her shoulder, like she was being controlled by it. She felt urged to enter his home, and held on to him as he led her to his front door and into his home.

"Here we are." He announced, as he led her up three short steps and then into a vast living room where he seated her on a large sectional sofa. She looked about her environment quickly and noted that this man was a rugged type of brawny man, from the bear rug replica on the hard wood floors, to the Moose's head hanging from the wall. There was a huge fireplace and an abstract painting hanging on the wall. There was not much else. "I'll go get you some water." And before she could look up at him he had walked away. She couldn't help noticing how his tight perky ass swayed in his denim and how his calf high Timberland boots hiked up one of his pant leg. He moved swiftly like a man with purpose and calculation and she was able to survey him in peace without being plagued by visions or pinched and jabbed by some controlling spider. The thought still seemed like a dream to her. Something she fantasized and she was curious as to how the whole thing would play out.

"Here you go." He said returning and seating himself next to her on the arm of the sofa and leaning in a bit with his left arm outstretched on the back of the sofa seat. Swallowing hard, Serena looked up at him and smiled.

"Forgive me. I know you told me your name, but I have forgotten." She hung her head, a bit shyly and feeling awkward. She knew all this other stuff about the man and the damn spider couldn't give her a vision to remember his name. She chuckled. How ironic. Some things just have to be done the old fashioned way.

"Vincent." Serena was jolted by the deep rumble of his voice and forced herself to look into his eyes again. "Vincent

Ratigan is my full name." Her smile brought one to his lips and they both locked in a momentary gaze. He reached for her glass with the water in it and placed it on the end table next to the sofa.

"Thank you. I think that was exactly what I needed. But maybe I should go now." Serena clasped her hands, trying to feel for the webbed texture that had her palm's stuff to the steering wheel earlier, and felt a slight panic as she realized that she no longer had the paper with the list of names on it, that originally drew her to this man's house. Sensing her discomfort, Vincent then got up and sat across from her in the loveseat so she wouldn't feel threatened.

"Why don't you sit a while longer? You were really out of it back there. Do you feel feverish? Are you faint?" He asked. His eyes narrowing and lines drew themselves across his forehead in genuine concern. Serena almost bawled over laughing, and forced herself to smile instead.

How ridiculous that this murderer would act as though he gave a shit? She couldn't comprehend how amazing it all was. Slowly crossing her legs she took her hair that had been loosened and knotted it on top of her head. She felt a sensual shiver go up and down her spine and blinked hard to shut of the visual of what came to her mind.

"Oh my Gosh, I think I really should be going." She stood and then placed her hands over her face to prevent herself from looking at him again."

"What? What are you doing? Are you sure you are okay?" Vincent stood and reached for her. She pulled away and then peeked from beneath her fingers. "If you don't mind me asking, are you under psychiatric care?" Serena only giggled and shook her head no. Then she laughed as she thought about Cathalina. Technically she was, and she laughed again. He had no idea. Regrouping and pulling herself together, she managed to calm her giggles and brought on an air of professionalism. The sensations between her legs were making her vulvas quiver and she squeezed them tight, sending sensations through her clit that immediately creamed her thongs. She tried to will the wetness to not stain the back of her skirt or run down her legs. Shit I have to get out of here.

"Mr. Ratigan, I am indeed indebted to you. You have really been kind. But it is time that I go. I have been out later than I anticipated and I do have some obligations at hand that needed to be tended to." Stumbling a bit, she gathered her strength and direction and walked toward his door.

"Well if you ever need an ear or a helping hand. You know where to find me." Vincent called after her. He didn't feel like asking her to stay again or chasing after her. He just wanted to watch as the fine specimen of a woman sauntered away from him and as much as he enjoyed the view, he was concerned for her driving to wherever she was destined.

"I am sure this woman is some crazy nut." He snickered to himself as the door closed behind him. "That's the last thing I need in my life right now, sexy or not. I have too much of my own issues to deal with right now, than to be taking on somebody else's" He grumbled under his breath as he prepared to go back and continue his evening walk. He tried to get Serena out of his mind for the rest of the evening. But he just couldn't. He was drawn to her vulnerability, her seemingly innocent disposition. And his night was filled with thoughts and dreams of her.

## MAN KILLER 9

Elizabeth got into her car and drove down the highway in Atlanta's rush hour traffic. She felt hot and bothered but couldn't help enjoying being in the sexual Mecca of this day and age. Yeah, her type could really thrive there, where there are more under cover down low brothers than anywhere else in the United States. The play she starred in was in its final week and she was getting antsy to have it completed. She pressed the CD button on her car stereo and relaxed as Jill Scott smooth grooves relaxed every tense bone in her body. Just as she pulled into a small pizza joint, her cell phone rang and she saw that it was from Serena.

"Hey sweets, how are you feeling these days?" The question was truly rhetorical, because Elizabeth knew the side effects of joining with the spider. Her black widow is always perched proudly in the crevice of her bosom and nestled discretely beneath her cleavage.

"Liz, it's so good to hear your voice." Serena breathed, slowly trying to calm herself, trying to be and sound rational. "How are things going for you in Atlanta?"

"I am good. The play is almost over and I miss you guys. Things have been pretty quiet since your induction into the team." I wouldn't say quiet, Serena thought begrudgingly. I would say things have been nothing less than psycho.

"How have you been feeling? Is everything okay?"

"Well, to tell the truth, I have been feeling sort of

queasy." Serena told her, not wanting to divulge too much information. Liz was cool and everyone loved her, but she was afraid to tell them what she was experiencing. What if it was a side effect?

Elizabeth got out of her car and moved toward the entrance to the pizzeria. She was starving. But something told her to stop and listen to Serena. She could almost feel an eerie sensation come over her and her chest pumped twice as if her skin was ripping from her body. She knew somehow that it was spider connection. Serena is in trouble. The thought came her as though it was not even her own thought, and suddenly the pangs of hunger she felt came no longer from her chest and a strange kind of excitement almost gave her dress a flag pole.

"Sweetheart, have you been getting enough rest? You have only been indoctrinated a week. You need time to get used to the symbiosis." She tried to calm the stimulus that was causing her heart to race and her blood vessels to fill. She looked around, to see if anyone had seen her strange reaction to the phone call and then quickly dodged back into her car. "I guess I haven't slept much except for the day after the ceremony, but I felt good and today was my last workday for the week."

"Okay, so what are you doing now?" As she asked the question her hand subconsciously fondled her leg and massaged under her dress above her thigh. The ache she felt was not sexual, it was more like a warning of a threat. She took her bulging shaft into her hands and tried to quell the false urges that had grown within her.

"I am lying down in my bedroom. I am about to take a nap. Jason is here with me. I am safe. I just really wanted to say hello." Serena lied, but she didn't realize that the communal connection they had would send waves of uncertainty through the phone letting her peer know that she was shaking; uncontrollable tremors as she curled into the fetal position on her bed, and juices of unknown desires ran down her legs and saturated the sheets.

"Okay Serena. Well it's good to hear from you. I will be back in Miami next week. The play is wrapping up its tour and I am happy that I am not far away from home." Serena's soft chuckle sent a serge of blood to her already fortified erection. At the same moment, a web of confusion filled Elizabeth's body and almost made her scream from the bite the Black Widow unexpectedly administered to her bosom.

"What the fuck was that?" The words came out of her mouth before she could register the thought.

"What happened? What is it Liz?" Serena asked, her voice now loosing its cool and her fear seeping through the telephone line.

"It's nothing. Hey Serena, I gotta get back, so let me go get something to eat and I will touch base with you again soon." Liz rushed off the phone as though it was contagious and threw it on the seat as soon as the last words were out of her mouth.

"What the hell was that about?" she asked herself, speaking into her car as though she would get a response. But the only response she received was the throbbing ache of her penis. She yanked at her dress and unbuttoned her bra to see where she felt the bite. The Black Widow tattoo on her body had made an uncomfortable realignment from facing down into her bosom to facing up with its legs sprawled as if it was ready to jump from her body.

She picked up her cell phone and dialed Cathalina's cell phone number. She couldn't wait to return back to her suite to make such an urgent phone call. She needed to let Cathalina know what was going on. It rang out, so she sent a page with their special code requesting that Cathalina returned her call. Then she tried her home an as a last resort tried her office.

"Dr. Shakhar."

"Working so late?"

"More like thinking and planning." She chuckled.

Cathalina wasn't sure if she should regret what she shared with Cleo or not. She needed to focus on what happened to Lara, she couldn't believe that she was dead. How was she going to explain that Lara was gone to Elizabeth and Serena? Cleo knew now. She wasn't sure how Cleo was handling Lara's death since she was so focused on the fact that Detective Taylor was hitting on her. She hadn't taken Cleo's calls and Cleo was blowing up the phone. The last time she spoke with Serena, she sounded as though she was in a daze.

"Is everything okay Cathalina?" Elizabeth placed the phone closer to her ear and tried to listen to their recruiter with more than just her ears. She sensed a form of distress. She couldn't place her hands on it, but it was weird that Cathalina sounded out of sorts.

"Yes dear, all is well. But tell me, how is your show winding down?"

"It's coming to a close nicely, I am happy to say. I am tired of it now. I miss home." Her voice trailed off, but the true intent of her call had not left her mind.

"Cathalina, I spoke with Serena a moment ago. Is she adjusting well to the Brazilian Wandering Spider?"

"Why do you ask that?" Cathalina was now alert. Elizabeth has struck a nerve.

"She seemed not altogether there. I sensed that she might be torn somewhat, deciding, not adjusting well. I cannot really tell, but something is going on."

"We should be meeting up tomorrow as a group. The

only person missing will be you. But we will fill you in later." Cathalina informed her ready to get off the phone and go find Serena.

"Thanks for the call Liz, You are wonderful and I miss you."

"Okay, I will be home next week. I am anxious to see how Serena has acclimated herself to the spider." They both silently acknowledged the same wish, and then disconnected the call.

\*\*\*\*\*\*\*\*\*\*

The pangs of anger and desire that Elizabeth felt that were being transmitted by Serena were overwhelming. They were becoming connected, but why the connection with her and not Cathalina? She wasn't sure, but she knew she had to get back home. She didn't get out of her car nor did she ever get her meal. She had become transfixed on the emotional pull from her spider sister. She was always very calm and in control, so much more aggressive with predatory lines stronger in her than the other ladies, maybe because of her testosterone level.

She drove back to the Hyatt where the cast for her play stayed and rushed to her room. She needed to alleviate the pressure of what was building in her; she couldn't get her erection down.

When she walked into the lush double suite, she heard singing coming from the opposite end of the room. Her roommate was in the shower. She always loved to hear her sing the show tunes as though in a rehearsal every time she took a shower. She also knew that Francesca had a crush on her. She was the leading lady and Francesca was Elizabeth's under study. She sat on her half of the room, trying to will her huge penis to quell itself, but the images that Serena were sending through her were violent and hungry. They sent surges of electrical quality through her and she needed to quiet down. She didn't want Francesca to come outside and see her like this. A twelve-inch dick on a beautiful Asian woman would be hard to hide.

    She lay back on her bed and tried to masturbate the pain away, tried to seduce herself into letting go. But Serena had captured the essence of a powerful man with a dark aura, something that repelled the spider and drew him as a source of their cause. That kind of connection was something she cannot let go of and she was so shocked at the vivaciousness, the clarity, and the awesomeness of the emotion. Damn I didn't know she would be able to do that. The premonition was right. Maybe Cathalina was right about her. She is to be the Spider Queen. Serena is transmitting sensuality like she couldn't believe.

    She heard the shower cut off and Francesca stepped out. She looked at the flagpole her dick was putting up and grabbed for the sheet to cover her embarrassment. This was her insecurity, knowing she wasn't a real woman. Having this part of her was a source of her shame, not really able to have a relationship with a man.

    "Liz, I didn't know you were here." Francesca told her after composing herself from her initial surprise. Liz never returned to the room that early, so she was taken aback some.

    "Sorry if I startled you Fran, I just came in and am feeling a bit tired." She lied, faking fatigue as she yawned, stretched her hands above her head and turned on her side. Damn, I thought she had never been with a man. How in the world could she transmit this shit? She fought with the desires that forced themselves on her and she wondered if the others could feel it too.

    "Hey what's wrong?" Francesca came and sat at the

edge of the bed and reached out for her leg and gently caressed it. "You look like you have seen a ghost. All the blood has left your face." She said, stretching her long frail body alongside Elizabeth in sisterly concern.

They had chatted like this numerous nights, and it was no big deal. But the image of Francesca's damp skin and wet black Shirley temple locks were wrecking her cool.

Francesca smiled innocently and her big blue eyes sparkled as she anticipated what Elizabeth would talk to her about tonight. Their time together was winding down and she knew she would miss the gorgeous Asian beauty wrapped in black chocolate. She wished that she didn't feel so distant from her and wanted on so many nights to hold her. But

Elizabeth always kept her at arms length. While the rest of the cast, frolicked erotically together and mixed and mingled, she had no stories or memories to share with the group as they gossiped about hot nights spent making it hotter.

"Please." Elizabeth barely uttered on a ragged breath.

"Please don't do that." She sighed; placing her hand on top of Francesca's to stop the fluid gentle movement of them up and down her thigh.

"I am sorry." Francesca blushed. Feeling rejected she began easing herself up to go.

"Francesca, it's just that."

"I know. You don't like girls. I feel so stupid." She exhaled and raised herself on her elbows to remove herself before she lost anymore of her pride. As she did so the towel that was casually wrapped around her bosom loosened and Francesca's beautiful cantaloupes bounced joyously at their release. She reached to cover them, but Elizabeth touched her hands, stopping her. She shuddered from the ripples of desire that found their way through her body and if she had made any progress on quelling her hardened penis, she was duly exposed now. She couldn't hide it anymore.

"You are so beautiful." Came the husky sensual sigh from deep inside Elizabeth's throat. She inched her way closer to the woman whose naked body screamed for her. The towel barely covered her thighs as it fell and revealed the close trimmed hairy mound of the Eden she hid between her legs. Francesca smiled a pleasing smile. Her eyes danced with curiosity and willingness. Hope filled her as her breaths became rasped and short and her chest heaved up and down in anticipation.

"You think so? I mean, I didn't know you..." and before she could finish the sentence, Elizabeth closed the gap between them, her left hand reaching up to Francesca's face and pulling her down toward the bed and her right hand finding her waist as she pulled her to meet her desires, turning on her back and allowing Francesca's body to slowly slide on top of hers.

Suddenly there was a gasp and a shudder. Francesca jumped to her feet and her eyes bulged from her body.

"What the hell is going on here?" She asked. "What are you?"

"I tried to tell you but..."

"What do you mean you tried to tell me? Am I that difficult to talk to?"

"No it's nothing like that all. I have always had this problem and..."

"Problem! You call that a problem? You are a chick with a dick. That's not a problem that's and atrocity!" Francesca exclaimed frantically. She paced back and forth and then ran to the bathroom to find her clothes.

"You are the one who wanted to get laid, now I am an atrocity? You don't like dick? You don't want it?" Liz yelled walking over to the other half of the hotel suite to where Francesca was hoping to get her to calm down.

"Of course I like dick, I just didn't think… I mean I wanted to be with you."

"Well, this is me. And if you like dick well then I have got one. So what's the problem?" Elizabeth yelled and as she got closer, Francesca closed the bathroom door.

"That's just not normal. That is not normal. It's huge." She screamed. "I will scream rape if you come in here I swear."

A wave of shame and embarrassment swelled within Elizabeth. She knew this would happen. She had hoped that since Francesca was insistent on coming on to her that she would find it as a delightful surprise. But she was wrong. Sad tears welled in her eyes as she stood outside the shut bathroom door hearing Francesca panic on the inside. Her erect penis grew limp and hung down her clean-shaven sexy feminine legs. Her vagina throbbed from desire.

"Well if all you wanted was a pussy I have got one of those too you confused bitch." Elizabeth yelled. Her anger getting the best of her and then she stormed away.

"Get away from me you fucking freak. Get away!" She heard the frantic screams like a trapped animal emanating from the closed bathroom door. She walked over and began packing her things. She had to get out of there. Francesca was no doubt going to cry wolf and then everyone would know what she was.

Suddenly she heard the door to the bathroom open so violently that it shook the room and Francesca came storming out.

"Okay then, I am game." She pouted. Her breast perking to the occasion, as she slowly slipped her fingers in between the tartness of her legs, her pubic hair glistened with moisture as she rubbed furiously at her hot spot and then reaching for Elizabeth's hand, she pulled her close. Elizabeth was mesmerized by the transformation, so she followed Francesca's lead, allowing her to replace her hand and guided Elizabeth's fingers into the depths of her oblivion. For a moment Elizabeth closed her eyes. Captivated by the wetness of her, the erotic sounds of sensuality she emitted from the pit of her abdomen caused her shaft to rise again.

Francesca moved into her, filling the electrified space with hungry desire. Draping Elizabeth behind the nape of her neck with her hand she forcefully pulled her toward her. She stuck her tongue inside of her mouth and allowed their lips to do a tantalizing eager dance.

Francesca's mind was filled with all the fantasies and freaky longings she had ever dared to imagine and squeezed her legs tight almost cutting off the circulation of Elizabeth's hand when the juices for her desires dripped shamelessly down her legs. With each thought of Elizabeth ramming her dick up every crevice of her body, she felt spasms like electrical bolts shocking her head back, arching her spine, rotating her hips and pressing herself into Elisabeth for deeper penetration. Just as she reached for Elizabeth male piece, she felt the stiffened tension of her lips and her hand move away, sliding her finger from her tart and the movement of air circulating in between them.

"What are you doing?" Francesca yelled "Why the fuck are you stopping?" Elizabeth just looked at her, and using both hands, holding her at a distance so she could quell her desires.

"I am sorry Francesca."

"Sorry? What do you mean sorry?" Francesca wrestled her hands free of Elizabeth's grasp.

"On top of being a freak now you are a tease too?"

She was stunned and hurt, but Elizabeth was shocked. She never would have guessed that this woman had this violent nature in her. She turned her face away awed, her body succumbing to the pressure and the heartache of being so verbally smashed.

Then suddenly she felt a lightening fast sting on the side of her face. It happened so fast that she didn't know what hit her. Then she placed her hand to her cheek and felt the burning fire scorch her. As soon as she turned to look at Francesca, Wham! Another one, blending the rouge color on each cheek to match.

"How you like that for leading me on."

"You are fucking nuts." Elizabeth seethed from between her teeth. She couldn't believe that this woman was doing. Had she lost her mind over a piece of ass? Was it the rejection? Damn!

She had barely recovered from the shock of being slapped twice, once on each cheek, when she heard the screeching owl of a siren and the waving banter of a mad woman rushing on her. She ducked just in time and fell on the backwards on the bed, her suitcase coming undone and her clothes flying in every which direction. Francesca went tumbling into the wall and smashed her face.

"Now look what you did." She yelled at the top of her lungs and attacked Elizabeth again. Elizabeth placed her hands over her head to stop the hit she knew was coming and yelped when she felt her back snap and her knees defensively pulled closer into her abdomen. She almost laughed at the absurdity of it all. Was she really being assaulted for saying no to a woman? But the thought didn't stay there long. She had to protect herself from Francesca and she knew how the story would go once it was all over, but as of that moment, it was all over anyway.

"Don't do this Francesca. You know that what you are doing is irrational and it makes no sense at all." She tried to reason with her.

"Now you are condescending me?" She balled her fists into pink knuckles and prepared to swing, but Elizabeth slowly crawled off the bed and stood on the opposite side of it to give them distance.

"We don't have to go where you are taking this. We can sit and talk this out." She laughed in her mind as she said them. Francesca was obviously not in a talking mood and there is going to be no way out but through her.

"Oh now you want to talk? What happened to all that deep logic communication I was dropping on you earlier?" She snickered.

"I just don't want to argue with you. You have been a good friend up until this point. I think we can work this out and go our separate ways with out this getting any nastier than it already had."

"Well you see that's where I think you are wrong. Things are already nasty, it's about to get worse. I mean, who the hell do you think you are? Coming on to me, teasing me and then getting on your high horse about not finishing what you started." She exclaimed in shock, as though the mere thought of not getting her Jones on was the worst thing that could ever happen to her.

"We are both adults here, and I think you are being ridiculously unreasonable. What do you want to do? Rape me?" She said it as a rhetorical question, but the crazed look in Francesca's eyes and the way she was heaving, her balled fists turning pink and her knuckles turning white from the bones rubbing against the skin, she knew that was exactly what was on the woman's mind.

She shook her straight black hair and her slanted Asian

eyes squinted tighter. She was beginning to get furious. Who the fuck did this bitch think she was dealing with? Her anger pained her so much that she could feel the fanged legs of the black widow gyrate against her bosom and its red alert underbelly mark burned scarlet to match the fury that had now built in her.

"Listen, things are about to get way out of hand." She used her hands to illustrate just how out of hand things would get by stretching them wide as far as her hands would go.

"You are not going to like it if you really pissed me off and I am trying like crazy to be understanding. You are gonna make me fuck you up." She warned. The spiders' venom was spreading like wild fire through her system. Francesca didn't wait to lounge again; she hurled herself at Elizabeth and started to punch her. Elizabeth blocked her face with her hands and her fingernails searched for and found the woman's jugular and temple. Her fingernails elongated and punctured her in several different places while her elbows criss-crossed and protected her face like an eagle's claw.

She felt the energy of this woman's spirit who had seemingly attacked her for no reason, and she drew on her fear, played on her emotions and allowed the spider to move through her. The screech that echoed from Francesca's lips almost made Elizabeth freeze in the very spot she laid on the floor, she removed her hands from over her eyes and saw that foam had gathered at the corners of this once beautiful woman's mouth. Her eyes had fallen back inside of her head and she couldn't make anymore sound.

She pulled her hands in and retracted her fingers but it was too late. Francesca fell to the floor and began convulsing. Elizabeth didn't wait. She got herself together, grabbed her things and ran out the door. The play was scheduled to end next week when she was to return to her family and friends, but the play ended in that moment that Elizabeth took the Amtrak train from Atlanta Georgia to Miami Florida.

## MAN KILLER 10

"Don't go Liz," Francesca pleaded weakly from foamed lips and bruised face, neck and temples. She couldn't hear, she couldn't see. She felt paralyzed. "Please come back." And she felt a tear escape and fall from the sides of her face. She pulled her body to the door of the luxury Hilton and kicked at it with all her strength. But her strength was gone and she could not muster enough energy to kick hard enough. The she started to laugh.

She slowly recovered consciousness as the persistent knock at her room door brought her back to the world of the living. Her head was aching and she felt numb all over. But that was nothing compared to the severe cramping she felt in her abdomen, her spine felt rigid and she was nauseated and perspiring profusely, could barely breathe and trembling. She couldn't understand what was happening to her. She couldn't answer the door.

"Elizabeth, Francesca. Is anyone in there?" Came one focused voice amidst a pandemonium of voices outside the door. She tried to answer, but the words were only in her head. She couldn't speak and she was loosing a grip on reality.

"Somebody answer this damn door now or we are coming in." Came a man's voice she vaguely recognized, not because she didn't know her stage manager, but because her mind was taking leave of cognizant thought.

The banging went on insistently until the hotel security was called and the door was programmed to unlock. The casts of the traveling off Broadway play rushed into the opened space to see a naked Francesca curled at the doorway.

"Oh God, is she alive?" Frauline asked terrified by the foaming puke that oozed from the corners of the woman's mouth. But she couldn't help thinking how great it would be to finally now be in a position to play the understudy to Elizabeth, whose position she truly coveted.

"Get the police. Call an ambulance." The stage manager yelled frantically, and the hotel management put the emergency dispatch out to the hotel room. Everyone looked on horrified at the scene unfolding before them and gawked in awe as the medics whisked the stupefied Francesca away.

\*\*\*\*\*\*\*\*\*\*

Francesca was in a coma for four days as detectives swarmed around the ICU unit in wait of her recovery to question her. They had plagued the doctors with questions of why this had happened. They were a permanent fixture at the hospital for three days, surged by curiosity of this strange occurrence of a woman seemingly beaten and abused by another human being, yet they are being told by expert that this woman was reacting to some strange poison of a Black Widow Spider. The very concept of it was strange to them

"So what have we got?" Homicide detective Minto asked as she approached her male peers who all stood in recognition of her professional status and her uncanny beauty.

"We spoke to some arachnid specialist who insists that this lady had come into contact with some special type of Black Widow Spider that's indigenous to the Southern Florida region." Detective Vile told her as he fidgeted with his hat and fumbled to find his words, awed by her mysterious eyes. She was something special and she is the only woman on the special homicide investigation unit. She was young and busted her ass and she didn't play. Her mystery captivated them and she knew her stuff.

"So is she awake yet?" Detective Minto queried, her eyes slowly lingered on each of the three men and then passed them nonchalantly as she sought out the answers to her questions.

"They said that she has come out of the slight coma and her fever had subsided, the level of venom in her system doesn't make sense. The arachnid expert said there is no spider in the world that could administer the quantity to her system that they are saying she got, unless it was the size of a human being." Detective Humdrum added, giving her all the information that they had.

"And that once they have checked her brain waves to see if she is cognizant then we could talk to her." Chimed in Special agent Devout. He smiled broadly at her approval when she nodded and walked away.

"Hey man I think she's into you." Vile chuckled, giving Devout a high five and a playful shove.

"You must be drinking man; she ain't into nobody but her job. That's her man and she probably wants to keep it that way." He stated, pushing him back, wishing with all his mind and heart that the smile she gave him were more than just a appreciation of professional passing on of information.

All three men looked after her as she sashayed her round perky bottom away, wearing the hell out of some Guess fitted bell-bottom jeans, spiked cowboy boots and a white dress shirt with a collar and a neck tie. She had an eclectic style about her that was unique and all her own. She wore her hair short in African Kinky knots on the top of her head

# Man Killer

like little round knitted sets of yarn. She was black and beautiful. They looked on and drooled until she reached the corridor and was about to turn. But she didn't. She turned back and walked full speed back toward them. Something told her to go check on this woman, a natural intuitive instinct she had always had about people but she didn't know quite what was propelling her this time. Just a hunch.

The three men, almost in shock at her abrupt about face stood transfixed. Watching the graceful six foot one inch woman, strut toward them in her boots that gave her at least an added two-inch boost and her necktie that sported little yellow smiley faces.

"Let's go." Her directions were a concise and direct.

"Where are we going?" Devout jogged to catch up with her as she sped past them as though she knew the exact location of what she was looking for.

"Where is her room?" Spinning on Devout stopping him in his tracks and almost causing a back-to-back collision where Vile and Humdrum stopped short of running into the backs of each other.

"You are standing in front of her room." Devout told her and pointed at room 912 with almost shaky hands. He couldn't believe it. The woman had practically followed a trail like a bloodhound and stopped exactly where the trail ended and acted as though she didn't even know it.

She turned to look where the detective finger led and made a quick turn to pursue it. The men turned to look at each other. They were all in pretty good shape. Humdrum was about five foot nine inches and was in the army as a Maintenance sergeant before leaving and becoming a police officer. He was built thick and broad at the shoulders and very average looking. Devout was tall about six feet two inches, and stood eye to eye with Minto. But he knew that with her boots off she would be a good three inches lower than him. He smiled at the thought and turned to look at Vile, who was the only light skin or red bone among them. He was shy but smart, quick on his feet, easy to work with and was the youngest of them all. But looking at Minto made them all feel awkward. She was lithe and strong. Her muscles rippled like a body builder and her skin was as smooth as a baby's bottom. They all felt she could take them if push came to shove and gave her the respect she warranted.

Her reputation preceded her. She went straight from high school into the police academy even though she was accepted at Harvard, Yale, New York University, Rochester Institute of Technology, not to mention Spellman and all the top black universities that were dropping full scholarships at her feet and all the athletic offers she had for track, basketball, swimming and gymnastics.

The woman's stats were mind blowing. She went to the police academy and blew everyone out of the water, men and women alike. The FBI, CIA and all government posts recruited her based on her impressive IQ tests alone. She walked right into the top ranking team in any department she wanted and was paid more than the commissioner of police. But she wanted to stay in her community and to help her people. She was tired of those accomplishing running away and then calling themselves anything but black. She wasn't having it and she was going to stay and clean up her home. She was poetry in motion.

Just as she was about to turn the doorknob, the security alarm went off and there were nurses and doctors running everywhere. They rushed to the door pushing her away as well as the rest of the police detectives who stood fast on her heels.

"What's wrong? What's going on?" Minto asked perplexed at the conundrum that seemed to just have suddenly appeared.

"The patient is going into cardiac arrest." One nurse stopped to inform her. Then pushing by her with the others, pushing carts of equipment and medical paraphernalia's in through the room door.

"Oh my Gosh." Detective Minto panicked and felt a weird aching in her abdomen. She was suddenly trembling as though she could feel what was going on in the woman's head. She stood by the door with them in tow and watched as they brought the woman back to reality, stabilizing her and everyone breathing a sigh of relief. But just as she and her team turned to go, everyone jumped as Francesca's eyes suddenly shot open and she reached past the doctors, past the nurses, and stretched to Detective Minto.

"Elizabeth." She uttered, "Trust your instinct. You know." She whispered in a barely audible tone, her voice dropping a few octaves and everyone strained to understand what she was saying except Detective Minto. She heard, something told her that she did know. But knew what? She had never heard of this woman or this Elizabeth. What did she know?

"What is it? What did she say to you?" Devout asked as Minto turned and walked out the door. Francesca died and they left the doctors to determine time of death. As Minto was cleared from the doorway her feet gave way and she fell right into Devout's waiting arms, who led her to a nearby bench to sit down.

"Get her some water Humdrum!" He ordered and the detective was off to fulfill this duty, while Vile took his handkerchief and patted down the perspiration that beaded on her forehead.

"The woman doesn't even wear make up." He marveled as he looked at the white fabric in his hand that would have come back stained with colors had she been the average woman.

Her eyelids slowly lifted to expose beautiful deep brown eyes that seemed to sparkle when the lights hit them. Her chills suddenly disappeared as she eased herself up from Devout's lap. She was up on her feet and smiling thankfully at Devout. His heart skipped a beat and then began racing as he watched her eyes curl into a slight slit and then opened again when her smile disappeared and she began to speak.

"We have a lot of work to do. We need to call in the forensic team and the coroner's office to find out if the poison was the cause of death." She told them standing and then acknowledging Humdrum who was just returning with the glass of water.

"Thank you," She told him talking it, and in a few short gulps the glass was empty. "There is something very odd about this. Don't ask, I just know." Minto handed the glass back to Humdrum and walked away, again displaying her ass cheeks bouncing with joy at her departure.

Dyania Minto looked behind her and noticed the physicians and nurses departing the room of the newly deceased Francesca. She couldn't believe what happened right before the woman's death, but her life had been filled with many unbelievable tales since she was a little girl. She felt suddenly tired and weird urges that had followed her throughout her entire life returned with a vengeance. She thought her doctor told her they were under control, and for years they seemed to have been. But for the past few months, they had been returning steadily and increasingly more powerful. She needed to call home, call her parents.

She looked favorably at Devout who was still in the middle of this telephone conversation. From the moment she told them what needed to be done, he was on the phone spewing orders and getting the job done. She liked him. She nodded a light nod of approval and walked away.

"Have a good weekend guys. We will pick this up on Monday. A sistah need to get some sleep." She winked playfully and was gone so quickly; that they had to blink twice to appreciate the exit.

\*\*\*\*\*\*\*\*\*\*

Liz was ecstatic to be back in her North Miami home. She looked over her Collins Avenue condo balcony and closed her eyes and imagined the ocean water washing over and cleansing her. She still couldn't believe what had happened, that she had allowed herself to get caught in an incident that could be detrimental to her identity. She had to let the others know. She had worked so hard to protect whom she was, and look at what happened? She was chased off of the set of a show she had worked so hard to accomplish and become good at. All her life she had wanted to become an actress, and she had become well acclaimed within her own right. Now she had lost it all.

"Hello Cathalina." Elizabeth answered waiting for the third ring so that the caller ID could register the person on the other end. She breathed a sigh of relief since her psychologist and friend was exactly who she needed to speak with.

"Hello my dear, I just received your message. Sorry I didn't get it earlier." Cathalina had received her message earlier that night, and had wondered what was going on, but she was a bit tied up with Cleopatra and could not get away. She tried to keep the personal counseling of each member private and only shared what concerned her sisters.

"Is everything okay?" Cathalina asked, sensing Elizabeth's energy through the telephone and she could tell

that something was very wrong. Even though Elizabeth sounded like her normal calm and tranquil self.
"Well, things are not good Cathalina. I think I may have gotten myself into trouble."
"What kind of trouble Liz? You were away working. What would make you return from your job a week before it concluded? Does it have anything to do with us?" The phone went deadly quiet, and Cathalina felt her heart begin to pound against her chest. She felt the Brown Recluse, she sat in her Coral Gables office and stared out over at Biscayne Bay, she placed her hand at her chest in a subconscious attempt to hold her heart in.
"No Cathalina, it has everything to do with me. But..." her voice trailed off and Cathalina could hear her swallow hard. "But it will affect us." She finished, lowering her eyes as though Cathalina could see her pain and anger that she rarely allows to surface.
"Liz, come on baby, talk to me." She sighed deep and heavily, her mind going a hundred miles per minute, wondering what the hell was going on.
"Psyche!" Liz yelled, "I got ya!" she laughed exuberantly.
"What the fuck you mean psyche? Liz this is not a joke and I am damn sure not playing with you. Tell me what the hell is going on?" Cathalina demanded.
"Nothing is going on Cath, you gotta chill and relax a little. You are too uptight." Elizabeth counseled.
"What exactly do you mean by that?" Cathalina asked, being careful not to show her claws.
"Listen to me, I am not trying to disrespect you Cathalina, but you need to relax, go to the spa and take a break, take care of yourself. I feel mad vibes coming from you. A crazy sexual energy that seemed to be fighting its way

to be unleashed." She did feel the passion that Cathalina was emanating. She couldn't quite put her finger on it, but she felt that Cathalina couldn't handle her news right now. She had to get herself straight and figure things out before she goes jumping to conclusion. Maybe nothing is wrong anyway. Maybe Francesca is fine and just jonesing for a good fuck and that's it. But something told her she was wrong.

"Al right, I feel you sweetheart. But this is not the time for jokes or games Elizabeth. We have business to take care. Actually, we should meet. Some things have happened you need to be updated on." She decided to let the situation slide. Her gut instinct tells her that there is something Liz was hiding, but she didn't want to have her friend's homecoming a sad one. She had come and gone as they needed her, taking breaks in between shows and last minute travels to arrive back at her hotel by morning. She should be rewarded for that.

"How about we meet for a late breakfast. I will drive up to see you." She told her. "Hey, what about that nice breakfast nook on the beach on Collins Avenue? Is it still there?" Cathalina asked excitedly.

"I think its still there. Gosh, we haven't been there since, since..."

"Since I began initiating you more that a year and a half ago. It's been a long time that we have been friends."

"Yeah." Elizabeth acknowledged, allowing herself to drift back into the past to the times when she felt really lost and alone.

"They served the best prochuto and salmon slices, with toast and juice."

"The special." The both giggled together.

"Yeah, let's meet there. I cannot wait to see you sister. I have missed you." Cathalina laughter subsided in a low toned elation of friendship shared with someone she cares deeply for.

"Okay, you are on." Elizabeth laughed.
"Last one to The Nook is a dead spider!" Cathalina giggled and hung up the phone.
"Oh no you didn't just hang up on me. I live right around the corner woman." Elizabeth said to the beeping dial tone and hung up. The phone immediately rang back.
"I do know you live around the corner, but your slow ass takes forever to get dressed and go someplace, especially when you think you have the advantage." Cathalina bellowed through the phone lines.
"How the hell did you know I was thinking that?"
"Because I know you heffa. Now get dressed. I am out."

MAN KILLER

## MAN KILLER 11

Serena tossed and turned herself into frenzied sexual tension and her dreams could not let the image of Vincent Ratigan go. He held her captive emotionally and she could not understand why. Her dreams ran rabid and got progressively more stimulating from night to night. She would dream about his voice, his baldhead, his sexy lips burying into her snatch and she would emit multiple orgasms, the spider leaving her almost wrapped in a webbed cocoon every morning she awake.

She was awakened again, and she laughed at herself.

"I must really be loosing my mind. Soon I would have to check myself into a psyche ward for being delusional." She laid her head back to the pillow and snuggled to get comfortable, but as soon as she closed her eyes, the images tore at her mind again.

She would imagine little Latoya's mangled body, visualize him raping and killing child after child. She did not know and couldn't comprehend what to do with all those feelings, all those emotions.

"Jasssssssoooooon!" She screamed, jostled from her sleep and heaving in a mass of opaque mass and sweat. She was naked, chest heaving and horny.

"Yes ma'am." He was at her feet, with lowered eyes, holding on to her bedside awaiting her bidding or punishment. He never knew which would come to him each time she called. "Jason, Jason, oh Jason." Her tears streamed down her face and she felt violated all over again. That same little girl having sexual interaction without her consent of full knowledge of what is happening. She hated the feeling of being out of control but to enjoy it like this; she wasn't sure whether to be angry or happy.

"Jason," his name echoed from her lips in short raspy whimpers and when she reached her arms out to him, he crawled on the bed towards her. Scared to death of what he was witnessing as she emerged or was metamorphosis into something else. He wasn't sure what was going on, and feared for her life as well as his own.

"I am here Serena. I am here with you love." The consolation came sincerely and the wad of creamy secretion that she nestled in excited and terrified him all at once.

*********

Elizabeth woke up throbbing and couldn't understand she was suddenly immersed in urges she never had before. She had been sprung awake screaming every night with no one to hold her hand, sending her in spasms of overwhelming desires and chaotic thoughts. Her already guilty conscience was not allowing her much sleep, and the added effects of demanding sexual desires were not helping her at all. She would awaken with multiple puncture wounds of the black widow in a way that she never experienced before. As it the creature was violating its own hosts. But that was impossible.

She heard the phone ringing violently. She took a look at the clock and saw that it was three in the morning. She cringed with worry and frustration as to who would be calling at 3 am on a Saturday morning. She turned on her back and closed her eyes, ignoring the annoying sound of the telephone.

A few minutes went by and it rang again, refusing to be ignored. She tossed and turned, pretending that the ringing instrument was just a figment of her imagination. The caller stopped momentarily. This time, for a couple hours and Elizabeth smiled a sigh of relief and attempted to return to her slumber, but the caller would not give up. Elizabeth jumped to her feet and snatched the phone from its cradle.

"It's three in the morning. What do you want?" She demanded without knowing who it was, she had not even bothered to turn on the lights. She just wanted to be left alone.

"Liz, you bitch you. Why you didn't tell me you were back in town?" requested the drunken slur on the other end of the phone line.

"What are you talking about Cleo? It's three in the morning! I have been back only one week and we are meeting today at Sex Cells, what's the big deal?" Annoyed at the abrupt disrespect and the fact that Cleopatra was drinking and was obviously dismayed, she softened her voice and turned in to her next dear friend.

Cleo was aggressive and felt confused most times. She always had a need to hunt and destroy. Her father prostituted her and her siblings to his friends beginning when she was seven years old. She didn't understand why her older sisters and brothers were having sex with each other. He would force her to watch his male friends penetrate her ten-year-old sister and watch tears run down her face, as bloody screams were just a turn on. Her twelve-year-old sister was violated in every orifice she possessed and her brothers were raped over and over again by these men as well as forced to have sex with each other. She was allowed to lick and suck and touch him as he fingered her vagina and performed oral sex on her. It destroyed her when her ten year old sister, got tired of the whole thing and bit the dick clear off of one of her daddy's friends. He was so angry that he went and got his revolver and blew her head off. Then threatened said same to any of them who dared to do something like that again.

Poor Cleo was terrified, and pee herself as she watched the man bleed to death. Her father took the man, her two older brothers and her now only sister to the back yard at three am in the morning and buried him. The pedophile's body and her sisters were buried together. Their mother dared not fuss or ask too many questions, not that she was capable. Since he had her drugged up and turning tricks at the street corners to put food on the table while he ate, drank and fucked the life out of their family.

Cleopatra watched as the years moved from her being seven to eight and then nine years old. Three years she watched her mother shoot up drugs into her arms and did whatever her husband told her to do. Three years she watched her brothers and sisters as they began to enjoy the abuse and began acting up in school. No one cared for Ghetto children living in the worst drug infested areas of Tallahassee. Not even the police would venture there after dark. And even the animals were abusive of themselves and each other. One day she walked in on her older sister who was eleven years old at the time and her youngest brother who was eight years old having sex. Her brother's face was between her sister's legs and her sister had what looked like their mother's dildo, violating her brother's anus. He was bleeding and whimpering and the more he whimpered the more violent her sister became.

Cleo ran to the garage and got a bottle of kerosene oil and threw it on the both of them. Her father stopped her as she was about to light the match and burn them both. She

was scared and terrified by the ruthlessness of her family.
    When she turned nine years old, Cleopatra took her fathers gun and took them all out of their misery. She was found dirtied and disoriented in their back yard trying to dig a grave for the rest of her demented family members. She hadn't slept in days nor had she eaten. She had defecated and pissed on herself for days so it was caked to her body with every new release. She had gone temporarily insane and was admitted to an Insane Asylum until she was nineteen years old. She was released into a world she had no idea about and found her way to Miami with the only talent she had.
    "Are you okay Cleo?" Elizabeth asked again more softly hearing the woman's sobs in the background.
    "Yeah, I am fine. I have just been missing you is all. I am really excited you are home."
    "Thanks Cleo. I know you were holding down the fort for us all here. How have you been?"
    "Drama girl, you know these men are no good. If it wasn't for their money and their dicks I would get rid of them all." She snickered. Elizabeth understood and smiled with a light chuckle so that Cleo would know that she understood where she was coming from.
    "You know it's not all like that now, don't you Cleo? I mean, not all men are bad, just like not all women are good."
    "Are you trying to insinuate something woman?" the intensity of her sudden anger flashed across the phone lines and stung Liz.
    "I am not trying to say anything my friend." Elizabeth backed down softly. She knew that this was a touchy subject for Cleo. They all knew each other's stories to some extent. Only Cathalina knew them all in detail and there was a certain level of confidentiality amongst them all.
    "I am just saying that, women are sometimes just as

worthless as men. Good and bad in each sex of the human race. That's what makes eradicating one or the other so damned hard. Or I would be out there with you on a beheading hunt. You know that don't you Sister?" Elizabeth tamed her voice and used their friendship to bring Cleo off of her defensive horse.

Again she heard the sobs and her heart ached for this woman whom she had known now for a full six years. She worked in Sex Cell for a long time before she met Cathalina and began seeing her. Cathalina was Cleo's prized commodity and she wouldn't let any of her workers or patrons near her. Cleo and Cathalina met and became friends ten years ago, so their friendship had survived and seen much, and it was clear that Cathalina was partial to Cleopatra's feelings.

"Cleo, baby girl, I will see you soon okay. Save a nice big hug for your little 'Nina' okay?" Her giggle was contagious and Cleopatra began to laugh. She always loved when the submissive came to see Elizabeth back in the day when she worked for her. They loved her diverse sex organs. Cleo called her 'Nina' because on the street, that's the name of a 9mm gun. Cleo said to have sex with her was a dangerous and deeply erotic thing. She always got her man or gal and if she wanted to, she could let them walk out without their wallets.

"See, I knew I could make you laugh."

"Yeah Nina, you were da bomb, always was and always will be." Cleo told her as she drifted off into her thoughts. Elizabeth was special and she hoped she knew how much she meant to her.

"So how about we go get some sleep. I will see you soon." Liz smiled her way through the call, she had to go lay down. Her dick was as hard as a rock and she needed to jerk off.

"Okay Nina. Good night." Elizabeth blew her a kiss and hung up the phone.

\*\*\*\*\*\*\*\*\*\*

Elizabeth got off the phone and headed to her bathroom. She spread her legs and stood over the toilet seat with her throbbing sex in her hand. She picked up the porn magazine that hid in the center of the magazine rack and placed it on the toilet bowl, turning the page as she gently massage the shaft of her desire. The moans came slowly as she imagined how good it would have been to place herself in Francesca's pleasure center. Gaining momentum she imagined withdrawing herself as Francesca took her twelve-inch weapon all the way down her throat without even gagging. Her pants came in rapid spurts and her breast heaved, perspiration beading on her forehead as she prepared to orgasm.

"Humm yes. That's it girl, right there." She spoke to the imaginary bobbing head that took her love stick into her trachea and shoved herself in and out of her hands as though the soft moistness of a woman's lips propelled the building desire. "Don't stop, don't stop," rasping voice begged the naked woman in her mind to take her in deeper. "Yes, Yessssssss, Yessss!" she breathed, as her ejaculation squirted into the toilet bowl blending with the water and making it creamy murky where her cum fell.

Drained from the experience, she pulled herself together and sighed deeply. It's been a while since she had been intimate with someone for her own pleasure. A while since someone had accepted her for who she was and allowed themselves to taste the advantage being with her would present, especially if that person was a man. But things have not gone in her favor. The only physical contact she can recall is when she was punishing a perpetrator, but that's not fun, its work. Well, sometimes its fun, she snickered and thought to herself as she took the washcloth down and wiped herself.

Slipping into a silky black gown, she got an elastic strap belt that is about the size of a thigh gun holster. She put her crotch less panty on, because those were the only kinds that could make her feel like a woman and let her penis hang. She took her now flaccid member and allowed it to hang against her soft inside thigh, then took the strap and band it against her legs so that when she was dressed like a lady, all you can imagine between her legs would be a vagina. The only problem was that it hurt like crazy if she got excited, that's why she masturbated first.

Wrapping herself into her black silky negligee she slid herself under the covers and closed her eyes.

"I cannot believe it's almost morning." She mumbled as she turned to her lamp on the nightstand and turned it off. Elizabeth had nightmares about Francesca that night. She knew something was wrong. She sensed it. She didn't know exactly why her body began to tremble and perspiration involuntarily formed on her body, making the bed sheets feel as though she was under water and couldn't breathe. She couldn't understand why the night gown that made her feel sexy only hours before, transformed into a death garb. But when she awoke, the black widow spider plastered in the center of her chest and between the mounds of her breast was hung upside down, where the red hourglass that is its signature mark bled red and drops of blood beaded around it like sweat.

"Oh my gosh, oh my gosh." She squealed to herself.

"Something has happened." She ran to the phone and began dialing Cathalina's number. But then she stopped.

"No, I am being paranoid. I can handle this." She consoled herself. "I cannot keep running to Cathalina every time I think something is wrong. Every time I get myself into some fucked up situation she has to get me out of it. Nothing is wrong. NOTHING is wrong." She stated firmly, and then placed the phone back on its base.

She began laughing, laughing so loud that she could hear herself echoing in the early morning dew. She walked to her balcony and looked out across Collins Avenue to the rising sun coming over the horizon of the ocean. "God you are so amazing, so powerful, and so awesome in all your glory. Just look at you go with your bad self!" She praised and placed her hands to the heavens and began to cry.

Denise Campbell

## MAN KILLER 12

Cleopatra hung up the phone and turned around to face the mound of molting fetid bodies piled behind her. She had been collecting them for a week, ever since Cathalina allowed her to taste the sweet succulence of her nectar once more. She didn't understand why she had gone out on her own, why she was uncontrollably propelled to destroy. She felt better than she had since Serena came into the picture. Better than their mutual goals and plans.

She choked and began vomiting again as the smell gained in intensity. She had to do something. This was her workplace, her business. A dungeon yes, but the fact that she had brought the decaying bodies to the underbelly of her home, dug deep on the underside about three levels beyond the main floor where the rooms and her girls worked their feminine and devious magic with their bodies for money. She took them to the level where she kept her pets; her alligators that she knew didn't judge her and would enjoy the appetizing rotten semi-decaying pieces of flesh. She could have concealed her wreckless hands along time ago, but she refused to allow the gators to partake of her kill this time. She wanted to see them decay and molt. Their jawbones becoming decomposed and slimy with teeth structure exposed. Eyes sunken and bodies wrapped, warped, broken, and dismantled. It was obvious that something strong and powerful had gotten to these people. She looked at the bloody gross mass of missing body parts on mismatched bodies and half eaten body members. Her stomach churned with disgust and hunger as she began regurgitated the day's meal. Seething and writhing white footballs compiled thousands of maggots.

"Madam, Madam," Came Natalia's frantic call from the second floor. She knew she needed to meet her quickly before she got any closer and smelled the stench. Natalia knew that no one was allowed pass the main floor without specific clearance, but she just couldn't help it. She understood that she was special to Cleo and felt she could break a little bit of the rules.

"What is it Natalia?" Cleo suddenly appeared at the second landing to the curving stone stairs that looked like a dragon's lair. The walls were unfinished and rocky, cobwebs and molds made the place realistically spooky to say the least. Natalia s wrinkled her nose like a rabbit's and moved it around awkwardly. She didn't want her Mistress to see her so openly put off by a scent. One of the lessons Cleopatra always taught was that smells came in all variety, and that the customers are also varied. If they couldn't control their noses then they wouldn't be able to control their pockets.

"Madam, Joanna and Fatima are at it again."

"What is it this time?" Cleo asked, in a surprisingly cool and calm voice that scared Natalia. Cleo would normally burst forward yelling and into action.

"Oh it is the usual Madam. A man."

"Really, what is so special about this man?"

"Money Mistress and this is the same man that they have fought over for months. He is always saying the same thing. How he gets a way with murder."

"Murder." She pondered mischievously. "I wonder what the pull is to him?" She asked herself dazed, almost gliding her two hundred pound body up the spiral dungeon's rocky stairs.

Natalia lingered behind her, curiosity pulling at her to go check where the foul smell is coming from and eyed Cleopatra as she made an exit. What could smell so horrible, Natalia thought to herself, pinching her nose to stop the odor from forcing itself upon her. She looked behind her again and heard the upper level door close, and then she began creeping down. Not seeing the slight trail of blood on the stair, she slipped.

"Shit!" She exclaimed as she tried to regain her balance. "What the hell does she do down here all the time?" She asked herself out loud. As she made her way down the stairs, Cleo stealthily crept back through the door leading down the spiral stairway to her private dungeon. She watched Natalia as she coughed and gagged as she neared the stench of the week old dead bodies. It was very dark and she could not see it. But she knew there something rancid there. She was taken aback as her feet neared the landing and touched something soft. She squealed and looked cautiously behind her to see if anyone heard.

Cleo watched the woman who had become her most trusted whore, her money make coochie. She wanted to see what she would do, how much more she could trust her. She swung her big bodacious body behind a stair crevice when Natalia turned around, then peaked her head back out as the woman stood still, not knowing what to do then ascending the stairs backwards.

Cleopatra speedily crept back out of the stairway and walked a little way down the hall, then turned back and made her way bumping into Natalia making her way from her secret place.

"Madame, did you see them?"

" No, actually I had something else to take care of, so I

# Man Killer

sent Hercules to settle the dispute."

"Hercules, why did you do that? He would kill somebody!" Horror wrote itself on her face as she thought of her friends.

"Well, you know my rules Natalia." Cleopatra said drawling her name in an Italian accent. She loved the way the woman's name sounded coming off her tongue. "I don't want fighting over money or dicks. We can get both and we are all above it. We are family." She told her calmly. Then glided by her and opened the door to her special place of solitude. Natalia gasped. She knew what this woman was capable of; she was starting to become concerned that she didn't know just how much this woman was capable of. Her instincts told her to beware.

"But ma'am, they were two of your best girls. Did you tell Hercules to take it easy?"

"How dare you question me? Would you care to be in their place?" Cleo scorned red burning in her eyes, the scales on her back rising, her shoulders stretching. She was already stressed. She felt sexual urges and desires she wasn't sure were hers. She felt that Cathalina was ignoring her since she re-sampled the goods, now her slaves and her workers over were stepping their bounds. Even from Natalia, she was not having it today.

"I didn't mean to say anything wrong Madame, I was just concerned." She lowered her eyes apologetically and stepped to the woman to receive whatever wrath she wished to bestow upon her. But Cleo just turned and walked away from her. She didn't want to hurt Natalia. She just wanted her to know and remember her place at all times.

"I am expecting the gang. Let them down here when they arrive. Tell Hercules to bring the man my girls are so infatuated with. I want to see just how murderous he is, and what he is packing in his pants to drive my sisters wild." She snickered at the thought, but felt herself building moisture between her thighs at the thought. Now she knew something was wrong. She never gets excited over the thought of a man. Natalia, smiled quickly at the thought of seeing Elizabeth and Cathalina. She had heard so much about them both. These ladies are legends. Vices have been trying to track them for years when the first string of murders and missing people went down. No one connected them to anything. They were so cool and swerve.

*The Gang!* She thought. Now this should be interesting. All those talk about Serena who has stepped in on Cathalina. She hoped she would be there too. Her stomach knotted with the assignment. She rushed off with butterflies tingling her in stomach and her mind racing

\*\*\*\*\*\*\*\*\*\*

Cathalina knew that this day would be hard. She knew that after what she shared at the Ft. Lauderdale airfield with Cleo that she would expect more. It could never be just about the moment with her.

"Serena baby, are you ready girl?" She asked as she kissed the woman on her forehead. She relaxed in the back of the black car she decided on for transportation to Sex Cell.

"I am okay Cathy. I just keep having these dreams and headaches. It hurts." She confessed. "Sometimes I want them to stop, sometimes it's as if my mind is bombarded with things I have done in my past, and from a life I know I have not lived. Yet, it feels so real."

Cathalina snuggled closer to Serena and placed her arm around the woman's shoulder. She then gently touched her temple, urging her head to find a resting place in the crevice of her chest. She felt her heart beat as Serena recounted the dreams, the fantasies, and the spider's anger, not to mention the vision. She knew there would be some side effects, a consequence to Serena being inducted with the Brazilian Wandering Spider. That spider was the most deadly. They had no idea how it would interact with her system. She was excited and scared all at once at the prospect, but for now she just listened.

"It's going to be okay Honey. I know this all new, but its so exciting. You are the spider queen. Now we will meet for the first time as a family. Today we will understand how we are tired together as a unit. Today we will map out our journey and you will become stronger, and more powerful as you learn your way around you symbiosis." Cathalina smiled widely, thinking of all that she had worked for to get to this day, this moment. The side effects are an extra benefit. "You will become," she stopped herself to make a correction, "no; you are the SPIDER QUEEN, our leader. Our Queen bee and we are at your disposal for anything you need us to do within the ranks of our association." Cathalina's voice was soft, motherly, comforting and totally in control. She needed Serena to adapt to these skills quickly, adapt to her new body.
Serena curled her legs under her and snuggled closer into Cathalina, listening to her map out her destiny.

"How long before we get to Liz?"

"We are close now. She will be waiting outside for us, and then we will head to Cleo's. She is expecting us." Her voice dipped a few octaves at that moment, the thought of Cleopatra waiting for them. If Serena gets anymore powerful, she would be able sense character and anticipate behavior. She didn't want Serena to become too aware of what is between her and Cleo, at least, not yet. She wanted Serena, she needed her to love and depend on her as a partner. But she knows that no matter what, Cleo will be a problem.

"Make a left here." Cathalina uttered instructions for the Limo driver to exit off on Collins Avenue and to enter the approaching estates. "This is it, have the guards buzz us in." She told him.

As they pulled up the Elizabeth's condo, they say the black woman with her full round face smiling brightly at them. Her evenly whitened teeth shone with joy as her eyes come to an almost full closer. Her straight long black hair fluttered in the slight breeze that coiled her long flowing white linen dress between her legs and curving around her body.

Cathalina exited the vehicle and dashed towards Elizabeth.

"Woman, what a sight for sore eyes you are. You are even more beautiful today than the day I met you." Cathalina complemented, spinning her around to admire how well she put herself together, and then hugged her again. "No one would ever be able to tell you are packing a twelve inch weapon between those gorgeous legs." They laughed heartily and pulled away from each other with a smile.

"I missed you Cathalina. I felt like I was missing apart of myself being away from home." Sadness came over her as she thought back to Francesca. An eerie feeling enveloped her and she cringed. Oh gosh I hope she is okay she thought.
Noticing the change is Elizabeth's face Cathalina became concerned.

"Is everything copasetic?" She asked, searching Liz's eyes for the answer. Perking up, Liz put on a great big poker face and shook her head yes.

"So can I see our new initiate? I want to see how she has bonded with her soul mate." Liz commented and walked toward the other side of the Limo where the driver stood with the door waiting for her to enter. While Cathalina slipped in on the left side where she exited and back next to Serena, she was now sandwiched with Elizabeth and Cathalina on each side of her.

As the women settled into the comfort of the seat ready to make the forty five minute trip from North Miami Beach to Miami where Cleo's spot was, they shared an electrified sensation that brought them to a sudden alert. The women sat up and grabbed the arm of the other so that they were huddled and began interlocking.

"Oh God, did you feel that?" Excitement filled Cathalina to the brim of overflowing. The sensuality she felt was beyond anything she had ever experienced. It was like having ten people massage, caress and gently kiss her body all over. Rolling her in soft rose petals and bubbling champagne that was as smooth as butter, wrapping her in a cocoon of love and delight as passionate urges throb between her thighs and dripped down her legs. She felt as though light was around her, the life after death kind of light with angelic serenade. The split second of transmission held her captive emitting an orgasmic sensation that was so profound she was speechless.

"Yes. What was that?" Elizabeth turned and looked at Serena who sat centered to her and Cathalina, she didn't say anything, but the startled horrific look on her face sprang fear within them.

"Its alright, she is probably just having another reaction." Cathalina soothed, making an attempt to calm the anxiety rising within them.

"Yeah but Cathalina, did you feel that?" Elizabeth was hard pressed to believe that Serena was making them feel this incredible. But the look on Serena's face didn't say she felt incredible, she looked to be in pain.

Another sensation jolted them back to the smooth leather upholstering that covered the seat in tawny brown. While they sat affixed to their seat, they felt another sensation, a thought.

"What was that?"
"What was what Cathy? I didn't feel that."
"No, not a feeling. Did you say something?"
"I didn't say a word. I thought you said it?"
"But Serena hasn't moved. She didn't say anything."
Cathalina was sure. But the voice did sound familiar to hers, though muffled and filled with rage.

Suddenly, Serena's back arched and her head fell so far back, Cathalina and Elizabeth grabbed her simultaneously to prevent damage to her neck. As they wrapped their arms around her back they felt huge humps rise upon them. Her face became distorted with pain yet; she still had not made a sound.

"I think you are over reacting Serena." Cathalina responded, not realizing that the words were not spoken to her but sent telepathically.

"I agree with Serena." Elizabeth retorted. "She is right. Why should he get away with it? That poor child must be traumatized."

"But he has not done anything wrong." Cathalina argued, thinking that she just really needed to get over to Sex Cell so they can figure out what's going on and where to go from where they were. Things were developing so fast and seemed to be spanning out of Cathalina's control. She knew this would happen but she is no longer the one guiding them. Something within Serena was.

He has not done anything yet. Was the thought that Serena transmitted back. But I can feel it. I know he will hurt them. Another violent convulsion and Serena was doubled over in the back of the Limo regurgitating the mountain of food she contained earlier that morning.

"My Gosh Serena what did you eat?" Cathalina asked as she and Elizabeth released the hold on Serena to cover their nose and mouth. The smell that was permeating within the limo was making them feel sick. They looked again, and saw that there were pieces of human body members that were half digested and rotting within her. The smell caused them to bulge and their thoughts become joined as one.

This man has been beating his wife senseless for the past four years. He has a few lovers, but that has not satisfied him. He is tired of his wife and children getting in his way. He feels trapped and wants out.

Cathalina and Elizabeth looked at each another and then toward the front of the car where there was an opaque glass soundproof partition that was up. They could see the driver but he could not see them. He could sense that there was something going on, a commotion. But it was not his concern. He had more important things on his mind.

"But how do you know this?" Cathalina asked, terrified and fascinated by the shared knowledge they were experiencing.

"What if you are wrong?" Elizabeth asked out loud. They were trying to be reasonable, but the sensation that Serena was sending them was not one of collaboration but action. They too felt unlike themselves as they were drawn and their thoughts and ideas melted with Serena. They could hear her telepathy, but they could not transmit back. Anger rose within them as her thoughts sent snapshot after snapshot visuals and sound effect of the day earlier.

"I am going to cut your fucking neck off!" He bellowed over the frail looking woman who cowered on the kitchen floor amidst pots and pans that had been thrown at her,

leaving behind blood drenched mouth and lips swollen to painful proportions. The woman grabbed her head and held a kitchen dishcloth to it in futile attempt to stop the blood. They cringed as the man pounded away his frustration at the woman. But then they were taken to the other end of the room, toward the staircase where twins sat huddled in tears.
"Don't hurt mommy daddy."
"We don't want mommy to be dead." They cried so hard that there were no longer tears but stained cheeks and puffy eyes on innocent little faces that have become used to abuse.

Their anger brew as Serena showed them what she saw and the spiders became testy, rustling on the various parts of their bodies as they grew within them.

"No, I don't think we should do this. Not here. Not in broad daylight."

"I am NOT asking your permission Cathy." Serena bellowed, words cascading from her lips for the first time since they got inside the car.

"I am not being disobedient Serena. I just think we should be strategic." The reason coming from Cathalina was hard to deny, and Serena's respect and admiration for her, caused the anxiety of the Brazilian Wandering Spider to quell and relax.

"We can do this another way. We know who he is now, and where he lives. Let's just get to our destination and take care of this later."

But he intends to burn his home down tonight and cover it as an accident to collect the insurance money. Two years ago he took out life insurance on his entire family. This man will hurt his family before the day is out. Was the thought Serena tried so hard to lock from her mind. The children looked to be the same age she was when her father decided he wanted more from her.

"It will be okay Serena. Please trust me. I have not steered you wrong."

Serena turned slowly and looked at Cathalina. Her eyes were wide and murderous and her skull widened and cracked with coagulated ooze forming on her face like sweat. She felt for a minute that Serena did not trust her. In that instant, she thought Serena would attack her. But Serena returned her gaze toward the front of the vehicle where her interest sat, stuffed in his black suited uniform, his thick eighteen-inch neck bulking from his choler.

Then Serena sat back. The sensations begin to temper and fade as Serena saw the reason in Cathalina's words. Elizabeth was still on the defense, ready to do as Serena commanded. Her fingers already elongated into poisonous talons, her mind not strong enough to sustain another image from Serena without action. Elizabeth's alertness sent a surge of arousal through Serena and the thought was as out of her control as the desire to defecate.

There was a loud crack and the partition was shattered into a multitude of glass pieces and before the driver was able to react, Elizabeth's talon had stung his huge neck and left puncture wounds the size of a quarters on him. Shock and adrenaline budged his eyes from his body and the color was drained from his face. But instead of becoming even paler, the Venezuelan man's face turned black as the tar that's used to cement the streets. The poison was intentional and angry. He was dead on impact and the vehicle speed out of control on the 1-95 causing cars on either side of it to come to halting stops, screeching and spinning as the limo quickly regained control when Elizabeth slipped nimbly to the front seat discarding of the body as she calmed down from the rush and felt her body tingle as with the medley and after effects of getting off a

roller coaster ride at Walt Disney World
.

\*\*\*\*\*\*\*\*\*\*

"Hurry, let them in." Bellowed Cleo when she saw the banged up Limo pulled up to the beautifully established looking day spa. The outside fascia eludes any suspicion about what goes on under the three tiers leveled dungeon specializing in BDSM. Natalia put on her best professional smile and walked briskly through the front door and into the posh waiting area, where unsuspecting clients awaited their manicures and pedicures, reading and listening to smooth jazz.

Cathalina hugged Serena close to her and Elizabeth ran behind them. There were a few suspicious stares at the unkemptness of the women who arrived and were ushered in behind the closed doors leading to the spa quarters. They received a few undesirable stares from those who thought they had skipped the waiting area and were receiving preferential treatment, but the most that happened were a few crossed eyes and hissing of teeth.

"What happened to you guys?" Cleo questioned, looking Cathalina up and down with a nonverbal, I told you so, and waited for a response. She waved Natalia away with the flip of her wrist and the woman knew what to do.

"It's a long story Cleo. Can we get away from here and go into The Cave to have this discussion please?" Cathalina snapped. She was in no mood for Cleo's barking ignorant ways.

"This is not the time to get all high and mighty on me Cath." Cleo spat. "I am the head bitch in this place." She clenched her fist and stormed off. "What? Aren't you coming?" She turned to look at the stunned faces behind her. She didn't see the piercing look that Serena gave her, nor the way that Elizabeth's spider perched on her chest in preparation to launch. Her anger was all she saw and felt and at that moment, she didn't care what any of them thought. Especially Serena.

"I would keep walking and cut that temper down if I wore you Cleo. This is not the time to act butch. You don't know what's going on and you are going to put yourself in harm's way if you don't chill." Cathalina warned calmly, and then smiled, hoping that Cleo would pick up the hint. She felt Serena temperature rise and her body shuddering. She knew Cleo was about to put herself in immediate danger.

"Whatever!" Cleo stammered as she walked off, leading the way to their specially established place at The Cave. Once they were all behind closed doors, Cleo pressed the hidden button on the wall and the huge steal door slowly pulled shut behind them.

"Cleo listen, things have changed. There have been some advanced reactions to the spider initiation on Serena that we don't know about. You need to be…"

"I don't need to be or do anything Cathalina. That's what you all don't seem to understand. I am so tired of everyone running around talking about Serena this or Serena that. Who the fuck is Serena?"

"Cleo please calm down." Elizabeth begged. She was on telepathy communication with Serena; she was now bound by her command as they pledged to follow whoever was initiated with the Brazilian Wandering Spider and whoever the spider chose to assimilate with. Serena passed. She survived. The first to have done so in the ten years that they have been trying to find a leader to guide them and since Elizabeth joined, at least three women died in the quest of accepting the Brazilian Spider. But Serena is strong, and she is now pulling their strings and forcing them to do her bidding just by her

sheer will.
"Why the hell are you too acting all scared of this bitch all of a sudden? She has never even been fucked and is so naïve its not even funny. We are the elders here. Not her. We are the leaders here. We tell her what to do!" The minute the words come out of her mouth Elizabeth had leapt to her side in one giant stride and had grown spiked talons in preparation to strike.
"Please Cleo." Elizabeth begged, not able to control what she would have to do if given the command.
"Serena is our queen Cleo, please calm down. She will not hurt you. You are our guardian and provided us a safe haven." Cathalina used her calming techniques to stroke Cleo's ego, but the woman was so enraged that the entire time she spoke Cathalina held Serena to her bosom like a brand new vulnerable baby. That she took her side and defended her, as though the other night didn't happen. As though they were not friends and lovers way before Serena was even a thought."
"Fuck you Cathalina. Fuck all of..." Her eyes bulged with terror as she watched as though in slow motion the way Serena began to shake. It happened almost instantaneous.
The woman fell to her knees and then was suddenly on all four of her limps, simultaneously, she grew legs and her head reared in anger, Cleo's jaw fell opened when Serena belched and a thick white glob came out from her mouth plastering Cleo's mouth shut and jolting her back so hard with such force, that she was flung to the wall and all two hundred pounds of her hung from her head, where only her mouth was paste shut with the webbed material and her arms and legs flung wildly in an attempt to release the grip on her.
Elizabeth and Cathalina stepped back respectfully as Serena warned them not to interfere. Serena spat again, and used the

blobby material to restrain Cleo's hands and abdomen to the wall and then released the hold on her mouth. Serena knew she wouldn't scream. She would be curious. Besides, no one could hear them in there. Now listen to me. I have nothing against you. We are working together and right now you need to shut the hell up and let's take care of business.
"But, but…"
No buts Cleo. This is the way things are. I didn't ask for this either yet here I am. Don't I look fucked up? I hate my life; I hate the man who did this to me. I wish I knew where he was so I could rip him apart.
"Serena, we are all hurt, don't hurt Cleo. She is a victim in this too, just like the rest of us." Cathalina jerked back the tears that threatened to invade her eyes.
"Life could be so much better." Serena diverted her attention from Cleo and turned to look at Elizabeth and Cathalina, who stood by her side. "Look at us. W are accomplished, educated, successful and beautiful women with careers and assets that made us the envy in everyday life. But what kind of life is this that we are living? Look that this disgusting monster that I am becoming. The hatred and rage in me is eating me up and consuming me to the point that I can no longer think about anything but destroying the very idea of the bastards that do things like this to people like us."
Cleo snickered cynically at Serena's pain, and with the thought she felt what seemed like a tongue lash out and stung her hard making her scream out. But it was a phantom thought that reprimanded her.
"How? What?" she couldn't complete her thought instead she looked to Cathalina for support but Cathalina only looked away. She was at Serena's will.
She tried to tell you, but you wouldn't listen. We have worst things to worry about than each other. There are predators out

there destroying our innocence. Taking away our rights and our choices by compromising us, some, before we knew any better, and others become victims. You know this Cleo. Why do you have to be an ass all the time?

"I am not afraid of you Serena. You need me, not the other way around." Cleo found the courage to retaliate. "Listen to you, you are weak and foolish. You think that life out there is good? That somehow if this had not happened to us we would have been living this fairy tale life with love, husbands and children and shit? You have definitely lost your fucking mind."

Those words cost her. As soon as she said them Serena sent out a high-pitched yelp that only affected Cleopatra. She could not protect her ears with her hands as it was bounded by web and her screams came out with excruciating pain. Serena did not stop. She linked with Cleo's mind and began showing her what Cathalina wanted her to know.

She emitted image after image of her transformation when she killed Marcus Cummings, running into Vincent Ratigan and the serial string of rape and murder he got away with. She showed her what it felt like sensing Elizabeth's discomfort and emerging transformation, on what happened in the limousine on their way there. Cleo screamed in pain as the vision of what had happened between the women over the past week pierced her mind. The sound that Serena sent with it burnt her ears and blood spilled from them. She felt the rapture of her eardrums and passed out when Serena stopped. Serena turned to Cathalina who now had tears in her eyes.

"Now she knows." She said and fell unconscious to the hard stone floor. The minute Serena fell, Cleo was released and the trance that Serena had them him was lifted.

The excruciating pain she felt had her doubled into the fetal position, aching and screaming at the top of her lungs. Elizabeth ran to her, and gently placed Cleo's head into her lap. She was so frightened she was shaking.

Cathalina began to wail in a way that she had not cried in years. She felt her anger bubble to the point of not knowing what to do. She stood up and began banging on the walls so hard her nails broke, her knuckles scraped and bled. She couldn't stop the agonizing torture that she had suppressed that have been released through Serena's words, her thoughts, her grief.

"Oh God Elizabeth, what have we done? What have we become?" She asked in her despair, pain dripping through her pours as she became drenched with sweet and her fingers bled from the self-torture she inflicted upon herself. "We have become monsters. I hate these no good pieces of crap that did this to us, to me. Oh God why did you let this happen? Why? Why? Why?" She screamed now, wailing, getting angrier, more resolved to go out and finish what she started.

"Cath, it's not our fault. It's not our fault." Was all Elizabeth could say as she rocked the terrified Cleopatra in her lap. She remembered back when she was ten, learning and understanding how different she was. Finding out she was a freak, and saying those words were all that kept her sane.

"That's right Liz, this is not my fault, and I refuse to let them get away with it. They made me like this and I will move heaven and earth and I will not stop until they pay."

## MAN KILLER 13

As soon as Cleo brushed her off, Natalia took her queue and ran to the front of the spa, jumped into the limo and drove it around the back. She pressed the password hidden behind what looks to be over grown wild ivy that had spread on the back of the building and a door appeared in the impeccable seamless wall. Natalia drove into the third level down and ran over what sounded like crackling bones and that same stench from earlier that day when Cleo caught her coming out.

She held her breath and her nose at the same time and cringed with repulsion at what she stumbled onto. She didn't stay long; she didn't want to miss what the team was there to talk about. She knew Cleo's secret hiding places and all the passwords to get through. She sensed that Cleo had some idea that she had access to her private domains, yet, she did nothing about it. No matter. She had to get back to the other women before she missed anything.

She had heard so much about them from Cleo that she felt she was among luminaries. She didn't take the back entrance out, she stepped over the dead decomposing body members and walked along the edges of the pond where Cleo kept her "pets", then rushed to the spiraling staircase where she was almost caught by Cleopatra earlier and made a discreet exit. She looked around and headed to the only place she knew Cleo could have taken the others. She had been preparing for it all week. When she rounded the bend she over heard Cleo yelling at the others, asking them what had happened and yelling at them for their recklessness. She hid until they walked into the cave and then she snuck in behind them.

They were so engrossed in their conversation that they didn't realize that they had been followed. Natalia could barely keep herself still when she over heard the women's conversation. She almost screamed when she saw the transformation that Serena underwent and past out behind a piece of rocky structure where Cleo had a secret passage door that led to the storeroom where she kept her toys, condoms of all variety and flavor and torture equipment for what she called, "special cases."

When she revived, she saw the two women passed out on the floor and heard Cathalina's ranting. She snuck out and decided to take the rest of the day off. With all the commotion and everything else, no one noticed that Natalia was missing for the rest of the day.

\*\*\*\*\*\*\*\*\*\*

Natalia swerved through traffic like a mad woman in her little Minnie Cooper. The small vehicle slithered and pushed its way through traffic so fluidly Natalia felt she was flying. She had to slow down so that the state troopers didn't pull her over. This was all too weird and good to be true.

As soon as she pulled up to the great gates, she pulled the small car to the side and hid it as best she could among the huge trees and over run ivy plans surrounding the premises and took her shoes off. Since she was wearing short shorts and above the navel cropped t-shirt, she was dressed perfectly for what she needed to do. Natalia's adrenalin pulsed through her as she slowly scaled the walls to the twelve-foot gates guarding the semi-mansion and reached the other side safely, not withstanding a few bruises on her knees, legs, thighs and arms. Her tan shirt was smeared stain with the green plan as she tried to brush herself free of debris.

She crept to the huge windows and tried to peer in, but the frosted opaque windows gave her little leeway to be nosey, so she decided on the next best thing. If the rumors are true, then she could definitely work her new plans.
She walked up to the huge Roth iron gates and studied the doorknocker that looked as creepy as if it was alive. The huge iron spider, delicately crafted, etched and edged in all the right places where to even look at it her skin crawled.

The eight-eyed creature stared at her with thick-perched talons that appeared to move with each knock to announce her arrival. On the fourth knock she waited patiently for an invitation it. It seemed to be taking forever.

\*\*\*\*\*\*\*\*\*

Jason looked through the windows and starred back at the beautiful petite stranger that was peering back at him. His heart raced in shock, as there had not been a visitor to that house unannounced in years. He was not sure what to do, but he ached for company and his loneliness got the better of him.

Jason ran to the door that lead to his private hallway and domain. He had grown accustomed to not wearing much around the house, but for the first time since tragedy befell him in association with his acquaintance with Serena, he would finally be given the chance to feel free, like a man, admired by a woman who didn't know his plight, for him to not be driven to the ground through mental, psychological and physical abuse. His need to see someone outside of Serena and her crew, his curiosity to why she was there, his need for company, propelled him forward, finding a white collared shirt with breast pockets that buttoned down in the front, and then released his locks so they fall to his shoulders. He reached for some khaki he had not used in more than two years and house loafers. His thoughts raced as his mind's eye went over the casual and messy look of the beautiful olive complexioned lady with bright green eyes and flowing straight brown hair, as he rushed back to the front door, hoping and praying that he had not been gone too long and that the reprieve to his solitude was still there. Relieved, he opened the door as slowly and casually as possible as not to appear anxious.

"Good afternoon. Can I help you?" He asked, his voice almost cracking as the open door and sunlight streamed down and illuminated more the beauty that stood before him.

"Hi, I am Natalia." She extended her delicate manicured fingers to him and waited for him to take it. Yes. She thought to herself excitedly the rumors are true so far. She lives with a man. Wonder if he is really a Eunuch? She smiled brightly at him as her excitement grew. So far so good, now she has to get inside.

Jason still uncertain as to whether it was a good idea to let her into the house or not, looked at her extended hand suspiciously and then returned his gaze to her eyes with a crooked smile. He knew that in light of all the things that's happened recently, Serena would not be herself and there would be no telling what the results would be if she found out he had female company in her house while she was out.

"How did you get in here?" He asked amusingly. He knew it must have been hard to get over the gates and it's a little walk to the front door. "You look like it took you quite some effort." He smirked. He had not felt like this in years. Speaking of his own will, apart of his mind released and was almost screaming the old Negro spiritual song, "we who believe in freedom shall not rest." He could almost feel himself do the jiggle the way the old black stars used to with painted black face back in the days in the movies.

"Are you Jason?" Natalia asked, wiping the smile from his face as fast as one might blink an eye and totally shattering his moment of freedom in thinking there was a stranger who did not know him. He hung his head and slowly began closing the door. "No please don't do that. I have news of Serena." Seeing that she caught his attention she pushed on. "May I come in please? I promise I am harmless." Her smile brought the sunshine back to his heart and the mention of Serena's name made him clenched and unclenches his fists nervously.

"Yes please. I am sorry. Come in." The door was again pulled open and Natalia slipped in.

"Wow this is gorgeous." She mused, "It must be so great living in a place like this. I have heard so much about Serena's home." As though it was some strange kind of living shrine, she jabbered on and on as she spun around in circles with her head to the high cathedral ceilings.

"Would you like to tell me what you came here for? It must be important if Serena sent you." Jason interrupted her admiration of the house that he had grown so accustomed to and felt so much pain in, that he no longer could see or appreciate the beauty that was embedded throughout it.

"No. I mean, it's not what you think." She closed her eyes and placed her hand to her throat and coughed. "May I have something to drink please?" She asked, stalling for time, and wanting a few more moments to look around at the exquisite luxury around her. She had never seen anything quite like it. Besides, she had no clue how she would get information out of him or get him out of the way so she could really look around. Damn he is off the scale gorgeous. She thought as she watched he leave her.

Reluctantly, Jason left the room to fetch her something to drink. He was almost afraid to turn his back to her, but realized that the sooner he got her what she wanted, the sooner she would leave. Lucky for him, Serena was picked up in a limo with Cathalina tonight and he knew something big was going down. She would be home her normal time, so he could relax a bit. As he poured the class of apple juice for Natalia, he decided that he too felt a bit parched and poured a glass for himself. Returning with two full glasses in his hands he extended the unused glass to Natalia and motioned for her to sit on the small vanity plush velour chair in a far corner of the room. There were not much furniture in the huge dining area and foyer, so there was not much furniture around for casual entertainment.

"Okay, now you need to tell me why you are here." Jason began immediately. Now that he was aware that she knew his mistress there was no reason to be coy. She was not here by mistake; she was here for a purpose.

"I work with Cleo." She began slowly, wanting to capture every reaction that he might have to her words. His face was stoic at the mention of Cleo's name and she wasn't sure if he knew of whom she spoke. "She always hangs out with Serena and Cathalina and she owns the place called Sex Cell." She began speaking fast. "I was there today. They came in all messed up, the limo banged up as though it was in an accident and I overheard something weird and Serena she turned into this weird thing…" The words began rushing out of Natalia's mouth so fast that Jason could barely understand her.

"Please slow down. What are you talking about and what do you want from me? There is nothing I can do about all this and if I were you, I would stay out of it." He warned, but he sensed that Natalia had something else in mind. She looked so scuffed up with the smudged dirt and plant stains and her face was soiled badly. Jason couldn't help it was be could hardly concentrate on what she was telling him, because he was being distracted by her beauty and the fact that he was actually sitting down, fully clothed and having a conversation with someone outside of Serena.

"One moment." He excused himself and made headway again to his private quarters. Grabbing a fresh white washcloth he dosed it in warm water and made his way back to where he left Natalia.

Thinking quickly as Jason made his exit, Natalia rummaged through her pockets to see if she had any emergency medication left in there. She found a couple dime-sized packages of roofies and ecstasy. Cleo always provided them with the top of the line drugs for clients, as some of their fantasies were to be raped or taken advantage of during role-play.

They liked to keep it as realistic as possible. Thinking quickly, she wasn't sure if she should put them inside his drinks or not. Since ecstasy was a small pill that's odorless and colorless, she decided to place it in his drink to detain, distract, and delay having to leave. She decided to drop it in his drink, if she could get solid proof, pictures, something, and anything of what she heard and saw tonight, she could sell it to the tabloids and stop selling her body for sex. Her parents would roll over and die in Alabama if they knew what she was in Florida doing for a living. They think she is an up and coming model, and at twenty nine years old, she is running out of time for a good career and excuses from keeping her parents from visiting her and having to show them who she really was.

Jason returned with the washcloth and gently reached to erase the smear from her face. She jerked back a little not sure is his motives were as obscure as hers, but then she smiled, and allowed him to wipe the dirt from her.

"There." He said, "Now you are as good as new." He chuckled and found sincere joy rumble up from him. He held the fabric in his hand and placed the glass of apple juice he was drinking on it, and then in three big gulps finished it. "I am sorry to rush you…"

"Natalia, that's my name."

"Natalia. It's nice to have your company, but I didn't expect you and that's unusual around here. So could you please tell me again how it is that you ended up here and if Serena sent you? I understand what you said about the accident and the other strange things, but Cathalina and the others are all big girls and from where I am standing, they take pretty good care of themselves.

"Yes, you are right, but don't you find all of this strange? I mean, if I didn't see with my own eyes I would have sworn it didn't really happen."

"I do think that you might have had a bit of hallucination. The story you recounted does sound very strange, more like something out of a science fiction movie. But I don't know anything about any of what you have said. Actually I feel somewhat relieved. I thought you were going to tell me something serious."

Natalia gasped at the blatant insult to her intelligence.

"Are you saying that I am making all this up? You must be really crazy!" She spat angrily. "Are you that whopped, dump, deaf and blind to not see what's going on around you? These people are a small cult group, they do weird stupid stuff that's causing unnatural things to their bodies and defying natural human law. They are talking about killing people and as far as I know, Cleo has already done in a few and that's a fact. And now you tell me that I have made the whole thing up?"

She knew he had to be lying. He had to know something. He couldn't just be living in this place with the one that they now call the spider queen and be ignorant of the facts. Natalia didn't have to fight with him much longer, because the known by many names including cherry, meth, scoop, soap, and fantasy and officially as Gamma-hydroxybutyric acid (GHB) began to take its effect, so she softened her voice and began roll playing as if at work.

"You are truly a beautiful vision, and I would love to help you, but this is very dangerous and I don't think you know what you are getting yourself into." Jason reasoned, looking at Natalia with tears forming in his eyes, his true pain and emotion showing themselves. "But it's so good to have you here. Thanks for coming."

"Its okay Jason, I have heard a lot about you and you are as stunning as I could have ever imaged." She sighed and inched closer to him on the small vanity chair.

"What would you want me to do?" He asked, his inhibitions beginning to give way."

"You don't have to do anything Jason. Just allow me to go look around. That's all. No one would ever know I was here." She cooed, allowing her sultry voice to soothe him, and he began to inhale the smell of her hair. The drug began sedating Jason and he wouldn't be able to stop her one way or the other. He relaxed as the drugs took hold of his system and began to caress Natalia's face.

"So smooth and soft." He uttered so low that she almost didn't hear him.

"Why don't you sit back and relax and let me just look around a bit. I promise I won't be long and I will be right back to sit and chat with you." Jason nodded in agreement. He liked the sound of her voice. There was a slight semblance of a southern accent but it was not very pronounced.

    Natalia inched her way from beneath Jason's amorous attempts and began her search. Soon he would be passed out from the drug and he won't even know what hit him. She knew she was on to something and she was not going to let his opportunity slip from beneath her.

## MAN KILLER 14

Dyania got up three days after Francesca's death and decided to go over her notes regarding what happened to the woman prior to her getting to the hospital. Everything was listed, including the cast, who found her and who was still in the show, that the show still had a week to go and that there was one person missing. Elizabeth.

"Elizabeth!" Dyania ran the word slowly off her tongue. "That's what Francesca said before she died the name Elizabeth." She jumped to her feet from her small office space in the corner of her bedroom and grabbed the phone.

"Yes Humdrum, I want you do go into the computer systems and let me know what else the original reports have to say about a member of 'A Woman's Wrath' cast. Her name is Elizabeth Chung."

"Is this another lead? Did you find out something?" Humdrum asked excitedly. He knew that her request could only mean that she was on to something, and it didn't miss him that she called him, and not one of the other detectives.

"Really Humdrum, you are over thinking this and asking way too many questions. Please just do as I ask. When I know more, I will be sure to clue you in." Dyania told him and hung up the phone. Feeling somewhat idiotic at the sound of the dial tone, Humdrum dismissed the idea that her calling him over the others meant any more than what she needed to have him do.

"My number was probably the first she could get a hold of." He spoke in silent reprimand at himself as he grabbed his jacket and rushed off to the police department.

"Maybe I will just give this to Devout to do, since he is so gun ho about her." His jealousy rearing its head, but deep down he knew that they all liked this woman, shoot; forget them, what about the whole freaking 56th precinct, and that may even include some of the female squadrons. He snickered as he turned the ignition in the car and drove off.

Dyania went back to the pile of the reports on her full sized bed and rummaged through them uncontrollably. She finally got a lead, a link to follow. Where is Elizabeth and why did she disappear the day of Francesca's death. She grabbed her notebook and wrote down a few scribbled notes.

*Roommate*
*All things packed and removed from hotel premises*
*Name uttered as last word from deceased, was the name of deceased roommate* *
*Home origin according to show Miami Florida*

"Damn why didn't I see this before?" She asked herself frustrated, throwing the papers back to the ruffled unmade bed and rushing to her closet where she found a pair of wrinkled denim flare bottom jeans, between the toes sandals and a tank top. She tried to put them all on simultaneously, then rushing through the door with her thoughts racing a thousand miles per minute. "I have to get out of here."

Then she stopped suddenly, a thought crossing her mind. So simple it almost went by as a blur. She stopped what she was doing and retraced her steps back to the telephone. She dialed directory assistance.

"City and state please?" Came the request from the

automated voice,
"Miami Florida."
"Please hold while we connect you to the operator." Dyania tapped her feet and wrenched her fingers as she waited for a live operator to pick up the call.
"Is this business or residential." Finally the operator was connected.
"Residential."
"Name of your party?" Before answering she grabbed the papers with the correct spelling of Elizabeth's name. She was so nervous she wanted to make sure she got this right.
"Elizabeth Chung. That's C-h-u-n-g." She spelt out for the operator.
"Thank you, one moment please." Dyania's anxiety felt like she was being pressed down by ten tons of steel. She couldn't wait for the woman to release her findings.
"Ma'am, I am sorry. I did find an Elizabeth Chung but the information is private and unlisted. Is there anything else I can get for you?"
"No, thanks for your time." She told her and hung up the phone. She was so excited she couldn't keep still. "That's just fine Ms. Operator lady, I will just go to the office and demand the number be released from there." She grabbed her keys, the papers and went out the door smiling

\*\*\*\*\*\*\*\*\*\*

Cathalina didn't know what to do with herself once they all left Sex Cell. Cleo was pissed, Elizabeth looked confused and out of character and Serena was wasted. She wasn't sure what was happening to them, what would happen to them from here on out, but she was scared and she felt as though she was totally out of control. She was not the one behind the driving wheel, and that would have been fine, but the person behind the wheels can't drive and that only adds fuel to the fire.

"Hey there pretty lady, want some company?" Came a rustic drunken voice behind her. She didn't turn to look around; she knew the kind of place she was coming to. The music was so loud anyway; she decided that she wouldn't even respond.

"Don't you hear a gentleman speaking to you?" Came the voice again. This time in her ear, the man pressing into her back. She could feel his penis ebbing into her spine.

"Listen, you are drunk, and I just want to be alone with my thoughts. Please go away." Her voice was nice and calm, but loud enough for the man to hear since he was getting up close and personal with her. She was hoping he didn't cause any trouble. She turned to look at the bar tender and called him over. "May I have another bloody Mary please?" Her smiled melted him and he felt as though she smiled only for him.

"Why, of course you can anything for the only lady in the house tonight." The bartender complemented her and she nodded a thank you and looked away. She thought the drunk was gone and so she turned to look at the dance floor, where men and women made carnal acquaintances and found love, sex, marriage and divorce all in one night, walking away strangers when it was all over.

"So, you think you are too good for me? You can talk to the hunky bartender, but you cannot smile at me?" belched the tall huskily build man. He looked liked he could have been a football player in his glory days, stretching up to about six foot five, a neck size about eighteen inches and broad thick shoulders. Except now, his belly hung so far below his waist it appeared his backside was on his front side. His pants hung below the crack of what should be his posterior, and he had more breasts than the average woman. Cathalina looked at him and laughed.

"You're serious?" She asked, not really wanting to get into anything but seemed to obviously have found herself into something anyway.

"What do you mean, if I am serious? Why all you bitches feel like you get some smarts and wear nice clothes, and process your hair that you cannot talk to a good up standing man like me no more?" He leaned into her, his breath reeking with liquor and something else that she could not recognize, and then it hit her. Smelt as though he had his face in between someone's legs only moments before and the blend of stench made her want to puke. He reached his had to the bar and the combination odor of his underarm with very poor hygiene and his fingers that was obviously initially scratching his behind made her gag.

"Listen, I am sure you are a very nice man, but I am going through some things right now. I want to disappear and be left a lone. Can a lady ask an upstanding man like you for her space?" She pleaded with the false good guy attitude this man was attempting to reason with but his intention soon came to light.

"Oh, now you want to play nice? It's a little too late don't you think?"

"Is this jerk bothering you?" Came the deep resounding voice of the bartender. Even with all the loud music, his voice came thundering through.

"Actually no. But thank you." She said to the bartender and then returned her attention to her suitor as the bartender walked away unwillingly to provide service to the other drinkers. "Where were we? Yes, I remember. You wanted us to go to the bathroom and do the horizontal dance like everyone else here right?" She smiled her voice soothingly intoxicating as she spoke. Her lashes fluttered as her deep dark skin radiated from her smile. Caught off guard the man didn't know what to say.

"Ah yeah, lets go to the john and do what everybody else is doing." He agreed grabbing her hand and pulling her to the location which he seemed to have had memorized. "I knew I had you pegged right. The goody two shoe type pretending you don't want to get jabbed with some real beef." He mumbled. Had it not been for Cathalina's hypersensitive earring at this point she would not have heard a word the man said, but she remained quiet, her anger building inside of her. Her thoughts tearing through her brain making her head hurt. Sure she knew better. Sure she was supposed to be the calculated, precise and ordered. She was the one in control and steering the ship. But things have changed, and she knew that it was only a matter of time before the volcano blew. Something was going to happen, and they might have to go underground again the way they did before when it was just her and Cleo.

A	ll she wanted was to be alone, she figured in a crowd of how many people she could disappear; get a drink without being harassed. But this wasn't the first jerk to come onto to her so aggressively, and frankly she had lost count, but she was tired of it and someone was going to get the lash back of that

The man pushed past the line of other men waiting to go into the bathroom. Some held their crotch to prevent themselves from pissing their pants and other held onto the next whore willing to give it up at a moment's notice. The man pulling Cathalina seemed to have garnered some bathroom respect, because no one grumbled or complain as she pressed forward, past them and into a toilet stall. She could hear moans and see legs held high at unnatural angels. The man ripped the top of her dress and buttons flew with her yelp.

"That's right. I like screamers." He looked at her what appeared to be an attempt at goo goo eyes and she heaved, bringing up nothing but dried air since she had not had anything to eat since the day before. This day was supposed to be a celebration of the joining of the three women, with dinner and wine. But it turned out to be tyranny among the crew.

"Oh so you like that?" Cathalina asked sheepishly. She knew his type, the criminal. It's about power, rape and abuse. This is not about sex or love or anything else. He wanted to have control over someone and she was going to let him think he is in control all the way until she has him where she wants him.

"Did I tell you to talk? Bend over so I can get a good look at that ass." Demanded the red neck slob who revolted Cathalina, but she was the one in control of this little drama enacting and it was going to go her way or no way at all.

"But daddy, I just need to taste that dick of yours. Can I smell it? Just for a second please? Can I just look at it?" She whined, and slowing inched her way to her knees. The bathroom guests, enacting their own drama sex roll began to pay attention to them. To her submissive behavior.

"Damn, usually he brings them in kicking and screaming." Moaned one man from a neighboring stall.

"Yeah." Came his partner, another male of a higher pitched voice. "She must be crazy or nuts because that dick got diseases that names haven't been invented for yet." He uttered between sighs of pleasure as his head banged against the toilet stall.

"She really gonna do him on purpose?" Whispered

one woman in the ear of her partner for the night.

"Looks like he hit the jackpot. Oh damn you feel good baby." He squeezed himself into her and pressed her back against the mirror almost cracking it.

"Yes! This is what I am talking about." Yelled the fat white man who felt like king of the toilet stall that night. He was getting it willingly, a history making event for him. Feeling extremely dominant his forceful nature prevailed and he yanked Cathalina's long hair back. She squinted her eyes and tried not to look at him as her anger swelled. She didn't let the hold on her hair stop her decent because she had one purpose and goal in mind. To show these disgusting dregs of society what a real woman was made of. She lifted the twenty five pounds of lard above his waist and found his pants buckle that barely held his pants up about his knees. She didn't let the pungent and foul odor that greeted her stop her either. She was so angry her black face had turned blue at just the thought of being placed in this position, of people like him always placing women like her in this position without their permission. He leaned back and allowed his hands to linger and roam over her ass and back, slipping his fingers down her underwear and allowing it to slide down the crevice of her behind, seeking out her womanhood. She clenched and squeezed her legs shut and received a heavy slap upside her head.

"Open up those legs bitch." He demanded. Whatever she was going to do she was going to have to move fast. She had nothing to loose now. This piece of dog shit was out of control and so was the rest of her life.

"Fuck it." She uttered under her breath and reached for his penis that seemed to have disappeared among the layers of fat that built his thighs. She had to bury her head under his stomach and between his legs to get there and feared suffocation. She sought out his member with her hands and as she heard him moan she knew she found it. She quickly pressed her face forward, moaning sounds of disgust that passed as desire. She took his penis in her mouth, ignoring the crusted blisters that she felt as he went in, ignoring the sores that felt as though puss was oozing from them as she pressed him into her mouth.

His body began to move and gyrate into her face, she almost gagged a few times feeling him inch is way in and out of her mouth. She knew she was contracting some form of STD from this man, but at that moment, even concern for her own safety was gone. She thought back to the moment she when she felt she lost it, when her right to be a mother was taken from her, to the women she counseled every day, to the perpetuation of this sickness that no one ever seem to want to talk about, no one want to acknowledge and women are forced to hide away like vermin.

"Enough!" Came her scream as she garnered all the strength she could, directing all of her rage, disgust, loathing, detestation and anguish to one central focal point, her teeth. In what seemed to be a split second she pressed her vicious oral tools as firmly and as tightly together and she did it with such forceful passion that she felt his tendons and ligaments in his male member sever from the man's body and was released into her mouth. She stood, feeling the blood run down the sides of her mouth and her teeth still snarled like an attacking animal. The man who stood before like a giant towered to the floor and exploded into screams so horrific and terrifying, it was heard outside the dance floor above the thundering music.

He held his penis-less crotch, his eyes closed tightly shut as he yelped, shrieking, rolling on the floor and writhing in unimaginable pain that only became intensified at the sight of his blood gushing all over the bathroom stall from the rupture of a major artery. The audience in the bathroom was shocked and was petrified at the sight of such fury, astonishment and disbelief gripped them. Disgust filled them as the stench of him shitting and pissing on himself and the blood that seemed to not have missed anyone that was within close proximity.

"She is out of her freaking mind." One man observed as he quickly buttoned his pants and the woman he was with ran behind him in horror. She stood, allowing her stained dress to drop back below her waist and down her ankles.

"You are nothing. You are a worthless piece of vulture that pray on the weak and the young. You should die." She seethed as she held his detached penis in her hand. She reached for the man's face that was still captivated and expressly pained. He moved so vigorously as though in a seizure that she found it difficult to get a hold of the man's head to keep it still. She wrestled with his agonized body for a few moments, but the anger that fueled her gave her indescribable strength. Finally, she opened his mouth and stuffed his penis down his throat causing him to gag. "Now, doesn't that taste good? Hum yummy!" she mocked.

"Take that rancid, decrepit useless piece of slab you call a dick and go to hell." Her voice was soft and calm. She stood there emotionless, watching, as the man's mutilated body jerked and convulsed as he was no longer able to breathe. Shock and fright traumatized him and she didn't move until his eyes rolled back into his head and all she could see was the white of his eye balls.

She pulled the front of her dress together to prevent anymore of her breast from being exposed and walked out as if nothing had happened. When she walked through the small club house, news had gotten around. The place was still and she had a path cleared in the center for her to exit. There were murmurs and whispers, and for some reason she smiled when she stepped into the fresh dew of the wee hours of another Florida morning. She could swear she heard cheers

*********

He was glad when she called. He hadn't heard from her since the last time she came by unexpectedly. She had been tired and worn and he could tell she had a lot of things on her mind. That had made her third visit and she was so stunning he couldn't take his eyes off of her. She wore off white linen shirt that flirted around her ankles and an off the shoulder top that showed off a wonderfully and intricately designed spider. He had never seen anything like it. It was exquisite. He remembered how she flinched and backed away when he tried to touch it as though he was about to hurt her. He couldn't believe that a tattoo artist was able to capture such details. It was stunning, and in some strange way, that too was some sensuously erotic allure.

They had spoken briefly and she claimed she was in the neighborhood and wanted to thank him for his help the first day they met. That was three meetings ago and her excuse was still the same. She wanted to thank him. The last time he almost lost control and tried to kiss her. He stopped him short but he could feel her wanting him, daring him.

"I must be loosing my mind." He chuckled lightly to himself. He didn't want to get close to anyone at this time. He had been out of prison and living a free life, somewhat privately for the past three years. No one had bothered him and he stayed clear of temptation. But how was he supposed to court a woman who said she worked for the Supreme Courts, as a judge none the less? She could snap her fingers and make his life a living hell.

"What am I doing?" He asked himself again. "Why am I nervously, anxiously waiting for this woman?" He walked to the refrigerator and took a jug of freshly made iced tea and poured himself a large glass over five cubes of ice. The air conditioner was blasting but he felt a heat surge he couldn't explain.

He clasped his hands and put them towards his face taking a deep heavy sigh. He was waiting for her now as she said she was on her way. When he first met her he thought she was crazy. Now, he wasn't sure if she was nuts or he was. He had become so drawn to her, the way she walked, talked, smelled. He couldn't get past it. He was a fiend for her as though she was a drug and he was an addict.

\*\*\*\*\*\*\*\*\*\*

Serena went through Cleo's wardrobe that she kept stacked with the latest styles and fashion paraphernalia's. She found a short sun dress that was a soft pink and slipped on a pair of pink sandals to match. She threw her ripped clothing from earlier into the trash and decided to call a cab. When she woke from her semi comatose state, she was alone in the conference room. Cathalina, Cleo and Elizabeth were all gone and she sensed that they were all off dealing with the revelations of the evening. It didn't go quite as planned, but they all needed their space.

She wasn't sure why she called Vincent. She knew what he was and who he was, that he was the very epitome of what she was fighting. The Evil they were all wrestling with. Yet, time after time, she found herself at his doorstep. The last time she thought for sure she would pass out if he kissed her. She didn't know if she had the strength to keep resisting him.

Her thoughts and her deferred desires were her worst enemy. She would feel like ripping him apart at the same time she felt like parting her legs so he could rip into her. She was a web of confusion and emotional contradiction.

"You made it." Vincent greeted her at the door when the taxi pulled up. She leaned in to pay the cab and he felt his heart race at the long sleekness of her legs. When she turned around, her auburn reddish hair bounced as in some secret celebratory joy. Her hazel eyes sparkled and again Vincent was forced to breathe deeply.

"Yes, I suppose I just needed to see a friendly face." Finally a sincere reason, at least she couldn't say she was in the neighborhood this time. She actually called first. He thought ecstatically with a smile.

"Is everything okay?" he asked, taking her hand and leading her through the house toward the back where she seemed to have become found of his back porch swing that was shaded by giant weeping willows and swayed by gentle cool breezes. She followed without reluctance.

"Had a little dispute with my friends, didn't quite see eye to eye on some issues." She sat on the plush cushion that seemed to invite her bottom from the first time she sat in it. She closed her eyes and wished and for a flicker of a moment she saw Jason's face. It startled her, but she brushed off the image and smiled at Vincent as he handed her a fresh glass of ice tea and sat beside her. He smiled and she nodded a grateful thank you. She looked out across his back yard at the healthy trees and beautifully manicured lawn in an attempt not to stare at his strapping biceps that seemed to bulged and flex with every move he made. The black fitted shirt he wore tapered into his chiseled waist that boasted an eight pack. His thick thighs contracted in his khaki pants that draped comfortably over his loafers. His smile took her breath away and she could almost already feel him inside of her she dreamt about him so much.

"Do you want to talk about it?" She laughed.

"Seems you have become my new therapist." She thought about Cathalina and where that venture led her.

"Looks like therapist comes in all type of packages these days, prizes, surprises and consolation prizes." She remarked sarcastically, thinking of how she went to Cathalina for help and where it got her. Now look at whose shoulder she chooses to cry on.

"And which one of those am I?" He looked at her with slightly arched questioning eyebrows that made his dark eyes dance with curiosity.

"I am not sure yet. But you will be the first to know when I have figured it out." She reassured him.

"I will hold you to that." He slightly leaned in closer to her and allowed their forearms to brush. "So you were saying about your friends." He changed the subject and simultaneously took a gentle loose hold of her hand as they rested between them on the swing. She took a deep breath and began to recount the evening as vaguely as possible.

"I just don't know if I am going to be able to go though with some plans that we made." She told him.

"What plans?"

"Can't say right now." She felt a tingling sensation on her shoulder that bore the spider and giggled with she felt the twitch between her thighs. She could decide what her body wanted her to do as she felt the grip on her hands tightened.

"Okay, but you are being very vague and its making it difficult to do my job as your psychiatrist." He joked.

"Don't laugh. Its not funny." Shoving him playfully with her forearm and as she turned to look at him she found herself face to face with his trembling lips and his captivating eyes. She couldn't pull away as she felt the space between them slowly closed and then the moment of truth when his lips pressed to hers. She began shake as the tremors of desires seized her. Enraptured in that passionate moment she was bombarded with images of innocent screams and tortured young bodies that were dismantled and discarded by this man, and in the same moment, her body longed for him.

The glass fell from her shaky hands and they found their way around his neck. In one quick swoop he had his hands under her and he cradled her like a baby lowering her to the hardwood floors that was the foundation of the porch. Their kiss became passionately intense and erotic. His hands found her thighs and explored them; rising beneath her short sun dress and causing her to feel for real what she had envisioned, powerful sensuality that had caused havoc on all of her senses now captivated her.

Vincent lowered himself on top of her and she felt the potent need rise between his legs forcefully and dominant pressing against her inner thighs. She spread her legs apart, her body begging him to fulfill all the visions that had tormented her for so many weeks and nights since becoming indoctrinated, feeling the desires of her subordinates, the erotic sensations of the women she had joined with.

He pressed his lips into her neck, her shoulders and chest, kissing trails of soft tender wanting everywhere there was an available free space. Using his teeth and tongue, he gently and sensitively removed the fabric that's blocking their bodies from touching. Becoming somewhat possessed Serena felt as though she was a fly on the wall of her own experience and allowed her body to become enthralled by the touch of a man who can really fulfill her in a way she had never felt.

She allowed her legs to fall apart, sending electrical urges like lightening up and down her inner thighs forcing her to arch her spine, pressing her breast into his chest, stirring a burning need in him and discharging deep guttural moans and groans from his lips.

"I want you." He uttered softly in her ear, "I need you Serena."

She moaned, not knowing what to say or how to feel. She was caught up and the desires were so overwhelming and intense that she was only able to sigh deeply, heaving into his hard chest. He took that as a sign of permission and quickly released his belt buckle, releasing his desire from its restraints and used his knee to part her legs. Slowly, he began moving into her, pressing his body so there was no space or even air between them. He grunted deeply feeling the tip of him press into the silky softness of her underwear, seeking to move it over, away from being a barrier to her Garden of Eden. The moistness of her panties gave him urgency and without using his hands, he was able to use his seek heat seeker to remove the restrictive garment. A cavernous unified mating call was sent from one to the other as the tip of him sampled the soft succulence of her.

She flinched and he paused to look at her. Her eyes were squeezed shut but her hips gyrated sensuously against his groin, urging him to continue. Gently, slowly, moving in rhythmic patterns of a fluid waterfall, he wasn't hitting her hymen yet, but the pressure between her tartness awoke in her pleasures and pains she could not fathom.

Her movements drove him crazy. What she was doing to him almost made him loose all reason and press himself deeply into her to satisfy the cravings they were both experiencing. But that look on her face. He knew what her body was saying and he knew that this might not be the right time. Damn I cannot even get through the entrance. He thought to himself, believing it impossible to have that kind of resistance at her age. In any case, he liked her and didn't want to rush her, so he began kissing her softly again, trailing her nipples through the fabric of her dress as she replaced the straps over her shoulders and going down to her belly button, pulling and yanking lightly as he neared the mound of her Eden. He used his momentum to ease his body down, allowing his face to rest between the crevices of her thighs and profoundly breathe inhaling the essence of her womanhood. He rested his head there as he caressed her forearms and thighs. Serena didn't say anything. She was glad he stopped. She had the feeling that she was about to hurt him.

MAN KILLER

## MAN KILLER 15

Natalia went back to Sex Cell and was totally intrigued, fascinated and overwhelmed by what she found at Serena's home. She sat in her dressing room preparing for the next shift and was sifting through tears, being distraught and confused. She held on tightly to the trinket she found, holding it to her breast and allowed the tears to flow down her cheeks.

"This just could not be possible. It cannot be possible." She repeated over and over again as if trying to convince herself of the truth of what she found or deny it, but it was eating away at her and she couldn't control the immense anger and injustice she felt that this woman was alive. The thought crossed her mind to call up her fathers people, the descendants, the members, the Clan to enact the pact of justice specified for revenge when her father died. That moment was so horrible and gruesome. They thought she had just faded away and became a dreg of society, but here she was, right under her nose.

Natalia thought of all the times she felt jealous, abandoned and not loved as well as her. She thought about how her mother and relatives would talk about the black trash that her father had embraced. Sure she was his whore, but so what? She got to live in his mansion, ate the good food, her bastard sent to the best schools, while she was the second hand, considered the "other" child among all his other white children. She was the one with the beautiful long hair that only a pure white person has. She was the one with green eyes and rosy freckled skin. She was the one who was white.

She remembered the pangs of hunger and beatings of despair that was bestowed upon her just because her mother was pissed at him and couldn't get what she wanted. She couldn't believe what she held in her hands. She couldn't believe what she had stumbled upon. She had gathered her things and ran straight out of Serena's house when she dug to the bottom of her foot locker and found the emblem. She was petrified to learn that she was her half sister, the black bastard everyone made a big deal of.

She ran to the small box of personals that she kept safe and traveling with them from Alabama. She took the box and walked back to her twin sized bed. Wiping away the tears from her eyes that clouded her vision, she curled her feet under her bottom and took a deep breath. She opened the box and rummaged through some trinkets and stones she had felt found favor in her and helped to guide her safely. As the path cleared at the bottom of the box, she was able to finally see the gold emblem tucked securely on one corner and hidden from plain sight.

She took it out with trembling hands and slowly brought it side by side to with the jewel she found in Serena's foot locker. As they neared each other, the striking resemblance to the other was uncanny and when placed together, they fit as if a puzzle displaying the crest of her father and his father before that, Klu Klus Klan and on the back the confederate flag. The parts that were missing filled in the gap of a noose hanging from an upside down tree and blood drops on the flag that she couldn't discern before. Some of the police who arrived at the scene were members of the Klan and had secretly handed it to her mother, who later handed it to her.

The crest is the heart of their organization and must be handed down only through the bloodline. There was no way she could have known there was another.

"Oh my gosh." She spoke out loud and looked to the ceiling to will the tears from coming again. "Serena Kowtow. It's her. She really is my sister." Suddenly Natalia was startled by a heavy knock on her door. She knew that only one person knocked with such persistence and insolence.

"Come in." She invited, quickly shuffling about and putting away her things before Cleo saw it. Cleo as a black woman has been the subject of many a taunting and teasing especially with her weight and she stood firm on the slavery movement and the need for reparations in this country. She couldn't allow her to know who she really was.

"Natalia, I waited and searched for you all night until 2am. Where were you? You missed a few appointments and I lost a lot of money."

Natalia had not been able to put everything away fast enough and tried effortlessly to sweep the emblem under the covers and out of Cleo's line of vision.

"I am sorry Madam, I had an emergency and I had to run out."

"What kind of emergency can you have without leaving a note? You have no family here. Are you seeing someone?" Relieved for the way out, Natalia began to laugh.

"I am sorry I didn't tell you before Cleo, it's just that its new and I wasn't sure he really liked me."

"Is that where you were coming from Natalia?" Cleo asked drawing nearer to the girl's frail looking form curled on the bed. "Is that where you were why your face and arms look bruised as if you had been in a cat fight and your legs are stained with green moss?" Natalia thought fast to attempt to get out of being caught with her pants down. She thought quickly, fumbling through her thoughts to come up with a feasible solution. Cleo had given her a way out.

"Well, ah."

"What are you hiding Natalia? This is simply not your style." Curiosity ebbing on her face causing her eyes to squint and pierce the girl's already torn and hurting heart, Cleo swayed her big Betty Boop body over to the small bed and used her hips to scoot Natalia over so she could sit beside her. Natalia tried to remove the objects from beneath the sheets before Cleo sat, but was unsuccessful.

"What tha..."

"I am sorry Cleo, let me get that." She tried to remove them quickly, but again was met with restraints and was unsuccessful. Cleo reached under her behind and pulled up the cold pieces of metal, each dangling from a piece of fragile strings that were old and worn and could fall at any moment from the weight the medallion.

"These are beautiful." Cleo observed at first glance, when the reflection of the emblem hit her eyes for the first time. She saw the raised markings and reached to caress them with her right hand. She held the two parts together and jointed them to read the engravings. It registered in her mind almost immediately the significance of the jewel. Her eyes sought out Natalia's and she searched them. Natalia could see the questions and she was almost certain that she now no longer has a job, but she would have to blame that on Serena as well. All of the ill will that had befallen her over the years she had blamed on the Negro bastard that stole her birthright and now she was alive.

"It's not mine. I found them."

"Found them? Where? These are solid gold and worth a lot of money, from the old days and the original KKK members. To get one of these you must have blood lineage.

"I...I stole..."

"Natalia, don't lie to me. You are shaking like a leaf and your eyes are red." Natalia was at a loss for words. Her emotions have betrayed her and she couldn't hide the truth of the value of the emblem from Cleo. Natalia by accident knew that Cleo had her doctorate in African American Literature and studies, specializing in US history from the days of slavery in this country. She had ventured into her Madam's private domain and accidentally bumped into her documents hidden in a box that was carelessly strewn in the corner of her dungeon.

"I am so sorry Cleo. I am so sorry." She began to wail, coving her face within the palms of her trembling hands.

"God, are you? You mean to tell me?" Cleo couldn't wrap the thoughts around her brain. She sat quietly for a moment and stared at the medallion. "It's broken in two." The words came out slowly as just an observation, and as her mind scrambled through years of studies that she long ago discarded and never thought she would ever use, it hit her.

Natalia swallowed hard and brought her hands down to her thighs. Her mascara had run so badly that her face seemed stained black. She took in deep breaths and decided she would not hide from who she was. Wasn't that what she wanted after all? To be recognized as her father's first born. The privileged one? The one to carry the bloodline and the history of her father's passions? How ashamed would they be of her now were she to continue to pretend she was not who she was?

"Cleo half of the Emblem belongs to me." She confessed as steadily as she could. She would be a woman and stand and take the consequences of who she was. Today, she would put aside her fear of Cleo in her profession and be a white woman who had power in her blood.

Cleo's face turned red, as the history of such a treasure

continue to unfold itself into her mind. The historian in her could not let it go. Her curiosity had to find out. How often was it that a black historian had the opportunity to examine up close and personal such an artifact, usually kept hidden and for secret private eyes only?

"That's right. In the event of the passing of a true Klan member, the medallion must be separated and shared between the two eldest children of that member's bloodline. It's the way they kept it secret and hidden for so many generations." Natalia was fascinated by Cleo's knowledge. She herself was not aware of such information and refused to allow Cleo to realize just how much she had on her.

"May I have those back." Natalia asked, reaching across the short distance to Cleo's hands.

"Not until you tell me who the second half of this belongs to, and why you have them both."

"I cannot do that. I will betray."

"Betray? You are worried about betraying someone other than me?" Cleo asked in mocked surprise in the face of the girl's insolence.

"You know better Cleo." Her confidence in what Cleo held in her hands grew. "You know who I am now and there is no need to play those games. With as much as you know, you understand that I cannot disclose anymore information to you."

"Okay, I could threaten you with beatings and pains so surmountable that you wouldn't care and then kill you. But that wouldn't give me the information I need. I will return these to you and walk away if you tell me who the other half belong to? Cleo was desperate. There had never been a time in what she learned the medallion was ever separated. It's the completion of two halves and they belong together. Apart, it looses its strength and power.

Tears again welled in Natalia's eyes and she turned away. How could she tell Cleo that a member of her close trusted group of friends carried the linage of one of the most hated and feared group of occult in history. Suddenly, she began to smile as she stepped outside of herself and began to think rationally. Cleo could become her confidant and even an accomplice. It was perfect. She would finally get the revenge she wanted.

"Okay then." Natalia agreed turning to face Cleo whose eyes lit up like a child's face on Christmas day. "I will tell you everything."

## MAN KLLER 16

Dyania rushed from the police precinct armed with Elizabeth's life history and the information from the files in Miami. She felt it was a stroke of genius that she thought to go check. When she sat at her small cubicle entranced in her research, Detective Humdrum, Devout and Vile sat back with stale coffee watching helplessly as a woman did the kind of work that would make a grown man cry.

Dyania was pissed when she arrived at the station hours after she had entrusted the information to Humdrum only to find that he only squabbled and griped about the project instead of actually doing it. She was not surprised when he turned his head in shame when she walked in and seeing him squirm under her heavy gaze made the others laughed heartily at him. He was so shamed that before she got up to leave and turned off her computer, he ran to the restroom lamely in order not to be subjugated to her snare again.

Rushing back home to her small apartment Dyania could not be more excited. She had to get packing. She couldn't believe all the unsolved deaths and strange occurrences being logged into the south Florida police computer systems. Why wasn't anyone curious about the whole thing? No questions, no aggressive research or investigation. She didn't need much as she was a tomboy. She threw jeans and sneakers into her heavy hiking backpack and grabbed her police badge, gun and a special necklace that dangled a pendant that was given to her as a gift from her parents when she was old enough to inherit it. She had never figured out the meaning of the pendant, but she treasured it as the most personal thing left to her from her parents. She went through her things and took her journal which she stuck to the far back of her bag where it was almost hidden. It was as though she was being propelled to Miami, as if she were to find more there than just following up on an investigation. Her instincts told her that there was something there that could explain some of the disturbing gaps of not only this case, but her life.

Catching the first flight out of Atlanta into Miami, Dyania did not waste any time. She called up the Miami Dade Police Department and asked to be forwarded to Sunny Isles Beach Precinct on Collins Avenue according to the location of the paperwork filed by Detective Taylor on the suspicious double suicide death in North Miami Beach. She was tapped her finger impatiently at the pay phone outside of Miami International Airport, waiting for the line to be picked up.

"You have reached Detective Jamie Taylor Sunny Isles Beach Precinct, if this is an emergency hang up and dial 911 or leave a message." The recording weighed on her patience and she didn't have time to wait for him. When the beep came on she was abrupt and to the point.

"Detective Taylor, I am special Homicide detective Minto. Contact the station immediately upon receiving this message. I am getting into a cab and heading to your department. Clear your calendar, we have work to do."
She hung up the phone with a slam and hailed the next taxi that came around the corner.

She gave the address and hopped into the back seat. She grabbed her pendant which was the symbol of the spider and held it tight. Suddenly there was an electrical surge through her and she had a vision of a spider that was also a woman. She shook her head a few times to clear the ridiculo7us image.

"I must be working too hard." She whispered and closed her eyes as she reclined back into her seat. Suddenly there were loud whispers and she couldn't decipher them. They came slowly then building momentum rushed though her brain like lightening. She tried to open her eyes but she couldn't. Then she saw the image of her parents, eyes frightened and opened wide with fear. "Don't go." Her mother, the voice of a woman she didn't recognize. She was too young when they died. But she knew it was her mother. She jumped startled.

"Everythin'es a okay?" Asked the Latin cap driver in broken English.

"Yes, I am fine thanks. Just a little thirsty." She told him and gently placed the necklace pendant back inside her shirt, tucked securely away from prying eyes. It seemed like forever before they arrived on Collins Avenue where it seems there were as much traffic as in the airport. She shook her leg anxiously as the taxi pulled up to what seemed like a very upscale shopping complex. She paid him and got out. She felt the fresh breeze from the ocean hit her face and reached for her sun glasses to block the glare of the beautiful Florida morning. Turning around to get her bearings she was immediately greeted by the sign and walked in.

"Yes can I help you?" The officer at the front desk greeted her.

"Yes, is Detective Taylor in?"

"He just stepped out. Is there something I can help you with?"

"Where did he go?"

"Excuse me?"

"Ma'am, I think the question was pretty clear." Her

voice was stern and agitated. She was beginning to loose patience with this paper pusher who was acting as if she was Taylor's bulldog.

"Listen, this is a police department and there is no time to play guessing games with people who have nothing to do with their time then harass people on their jobs." The woman sneered.

"Listen, officer…" she reached over to read the name on her tag, "Lopez shit head. I have no time for your games." She seethed. This woman had weaned on her patience. Her anger flared and she reached inside of her purse to pull out her badge and ID for the woman, who panicked and screamed for help.

Soon there were officers upon her, vehemently pulling her arms behind her back. Her nostrils flared ferociously and the adrenaline rush kicked up her anger a notch.

"Let me go you idiots before I have all your asses canned." And in one swift smooth motion, freed herself and simultaneously sent the two men staggering back away from her. "I am special homicide detective Minto. I was about to show this sorry excuse for an officer my credentials when she started screaming like a banshee." They all looked at her and then at each other embarrassed and seriously concerned for their jobs. The moment she said her name they were aware of whom she was. She was a luminary, a hero, a legend among them. They were thrown off by her narrow tall frame, her youthful hip look, gave the impression of a hip-hop girl from the streets.

"You are not the way we expected you to look."

"And what way is that you…" As she struggled to find words to described how she detested the treatment she received and their lack of professionalism in first finding out who they were dealing with. She suddenly realized why they had not followed up with the investigations she expected to have found in the records.

At that moment she could not comprehend the emotional stampede that over came her. Her head began to hurt and shake. Her eyes flared and almost squinted to a slit as if the light was bothering them. She balled her hands into fists and her lower lips trembled. She fought off the urge to punch the living day lights out of the three officers that have only made her entrance into North Miami more difficult than it had to be.

She turned to look at the woman who took one look at Dyania's faced and began to back up into the wall behind her. Her face was stricken with fear and she began to perspire. Dyania face turned beet red and so did the white around her pupils. She wasn't sure what was happening to her, but suddenly she could feel her thoughts transfixing onto the officers and she could hear their unspoken words, feel their fear and concerns. They weren't sure what was happening and neither was she.

Her mind began to transmit images of what she had always feared-Herself. Spiders crawled all around the police headquarters. Dangerous Brown Recluse, Black Widow Spiders, Scorpions, and other webbed creatures infested the place. She saw fear bleed from their skin as they were transfixed. The place became dark and the skies overcast. She slammed them with her anger as if her thoughts were words and they were able to feel every image, every pain, and every discomfort that she thought of or felt in that moment. Suddenly, there was a tap on her shoulder and she turned abruptly, her anger to now focus on the audacity who has dared to interrupt her. But she was suddenly calmed and her fists were released. When the other officers began looking around them in fear, she realized it wasn't something she experienced alone. They began brushing themselves off, stomping on invisible images of pests that where crawling under their clothes and open crevices on their body. They were released from the trance she held them in and ran immediately from her. Only he did not know what happened and looked strangely after them as they made their escape from the front lobby as though their lives depended on it. Her heart was beating so fast, she had to will it to slow down so she could breathe. She put on her poker face to not show the fear of what she had just experienced for the first time. She made a mental note to journal it. She has now escalated to another level of evolutionary state since her treatment.

"I am Detective Jamie Taylor. Is there something I can help you with?" He extended his hand in a warm greeting and Dyania relaxed. Still no smile on her face, she took his outstretched and shook it.

"Special Homicide Detective Minto."

"I see. I just checked in on my voicemail and got your message. You just flew in from Atlanta?" He attempted to make small talk, but soon realized she was not interested.

"I checked into the system and saw that you have a series of deaths where the coroner could not ascertain a tangible cause of death."

"Yes, let's go this way." He told her taking her by the forearm and leading her toward the back of the station to his desk. Dyania did not take likely to that. She planted herself where she was.

"Would you be so kind as to release me?" She smiled sarcastically as her eyes pierced his. Taylor stopped and stepped back a few feet away from her.

"I am sorry, my apologies." Dyania placed her hands before her and prompted him to lead the way.

"After you." She smiled and they began to walk.

Arriving at his desk Taylor explained to her the double suicide homicide that was so strange that they had no other way of listing it. It almost seemed as though to two people agreed to die that way.

"Well what about the incident on the highway, the dead man with spider venom in his blood." Dyania asked, not ready to let him off the hook.

"That was really strange. We had motorists who came into the local stations that day to say they witnessed a limo out of control on the highway, and then the man being thrown from it like a rag doll." He shook his head in disbelief. "His wife and family seemed relieved. The investigation showed that he was abusive man who terrorized his wife and family. Even threatened to kill them, but we know they were not involved as he was working that day for First Class Limo. We found the body but the limo has been missing."

"Okay, but during the autopsy, he was proclaimed dead before he was thrown from the vehicle right?" He looked at her and shook his head.

"I don't understand why you are here. This is not in your jurisdiction is it?" Taylor asked a bit perturbed. He didn't like the idea of some detective from another state stepping into his turf, gorgeous or not. And he was not going to give her the pleasure of letting her know that he knew who she was. As far as he was concerned, she was just another vice trying to show him up. Dyania reached into her purse and retrieved her cell phone.

"How about I let you speak to some special friends of mine. Not only will this be my jurisdiction, but it will be my turf too if you continue to fuck with me." She told him. Her smile was now demure and sweet and her eyes twinkling like the stars as she revealed beautiful even white teeth. Taylor rested his head in the palm of his hands and shook it. Then slamming his hands on the desk he looked up at her, defeated. His eyes glossed over in uncertainty but he knew she was not bluffing. This woman, even though she appeared to be much younger that he was and even younger than he expected, had a reputation that was as good as gold in the police force. He didn't want to be known as the one who went up against her. So reluctantly, he yielded to her requests.

"Okay, yes, the coroner did find it unusual that there was some sort of toxin in the man's blood, as though he was stung by some insect. We tried to cover it up because it didn't make any sense. I mean, what insect could be that powerful to put a grown man down? He was six foot, five inches and two hundred and twenty pounds. That spider would have to be big as all of freaking Texas to do that." He ranted.

He thought Dyania would be shocked and taken aback by the information. But she just looked at him. Intrigue building in her eyes and her face becoming more and more fascinated as his story built momentum.

"Why are you so interested in that anyway? A man being thrown from a limo is nothing for someone of your caliber to come all the way to Miami about?" He quizzed.

"It's classified." She stood to leave. "Who was the coroner on the case?"

"What do you mean classified? You come all the way here, put the fear of God into the department officers, demanded information and now, it's classified? Bullshit!"

"Who is the coroner on the case? You can tell me, or I can go find out on my own."

"Wait, I want in. I have some information that might help us. It's a long shot, but I want to be apart of this." His eyes searched hers with an irresistible plea. Dyania thought about it. She was a guest here. She didn't know Florida. He knew the place, could make her job a whole lot easier."

"Okay, tell me what you know." She asked.
"I'm in?"
" You're in!" Dyania smiled for the first time at his childlike enthusiasm for the job. She sensed that he was protective about his work and was not trying to impress her. She found that refreshing and felt she would enjoy working with him.
"Where are you staying?"
"Don't know."
"You stay with me. I have a large place, more than enough room. I am never there and the refrigerator is full."
"Well, I only need someplace to rest my head for a couple hours and shower. Okay, sounds good."
"Great let's go." As they walked out the officers who first met her when she came in, backed away and cleared the exit for her. They were not sure if they hallucinated or if she did something to them. There were no spider anywhere and after searching fruitlessly and spraying bug spray in every nook and cranny, they finally relaxed, but something about her brought back the unforgettable feeling of creepy crawly things attacking them. So they looked the other way and stayed out of her path until she was gone. Again, Taylor looked around at the officers curiously and wondered why the awkward behavior. He didn't think long on it.
"So what's the information you think can help us?" She asked as she got into his red 2005 Jaguar XK Series. She paused to admire the expensive luxury car and its premium import leather interior. "Nice ride." She admired.
"Thanks, I borrowed it." He told her putting the car in gear. She looked at him disbelievingly.
"Okay, its mine. But don't tell anyone. Women around here seem to only be interested in the kind of car a man drives. I work long hard hours for this."

"I understand." Dyania said turning to look behind are at the back seat. She nodded her head in appreciation. She didn't have to be offended of feel insulted by what he said. She knew who she was and what she had. It was nothing to her.

"Now, the information?" She was back to business.

"Her name is Cathalina Shekhar. She was the psychologist treating one of the suicide homicide victims. I know it's a long shot, but I just feel she is connected somehow."

"Well what are we waiting for?"

"There is one more thing. There is rumored that a woman fitting her description bit a man's penis off and choked him to death with it in downtown Miami. I was about to check into it when I got your message."

Dyania started to laugh. "What's so funny?"

"It just sounds ridiculous." She chuckled.

"Well, there is a dead man with a severed penis stuck in his mouth. Be he doesn't find it funny." Taylor grumbled defensively

.

\*\*\*\*\*\*\*\*\*\*

Cathalina could barely hold herself together once she left the nightclub. She felt high from all the cigarette smokes, drugs, marijuana and alcohol being served up in the place. Not to mention the extreme funk of everyone bumping and grinding the night away. She could smell the stench of death, blood and sickness on her. She couldn't stand still anymore.

She reached for the wall of the building to hold herself up. The world was spinning so fast she couldn't stand straight. She leaned over and began to puke. She was heaving so badly that she began to see blood coming from her mouth. She wasn't sure if that was the dead man in the bathroom's blood or eyes. Her eyes were bloodshot red and tired. She felt like crying but couldn't bring up tears.

She staggered to her car and threw herself in the driver's seat. Then she suddenly found her tears. They came first in small sobs, then full blown bawling.

"Why, why, why?" she banged her head on the steering wheel. "I tried. I did everything. Why am I here? Why this? Why now?" She heard the questions leave her lips and then she began to laugh. Her mind beginning to protect itself, bringing about her alter ego, the part of her that is strong, fearless and determined. She sniffled and searched her glove compartment for some tissue. She sneezed into it and wiped her nose.

"I am not going through that feel sorry for myself crap again. Been there done that. This is a different time, a new me. Cleo would know what to do." She smiled. She put the key in the ignition and headed for Sex Cell.

## MAN KILLER 17

Serena was glowing. She couldn't have been happier with the time she spent with Vincent. She felt so good that afternoon when she knew he could have gone all the way and stopped, that she was convinced he was her soul mate so she allowed herself to curl into a ball of female vulnerability and rest her head on his broad thick shoulders.

"I am glad you allowed me to take you home Serena. I would have been worried sick allowing you to take a taxi home by yourself this late at night." He leaned over and gently pressed his lips up against Serena's forehead, and her smile broadened. Her spider however, was in attack mode. She had been bitten more times than she could count anymore as she stopped listening to the spider's cautious attempts to bring her out of her euphoria. She no longer was able to hear the chaotic sounds like multiple voices in her head. Like her conscience, the voices had become muffled and the only thing she heard was the beating of her heart. She had never in her entire life, felt like this.

"Well, you make it impossible to fight you. You are just too persistent and I am too tired." Serena smiled up at him. "Besides, why wouldn't I want a hunk like you escorting me home?" When Vincent looked at her, she was smiling mischievously.

"What's that look on your face?"

"Nothing, I am just. Well, happy." She confessed

jovially and tightened her hold on his ample biceps.

"I never thought that after everything I have been through in my life, that I would be able to meet someone as special as you Serena. Thanks so much for giving me a second chance on life. Vincent's words pierced her heart and she never told him that she was a Florida State Judge, or that she knew exactly what his past was, or that she was destined to kill him according to the code of the organization of women she vowed to be loyal to.

For a brief moment she flinched nervously and the spider curled into a purr, sending endorphins through her body hoping to awaken her system with a shockwave of memory. But Serena's heart was not budging. She wanted this chance to find love. She was tired. For her, this was a glimmer of hope in her otherwise loveless future with a Eunuch as her companion. She didn't want to let this go. So she relaxed and listened to him tell her how special she was.

The words were like music to her ears. Vincent smiled at her silence and continued to drive. He knew there was something more to her, a secret he could not quite put his finger on. In prison he learned one important rule, never show all your hands and to keep a poker face at all times. That first day he saw her, he could have sworn he saw something move on her shoulder, and incest that pierced her skin and caused a small droplet of blood to ooze from her skin. He had shaken it off as a hallucination. Since that day he had been careful to watch again to see if he was going crazy. He felt crazy just thinking that what he saw was real, but he figured it wouldn't hurt to check. Besides, she had a very lifelike tattoo of a spider in that same location. He didn't stop making his intimate interlude with her because he wanted to. He saw it again, her tattoo moving, flinching, eyes focused on him as he looked back. His blood had curled and he was afraid. He couldn't get the look of the thing out of his mind. It was as though it understood, he wasn't sure if that was the same tattoo on her or something else that crawled on her but he felt as though if he went any further, the thing would attack.

\*\*\*\*\*\*\*\*\*\*

Cleo and Natalia sat outside Serena's home anxiously. Cleo couldn't wait to get rid of Serena. Finally her chance to be done with her, she was so nervous that she couldn't sit still. They had waited hours, she wanted to confront Serena and Natalia would be vindicated as the true daughter and recipient of the legacy of her father. They didn't have to wait much longer, as they watched the strange black Maxima pull up in front of her semi-mansion home. They gasped at the sight of Serena stepping out of the car with a man.

"I thought you said she was pure." Natalia chastised.

"Well if she wasn't before, she is a liar, and if she was, I guess she is not anymore." Cleo snickered. She could not believe her eyes, but then it occurred to her. Cathalina's precious Serena is a whore. Now she can with Cathalina back with this news about Serena and she couldn't wait. Her heart began to palpitate just at the thought of having Cathalina all to herself again, like in the old days. Cleo squeezed Natalia's hand as Serena pressed the code into her security gate and got back into the car with Vincent. They entered the compound and the gates closed behind them.

"Why didn't we go in?" Natalia whined.

"Because you idiot, they will know that we are following them. When I get my hands on her, I want her to shit her pants." Cleo seethed venomously. Natalia smiled at how vehement Cleo was toward Serena. She hit the jackpot with this one. She couldn't believe how easy this was going to be with

Madam Cleo at her side and then watched as the gates slammed shut and then drove away.

"Why are we leaving now after hours of waiting? This is bullshit." Natalia was pissed off. She was tired and nervous and anxious to get it over with. And Cleo was backing down like a yellow belly.

"Slow and easy wins the race Natalia dear. Slow and easy." She caressed Natalia's legs gently and smiled arrogantly.

"I don't know what the fuck is that supposed to mean. I have waited my entire life for this moment. You promised you would help and now you are spewing some shit about philosophy."

"You need to calm your fast little ass down Natalia. If we do things the way you want, we might screw the whole thing up and then you would be really angry then. Do you want to be caught and seen as a trespasser and go to prison for murder?" she turned briefly to check to see if she was making herself clear to Natalia.

The woman sat silently for a moment as if thinking about it.

"So what do you plan to do?" she receded.

"I plan to mess her up so bad that she won't even remember her damn name." Cleo smiled. She was going to make this hurt and she was not going to stop until there was no more breath left in Serena's body. For a brief moment, Serena sensed that something was not right. She turned to look back toward the gated entrance and cringed.

"Is everything okay?" Vincent asked, taking her hand in his and caressing her forearm.

"Yes, I just thought for a moment." Then she looked up at him. "Forget it, it was nothing." She smiled coyly and began to open the door. As usual, Jason was there waiting for her to come home, dressed in his loin clothe and ready to do

Serena's bidding. The shock on his face to see a man with her brought such horror to him that his impulse was to attack Vincent. Like a bulldog on watch, Jason flew at Vincent's throat and had him pinned to the wall, but Vincent was a big guy, and was much bigger than Jason pound for pound. He slammed Jason to the ground and began to pound away at his face.

"Stop this!" Serena demanded her voice a fervent echo throughout the vast house. The two men did not relent. Jason was fighting for his life. He had served her now for years and without her, he was nothing and he had nothing. He scarified to be with her.

Serena went to the staircase and pressed the button to the hidden wall and retrieved her cat of nine tails. She marched down the stairway and snapped it two times to get Jason's attention. Vincent looked up and was cracked one in the face by Jason and then kneed in the groin. Vincent rolled over on his back in excruciating pain and Jason jumped to his feet and began kicking him in abdomen and torso.

"Who- the- fuck- are-you?" He asked as his feet made contact after contact with Vincent's body. Vincent's moans and groans were painful and Serena cracked the whip several times but Jason was defiant and she had to lash out at him, clocking the whip into his skin and tearing away at the flash to get him to even flinch. Two more lashes onto his torso and legs before Jason stopped. His heavy breathing did not subside as he turned to look at Serena. His anger flared his nostrils and eyes burnt with fervently.

"Why did you do this?" His voice was so deep and low Serena almost didn't hear a word he said.

"Who are you to question what I do in my own house?" She responded, taking a move toward him.

"You are my woman."

"Your woman? What can you do for your woman? Can you fend for me, provide shelter, or fuck the shit out of me when I need it?" She steamed as she proceeded to face him.

"I gave you everything. I gave it to you the way you wanted it and I showed you love with the ultimate kind of love and sacrifice." Jason retorted, stepping into her face.

"Back up your disgusting no good stink breath out of my face." She demanded, appalled by the questions, the stance that he is taking.

"Oh, now my breath stinks?" His pride stung deep beyond his heart.

"I hate you. I have no respect for you. You are a stool for me to step on and a pot for me to piss on. You are not a man, you are garbage, something to be used and put out when I am done. Now BE GONE!" She dismissed, and as soon as the words escaped her mouth he slapped her so hard across her face that she turned almost as red as the color of her hair. She reached her hand up to snap the whip again but her hands were restrained by him.

"You no longer have permission to use me Serena. I am not your slave. I gave myself to you as a gift of love and you took me for granted and now, this is your true feelings for me. You no longer have permission to hurt me." His eyes were burning fire, and just when he raised his hand to hit her again, Vincent was up behind him, fighting to protect Serena from another assault. Vincent's strength and muscles were nothing compared to Jason's passionate anger.

"Don't you know never to fuck with a man who has nothing to lose and nothing left to live for?" He asked as he spun on Vincent and delivered another kick to his groin and flipped him over, twisting his arm behind his back and crushing his fingers.

"Serena, do something." Vincent yelled.

"She can do nothing. I have been living with her day in and day out. I know all her secrets and what buttons to push to make them work. Her transformation is nothing without the anger of sexual and physical abuse to fuel it. She cannot do shit in a situation like this. But I will show you what I can do." Jason was yelling at the top of his voice, and Serena sent her whip out again. But Jason grabbed it, pulling her to him as he sat on Vincent's back, bending his arm into unnatural positions. As Serena neared the burning furnace of anger that fueled Jason's rage, she began to sob. She had never seen him like this before. His soft gentle hands when he touched her, his passionate kisses and caress, his words of love and devotion to her.

"You are so damn naive Serena. Did you really think that is the way I was, harmless and stupid? I did that for you." He breathed into her face as she closed her eyes to prepare for his next assault. The thought of him hitting her brought the sleeping spider inside her alive. She began to morph and her body became lucid as she changed her human skeletal muscles. "That's it baby. This is how it must end. You started this, now finish it." He demanded, releasing Vincent's hands so he could use his fingers to plunge it inside of Serena's vagina.

"Don't you like that?" he asked still sitting on Vincent who managed to turn around to see what the mad man was talking about. "Oh, so you want to see the woman you are about to fuck. This is it, she, whatever the fuck that is." Jason pointed, and stood up so that Vincent could get a better look. But he did not release Serena from his choke hold. "See what she did to me? She cut my fucking dick off just so she wouldn't have a moment of weakness and say yes, to keep her precious virginity." He removed his loincloth and stood naked as the day he was born.

Vincent's eyes popped from his head at the sight of a black Greek God with no penis. They would love him in prison. He thought, but he was a killer, he had done some horrible things in his life. He had never seen anything like this, and as he watched his mind was already planning on what he could do with a woman like that. His instincts told him that he had hit the jackpot.

Serena could not transform to hurt Jason, her heart got in the way. Her changes came in spurts and she looked disfigured and horrible. Jason dropped her mutilated form to the ground and walked away, spitting at the site of her. Vincent reached out for her, and held her while she returned to her full human form. He was so fascinated he didn't know what to do with himself. He lifted her into his arm and walked right back out the door. He put her in the passenger seat and reclined it, then jumped into the driver's seat and sped out. When he got to the gate he realized that he didn't know the code. He looked to the semi-conscious Serena who whispered to him.

"Spider," and closed her eyes. Vincent opened the gate and took Serena back to his home. Jason stood at the door and watched Serena drive out of his life. He was filled with angry confusion and was not certain what was to become of him. He laughed eerily as he looked at his naked body.

"What life is out there for the likes of me? I have lived here for years with nothing of my own. No bank account, no contact with family or friends, I don't even own the clothes on my back." He laughed again, as cold reality hit him. He went to the staircase and pushed the button to the secret doors, releasing the chains from their hiding place. He went to the middle of the living room and began restraining himself the way Serena would when she was ready to have her way with him. Only, this time, he didn't just bind his hands and legs; he took one of the chained links and harnessed it around his neck. Holding the remote control in his outstretched hands he pushed the button so hard that when the chains began to pull, his neck was snapped, killing him instantly and his limps were stretched apart to almost falling from their sockets, torn flesh dropping fresh blood on her pristine floors.

## MAN KILLER 18

Cathalina groggily pushed herself up on her elbows to see what's going on around her. She felt the restraints holding her down and fell back into the small uncomfortable bed from fatigue and confusion. She shook her head wearily and tried to force her eyes open. She lay still attempting to adjust her eyes to the bright light, but one of her eyes was swollen shut and she became afraid. Her body felt sour and aching, her face felt swollen and her mouth tasted like dried up stale blood.

"What's going on here?" the question she asked more to herself than to anyone else. The words came out muffled. She couldn't see and was frightened when she received an answer.

"You are in the hospital Ms. Shekhar." The voice was feminine, soft, soothing. "I have been waiting for you to wake up for some time now." The female said again. Cathalina squinted her eye and tried to look again. She wasn't sure who was talking to her and she couldn't understand why this woman has been waiting for her to wake up.

"What happened to me?" Cathalina asked feeling around her body and finding the wires attached to her to monitor her heart rate and intravenous needles to administer medication.

"You were in a car accident two days ago. Do you remember anything about it?"

"I don't know what you are talking about. I don't remember being in an accident." Her one eye adjusted to the lights and she batted her eyelash until she was able to look upon the face of the tall beautiful dark skinned woman before her. Her slenderness added a harmless disposition, but Cathalina knew she was more than she appeared to be. She chuckled as the thought. After all, she had been specializing in picking out special people.

"It was pretty bad, you are lucky you survived it." Dyania moved closer to her and touched her hand softly, "are you in pain? Would you like me to get the doctor?" She asked. She felt a strange connection to Cathalina. She admired any woman who would stand up for herself, who refused to be victimized.

"Do you remember being in a bar nightclub two nights ago?" Dyania looked at Cathalina calmly assessing her as she pulled her chair closer so she could sit next to her, so that Cathalina wouldn't have to strain her voice to speak loud enough to be heard. "It seemed you had a very busy day before you ended up here." Dyania fixed Cathalina's bed sheet and smiled warmly at her. She felt so much more at ease and comfortable having made contact with Cathalina. When she and Taylor were called to the accident scene two days ago she suddenly felt that she had arrived at the right place. It was a strange kind of thing, sort of the way she felt when Francesca had held her hand. The held on to the necklace that was around her neck and squeezed it tightly, she hoped the woman would be okay.

"Is my doctor here?" Cathalina asked shakily, tears forming in her throat.

"Your palm pilot gave all the information needed to the ambulance team who picked you up. We also knew you were a donor just incase the situation turned tragic." Dyania told her.

"Who are you?" She finally managed to ask.

There was a soft knock on the door, before it was cracked opened slightly.

"Is everything okay?" Taylor asked before entering and gently closed the door behind him. "I see our patient is awake." He smiled as he too pulled a chair to the opposite side of Cathalina's bed then gently patted her hand as he took it into his. Cathalina looked at Dyania quizzically.

"Cathalina, this is Detective Jamie Taylor, and I am with a special homicide unit. I am Detective Minto. You can call me Dyania." She smiled again disarming Cathalina.

"I don't understand." Cathalina closed her eye and swallowed hard. She willed her thoughts and her heartbeat to be still and found the control to pull off a facade of confidence even in the face of such eminent danger.

"Do you remember me Cathalina?" Taylor asked forcing Cathalina to turn her head, bringing her attention to him. She shook her head slightly saying no, but she was fully conscious of who he was. "We met briefly. One of your clients, Lara Lopez was involved in what seemed like a double homicide/suicide. You identified her for me. Do you remember?" He asked again. He reached to look into her one opened eye but then gave up as she strained to see and tried to gain focus.

"Don't worry about it now Cath. Your doctor will be in to check on you soon and we will know how bad the damage is. We can talk later. We were just checking in on you as we have been doing for the past couple days." Dyania told her as she brushed a strand of hair from her forehead.

"Thank you." Cathalina said as she tried to muster a smile and wondered why she called her by her familial name. "Has anyone been here to visit me?" Cathalina asked her. She wanted to know if Cleo or the other girls knew what had happened to her. Just at that moment her physician walked in.

"Cathalina, haven't I always told you to take care of yourself?" He asked in chuckle. "Doctors do make the worst patients you know?" he commented to Dyania and Taylor.

"So I have heard." Dyania responded. She was in great spirits.

"How are you feeling Cath darling?" He asked as he took a small pen light and flickered it across her eye and then pressing gently on the swollen one.

"Horrible."

"So I would imagine." He told her as he checked her vitals on the machine and made notes on her chart. "But it seems you will live and live well my dear." He told her. He turned to address her guest. "I have to give her some pain medicine and some sleeping tranquilizers. I need to be alone with her now."

"Oh, no problem doctor." Taylor got up and placed his chair back in its original place. Dyania smiled again at Cathalina.

"I will see you tomorrow okay?" Cathalina nodded and closed her aching eye. Taylor and Dyania turned to leave and closed the door behind them after taking one more look in on her.

"So what do you think?"

"I think it's great that she is going to be okay. Once she is well enough, I would like to have a psychological evaluation done on her." Dyania walked towards the exit of the hospital and stopped when she noticed the candy machine. She loved chocolate bars and had not had one in a few months. They made her nightmares worst so she stopped.

"Now that's ironic." Taylor snickered.

"What is?"

"A psychological evaluation done on a psychologist."

He laughed heartily.

"Now you know that's just plain mean Jamie. Mean!" She laughed unable to resist the humor of it all.

"In all honesty though, I think you might have a point. What kind of psychological state can someone be in to bite off a man's penis and then stuff it down his throat while you watch him die? That's just deranged." Taylor reflected on the information that came in to them at about the same time they were called to the scene of Cathalina's accident. Just the thought of it had him pausing to grab and check his own manhood as discreetly as he could. Watching him made Dyania laugh again, the image of him vicariously experiencing another man's pain tickled her pink. She knew it wasn't funny, but she could hold back, from watching Jamie squirm.

"Exactly," Dyania said in between bubbles of giggles,

"According to some of the eyewitnesses, this man have raped so many women in that said same bathroom that its only a matter of time that he got a hold of the wrong one, but according to the coroner, this man stunk and had lesions on the exterior of his manhood. She must have seen all that." Dyania reasoned, and Jamie just continued to distort his face as the thought. It wasn't the blood and gore that bothered him, he was used to that. It was the idea of another brother losing what made him a man. It hurt him to the core.

"I understand what you mean though. A sane person seeing lacerations on someone's genitals wouldn't venture there, even fearing for her own life. Maybe something triggered her anger, maybe she went temporarily insane. Like Lorena Bobbitt." He chuckled again, unable to contain the mirth of the whole situation.

"Come on, let me buy you a cup of coffee and you can help me go over some of the information I came up with on another case I have been working on in Atlanta. It lead me here." She pushed her arm casually through his and began walking.

"Where are we going Detective Minto?" Jamie stopped in his tracks and turned to look at her.

"What do you mean? I just told you." She retaliated; seeing her good mood was being turned Jamie decided to save himself. He liked her this way, laughing, and in good spirits. He didn't want to see the woman who walked into his department two days ago anytime soon.

"No, that's not what I mean. I meant that you are a guest hear. You shouldn't be buying me coffee. Let's see. What time is it?" He paused to look at his watch. "It's only eleven thirty. That's breakfast." The smile that crept up on Dyania's face prodded him to keep going. "How about, I make it for you?" He paused to study her reaction. When the smile remained he continued. "At my place." He shrugged his shoulders nonchalantly to shake off just how much it would mean to him.

"Well…"

"I mean, if you don't want to its okay. There's a diner just around the corner." He jumped in before she could respond.

"Okay if that's what you want." She told him as she began walking again. "I guess you don't need to know what I was going to say then." She turned to look at him with a smirk on her face. Her full luscious lips curled into a smile and her eyes twinkling into the glare of the morning sun.

"If you were going to say no, then I you don't have to tell me what you were going to say." Taylor jogged the few feet to catch up to her as she picked up pace again, putting her arm back through his. "But if you were going to say yes, let me kick myself right now for putting my foot in my mouth, throw myself at the mercy of the court and ask you to ignore my male go and let me make you breakfast." He bargained. Letting him off the hook, Dyania stifled another giggle.

"So which way?"

"Yes!" Taylor exclaimed as he did the happy shuffle and took her hand gently. "Right this way."

\*\*\*\*\*\*\*\*\*

Elizabeth tried to reach Cathalina for two days and couldn't, then she tried Serena and Cleo. She was not able to reach anyone except Cleo. She was becoming frantic as her senses were going into overload. Her body was always on fire and now she was locked into Serena's every thought. She wasn't sure if she was just straight paranoid and loosing or mind, or if Serena had really gone AWOL.

"Oh God please, not now. Not now." She whispered into the telephone as it rang.

"Sex Cell, may I help you?" The pleasant receptionist asked.

"Cleo please?" She asked, trying hard to steady the telephone receiver. She waited when the woman put her on hold, but she couldn't hold much longer. She couldn't contain her nerves. Her hands were shaking so hard that she was banging the receiver against her ear. She put the headset back into its cradle and pressed the speaker phone button. She hadn't eaten or slept since that day of the meeting when everything went dreadfully wrong. Every moment have been painfully eroticized with passionate nightmares, she wasn't sure if she was dreaming or awake most of the times, or whether she was getting transmissions or loosing her noodles. She was tired, hungry, nervous and frustrated. She wanted to kill every and anything that moved. She needed to talk to somebody. She realized that Cleo had yet to come to the phone. She hung up and pressed the redial button.

"Sex Cell."

"Listen to me, get Cleo's big fat ass on the phone now before I reach through it and ring your damn neck." She didn't have to say it twice.

"Hold please."

"Who is this and what the fuck do you want?" Cleo was her natural same ol' nasty self. She was only cordial to Cathalina and didn't take nicely to anyone else unless there was something in it for her.

"Cleo, it's me. Something is wrong."

"Liz? Liz, are you okay? You sound like shit."

"How pleasant of you Cleo. Thanks." Elizabeth said trying to sound normal, let it roll off her back like it used to. But this time, she couldn't help taking it personally. After all, it was the truth.

"Soothing is wrong Cleo. I can feel it. Serena has gone AWAL and I cannot reach Cathalina." The moment she heard Cathalina's name she gained full interest.

"What do you mean you haven't been able to reach Cathalina? Did you try her at home? The office?" Cleo asked dread beginning to spread throughout her body.

"Of course I did all that. I wouldn't bother to call you if there were some other way." Elizabeth hissed.

"What are you supposed to mean by that?" Cleo asked defensively.

"Listen, forget it okay? Our girls are missing and that's the main concern. You can grill me later but right now I am freaking out Cleo. I cannot stop shaking. I feel like a drug addict going through withdrawal and I don't know if it's something that I am doing or if I am picking up something from Serena and Cathalina. I bled this morning when I went to the bathroom and I am aching all over as though I got ran over by a truck. Yet I feel like I could run a hundred miles right now from the adrenaline rush I am having. I feel sick. We are connected now and I cannot break this damn link." Tears began flowing down her face as she spoke. Her eyes were so misty she could no longer see and her voice was all choked up.

"Okay, are you home?" She could no longer decipher Elizabeth's words so she assumed that was a yes when she heard the goggled sound from Liz's mouth. "I am on my way. Stay there." Cleo told her and hung up the phone. As soon as Liz hung up the phone it rang again. She wanted to pick it up but couldn't. She was in no shape. Her voice was gone and her hands were trembling uncontrollably. She couldn't do anything. Then the voicemail picked up.

"Hello Elizabeth. My name is Detective Minto. I would like to speak to you regarding a Francesca Trivilani. You can reach me at this number..." Elizabeth's mind blanked out for a second and she didn't hear the number after the woman mentioned Francesca. She knew it. She was right. Francesca was dead and now they are coming after her. Heaven help her. "I would like to hear from you at your earliest convenience." She blanked back in to hear. "By the way, it seems you are friends with a Dr. Cathalina Shehkar. She was in a very bad accident and is in the critical care unit at Larkin Community Hospital in South Miami. Hope to see you there."

When the phone went dead, she was stumped. At first she couldn't find her breath and she was struggling to find her voice. She didn't know when it happened or how she found the strength or got the energy, but she knew she heard a loud wail, like a hundred screaming mothers in the throes of childbirth. When she realized the sound was coming out of her mouth she began wailing in shock and terror, and the tears flowed freely until they withered into sobs as she curled into the fetal position on her bed. The thoughts came in spurts. What was she going to do without Cathalina? She was their voice, their strength, she was their council. Who was going to rescue her? She couldn't leave Cathalina alone in the hospital by herself. Yet if she went, she would be arrested for sure. How would she survive?

    She wasn't sure how much time had passed but there was a loud thud thud thud at the door. She was jolted from her semi conscious half sleep and looked at the lock. It was four in the evening when she called Cleo and it was now six thirty. She pulled herself from her bed and moved shakily to the door. She wasn't sure who it was now and she was attempting to be cautious. Her brain was fried and she couldn't take another attack, she needed someone to talk to.

    She lifted the brass peephole to verify who it was, and for a brief moment she felt relief. It was Cleo. Cleo charged into the apartment and was filled with disgust. Apparently for the past couple of days Elizabeth did not find the need to shower or change her clothes. She reeked and she was falling apart. She was in emotional shambles.

    "Oh baby," Cleo found the love she had always held for Liz. "I am so sorry. Look at what she did to you; look at what she did to you."

    "What she who did to me Cleo?" Liz asked shuddering from an internal draft.

    "Serena, your so called spider queen. Where is she now when you need her?"

    "Don't blame her Cleopatra. We have been doing this long before she came into the picture. If anything, it's look what we did to her. What we brought her into and did to her life." Liz said, fatigue consuming her and she began to slide to the floor from Cleo's arms.

"Here, let's get to the bed." Cleo swooped her in her arms in one motion and carried her. Cleo looked at her with the love of a mother. She had groomed and raised Elizabeth from a teenager. When she discovered what she was, she gave her a home. Of course it wasn't the best of homes or the best of jobs, but it was what she had to offer. She allowed her to leave to pursue her dreams as an actress. Now look at her. Her heart tugged emotionally at the thought of Liz falling apart the way she was.

"Would you like some water? Have you had anything to eat?" Cleo looked around and picked up a few things from the floor and placed them in a pile on the floor. Elizabeth was immaculate. For anything to be out of place for her is unusual. She was apparently breaking things because there were broken glasses on the floor in the kitchen and water stains on the walls.

"Cleo, what am I going to do? I am in trouble."

"Don't worry sweetie, we are going to find Cath."

"No, it's not that." Elizabeth coughed her eyes burning and red from her tears.

"I don't understand. You are not in this alone." Cleo placed her hand around her shoulders for comfort. The smell of Elizabeth made her get up and walk to the bathroom to run the bath. She walked into the living room where the drapes were drawn and the lights were dark making almost look like night outside. She pulled the drapes open and slid the balcony doors open so the cool ocean breeze could circulate inside the North Miami apartment.

Cleo walked back to the bedroom where Elizabeth were and laid her out and began undressing her. She chuckled.

"I remember when I found you. You were almost as vulnerable as you are now." She stopped to turn off the water faucet and poured some bath oils and Epson salt in the tub to soak her.  She gathered Elizabeth's vanilla and lavender candles and lit them, aromatizing the environment.  She dimmed the lights and placed Liz gently in the tub.

"I am really in trouble this time Cleo, and nobody can help me."

"Hush now child.  I am going to put on a pot of tea, clean up the rest of this place and get to the bottom of this.  As she cleaned, she noticed that the voicemail light was blinking.  She probably haven't checked her message yet, she thought and directed herself to the nightstand where Elizabeth kept her phone.  She pressed the button and listened nonchalantly to the various messages from colleagues, her agent for new parts and friends.  When the message from Dyania popped up, Cleo almost gagged.  When she mentioned Cathalina she got light headed.

"Oh no."  It hit her hard.  She now understood.  Elizabeth was in trouble and they have connected her to Cathalina.  They were all in trouble.  Cleo finished cleaning as best she could, took Liz out of the bath and got her comfortable in bed.  She was sleeping before was able to even drink her hot tea. "That's all you needed baby girl.  That's all you needed." Cleo said as she walked to the Balcony.  "Now what am I going to do about Cathalina?"

**********

Dyania went over all the information that Taylor had to offer her.  She couldn't understand where the connection was with Elizabeth and Cathalina.  She shared with him the information on what had happened in Atlanta at the risk of sounding ridiculous.

"Amazing," was all he could say as he cleared their late breakfast plates and placed them in the kitchen sink.

"She was her roommate and the only one from the cast missing after her death. She is not being charged with the cause of death, but it's the only lead I have besides the victim uttering her name as she took her last breath." Dyania moaned a beaten sigh of confusion. She knew there was something more but she just didn't know what it was.

"So we have a man who died from a dismembered penis and then was gagged with it; a woman from a different state, Atlanta, whose cause of death was an over dose of spider venom; a man thrown from a vehicle on a popular Florida highway with said same spider poison in his system."

"Yes. But those are there different incidents at different times." The processing in Taylor's mind was on over drive.

"Then we have a case that seems totally unrelated. Your Lara Lopez, a patient of the good doctor who went insane and bit a man's genitals off. How the hell does all this come into play?" Dyania stood and paced the kitchen floor. The drip of the water as Taylor washed the dished caused a mental flow pattern in her head.

"Do you think there is a connection between those four distinct separate scenarios?" Taylor wiped his hands and walked over to her, stopping her by holding on to her forearms at arm's length.

"It's quite a coincidinki. I mean think about it?" She told him, pulling away and continuing her pacing path back and forth from the kitchen sink to the table. "What are the odds that the highway body was once the drive for Luxury Limos, that was rented by Dr. Cathalina Shekhar who when next seen was in an accident from extreme fatigue after biting off a man's penis then killing him with it, who just so happened to have been the attending doctor to your Lara Lopez who ended up dead in a suicide homicide situation and is a

friend of none other than missing in action Elizabeth Chung."
She sped her words off so fast to the point of breathlessness
and had to catch her breath when she was finished.

"Damn, I didn't even process it that way." Taylor sat down at the incredible burden of evidence just laid on him like a ton of bricks.

"It's all just too…gosh, I don't know." Dyania sat across from him, flung her hands on the table and dropped her head to meet them, gently banging it as if the force out more thoughts to make sense of it all. "I don't know why, but I am feeling it's all connected. Something is just not adding up." She finally said, piercing his eyes with hers. His mouth had dropped open at the revelations and all he could do was stare back at the youthful face of this investigative wiz. He couldn't believe her brilliance, her acute and keen reasoning ability.

## MAN KILLER 19

    Cleo decided to leave and allow Elizabeth to get some sleep. She needed to know that Cathalina was okay and to figure out their next move. She left Elizabeth's condo and got into the Honda Accord she borrowed from Natalia. As she plopped into the driver's seat, she reached for her cell phone and dialed for directory assistance.
    "Larkin Community Hospital," she stated into the automated voice activated service. She didn't wait for the number to be repeated. She hung up and dialed the number that was given to her. She was finally able to finagle her way through the automated system at the hospital until she received a live person who gave her the room and location of Dr. Cathalina Shekhar. She drove as fast as she could without being detected by a state trooper. She made her way through Coral Way Village, past University of Miami and onto to S.W. 62th where the hospital was located. She found the parking lot and headed into the hospital lobby. As fast as she could move with her heart beating faster than she could catch her breath.
    She stood breathless as she read the name of her most trusted confidante and the love of her life. She choked up as she looked through the small window opening on the door and saw Cathalina laid out. Her face scared and healing from the stitches they had given her, her legs in casts. She stifled

her tears and swallowed hard.

She turned the knob and put a smile on her face as she entered.

"Hey there gorgeous." Cleo said as Cathalina turned to look at her. She didn't want to give away just how horrible she looked. The scars, the swollen eye, the stitches, but to her Cathalina was still the most beautiful woman she had ever seen.

"Sweetheart!" Cathalina mustered as much joy as she could. She didn't think anyone would find her. No one knew she was there.

"How did you find me?" She mustered and then coughed. Her throat was dry and she reached for the glass of water next to her bed. Cleo rushed over to her aid and placed the straw in her mouth. Elizabeth is in a bad way. Spider senses I guess. Picked up that you were in danger and she is freaking out about a bunch of other stuff."

"Is she okay?" The evident concern in Cathalina's voice made her take her hand.

"She is okay. I just left her; I took care of her I promise." Cleo said, fighting the tears from blurring her eyes.

"Are you okay?" Cathalina chuckled softly, watching the hardness of Cleopatra's fascia melt away.

"Listen Cath, seems like we have some problems. Detectives are on our trail. They've been tracking Liz since she returned home from Atlanta. I don't know why. There is something she is not telling us."

"I know a woman and a male cop right? Been here with me since day one. If you hang around much longer, they will meet you. They come here like clockwork." Cathalina forced the words out. She knew she had to tell Cleo what to expect.

"Do you think they are going to find out? I mean, we

have done a lot of stuff over the past ten years, what will happen if..."

"Shuuu!" Cathalina mustered as much strength as possible to put her finger on Cleo's full thick lips. "I need to do something right now. You have to get to my office. Sooner or later someone is going to get there and start rummaging through my records. Delete all the files marked Man Killer on them. They are coded but it won't be hard with the police technology they have on hand to decipher it." She smiled when Cleo's mouth dropped open.

"You kept files?"

"Don't be silly woman. You are an entrepreneur; you have files for your organization don't you?" She took Cleo's nod as a yes.

"But..."

"Let me finish Cleo please. I am tired, and I cannot keep talking much longer. My throat is dry and I might pass out soon. Besides, it's only a matter of time before they bug my room." Cleo silenced her questions and listened as Cathalina continued. "Once you have gone through my computer files, I need to you go to my combination locker. Password is Man Killer, open it and shred everything in there. I have copies don't worry. They are hidden in a safe place; if anything happens to me the information will be destroyed."

"Where?"

"That's not important now. Do as I say Cleo, I have evidence on us to bring up things that would never be uncovered without it. About people and things and situations, you understand, don't you?" Again, all Cleo could do was nod her head. She knows that if they got their hands on her file alone, they would be closing unsolved deaths spanning a decade.

"How do I get back in touch with you?" She could not stop the tears now. The information and responsibility that's being placed on her without Cathalina beside her was overwhelming.

"I don't know. Tell the girls to stay away. Anyone who comes into contact with me will be questioned, I am sure of it. And they will look into all of your backgrounds just to rule you out of the equation." Cleo pressed her lips tenderly against Cathalina's with as much passion as she could muster without hurting her. She caressed her face and kissed her forehead.

"I love you Cath." She told her, resting her cheek against Cathalina's moist ones.

"I love you too Cleo." She responded, squeezing Cleo's hand with all the strength she could muster. "Now, do it."

"Do what?" Cleo jerked her face away from Cathalina's with horror in her eyes.

"You remember.? What we used to talk about years ago, just in case, when it was just us two." Cleo's tears turned to wails and sobs as she sniffled and reached for a napkin to blow her nose.

"That was a joke, we never intended."

"Desperate times call for desperate measures."

"But this is not it." Cleo was adamant not to listen to Cathalina's sickly ranting; she coughed on a sob and used the back of her hand to wipe her tears away.

"This is it Cleo, you promised me you would do this for me, and I made you the same promise. Were you lying?"

"No, but Cath, its going to be okay, we can fix this." "This is the way to fix this, it will close the ranks." Cleo dropped her head back to Cathalina's shoulders and grabbed her head, slightly lifting her from the bed, hugging and rocking her slightly.

"No, oh no, oh no, I love you so much Cathalina. You

are the love of my life; you have given my pitiful existence meaning and placed me on journey. You took away my pain and allowed me to see a bigger picture. You loved me. How am I supposed to live without you?" She asked. But she knew, that Cathalina would not answer. In her grief, she knew she had to respect what her friend asked, and as much as she tried, the reality of the situation was there obvious.

"Cathalina Shakher, I will never forget you." Cleo gathered herself and placed her broken neck back in its place on the bed. Cathalina's eyes were already closed as she hugged her friend, and her face was peaceful. Cleo leaned in and kissed her softly on the lips one last time, lingering there to carve the feel of her lips into her mind. Then she pulled away and walked swiftly out the door.

## MAN KILLER 20

    Serena turned blissfully in the comfort of Vincent's king sized bed. She smiled as she woke from her sweet dream.

    "Hey there sleepy head." Vincent kissed her forehead as he presented her with a breakfast tray of fruits and orange juice. "Hope you are hungry."

    "Famished." Serena laughed. "Do you have pancakes? Eggs?"

    "Of course I do. Would you like to get dress and come sit with me in the kitchen? We can talk as I cook." He offered.

    "Sure, I would love that."

    "Great. Take your time and get yourself together. Come and join me when you are ready." Vincent kissed her gently on the back of her hand, reached closer and brushed his lips against hers, then easing from the bed, took the tray and exited the bedroom.

    Cathalina sat up in the bed and surveyed herself. She wasn't wearing the sundress she had on the day before. Vincent had changed her and had her dressed in a gorgeous white chiffon night gown. It hung from her shoulders in spaghetti straps and flowed in layers to the ground, covering her feet and resting lightly on her curves. At first she was alarmed that he had changed her, but then her alarm turned to embarrassment and fear. He had seen her change. What's worse?

She looked around and noticed that there was a master bathroom adjacent from the bed. She gathered her garment and slid from the bed. Once in the bathroom she saw that things were immaculately set aside for her. A new toothbrush, towels and soap all neatly folded with a rose next to them. She smiled and felt a tinge of awkwardness.

"Is everything okay up there?" Vincent yelled from the foot of the stairs.

"Yes, I am fine. Thank you."

"Girl you sure are fine." He mumbled as he walked back to the kitchen to start the lady's request.

"Excuse me? Did you say something?" She yelled back as he headed away.

"Oh nothing, just missing you already, that's all." He smiled and continued on his way. As soon as he began to beat the eggs and set the table, Serena glided down the stairs to meet him.

"I didn't realize you were so immaculate." She admired. "Your home is beautiful."

"Thank you. It feels like a home now with someone as regal as you in it. It's never felt this good." He winked at her and made her shy away. She didn't remember everything that happened that lead her to being awakened in his bed. But she did remember the confrontation; the thought of Jason gave her a twitch of guilt in her abdomen. She wondered how he was, and how things will be from here after. Things are forever changed.

"Did I say something?"

"No, it's just that. Well, everything is so weird. This is not how I envisioned spending the night in a man's bed for the first time in my life." She told him shyly. The admission took Vincent off guard and she stopped serving up Sizzleen to talk to her.

"Are you serious? You have never spent the night in a man's bed?" He was filled with shock and honor.

"Yes, I have done a lot of things," she swallowed hard at all the foreplay, finger play, tongue play action she had participated in to justify and complete her actions, "but I have never had sexual intercourse with a man." Vincent had an immediate erection at the thought. All this time he was out there raping babies, killing, being a criminal, when he could have had all he wanted in one woman.

For a fleeting second, Serena felt his thoughts and jumped at his memory of killing children. The thought was so powerful that it pushed right through her emotional block and hit her right where it hurt. The spider in her blood curd and growled and then he touched her hand, endorphins kicked through her system and caused a drugged like reaction to her system. Smelling his testosterone didn't help and when he reached over and passionately pressed his lips to hers, she didn't resist.

When he pulled away, she was breathless. Her sex drive had gone into fifth gear and she wanted him to continue. But he couldn't. He kept seeing what she had become and he couldn't put himself inside of it, not yet.

"Come on, let's eat." He gently pulled himself away from her and moved back to the kitchen table, placing a place of eggs, Sizzleen and pancakes in front of her. Picking up a piece of the mean that is cut like bacon pieces but much thicker and less fatty, she looked at it as she turned it around in her hands.

"What's this?" She asked bringing it to her nose to take a sniff.

"It's called Sizzleen. It's better than bacon because its cured beef and turkey. It's much healthier." He told her.

"It smells really good." She smiled and took a big bite, "and it tastes really good as well." She told him. "I cannot believe I have never heard of this."

"Well, everyone is into the same mindset, if you don't look for something different, you won't find something different." He told her as he dug into his eggs and poured maple syrup on his pancakes.

"So how long have you been able to morph like that?" He blurted out nonchalantly as though it was just another change of topic. The question took Serena off guard and she began to choke. He jumped to his feet to assist her and she pushed his hand away.

"What are you talking about?" She flared as she gained some composure. This is what she was afraid of, what she didn't remember.

"At your place, when the guy there was attacking you, you, you…"

"I don't know what you are talking about."

"Oh stop the bullshit. Ever since the day I met you I knew there was something different about you. You didn't end up at my door by accident did you?" He asked, putting his knife and fork back on the place and smiling casually as though they were discussing the weather.

"I don't know what you are talking about." Serena insisted.

"Okay, I came to your house and saw a man who attacked me for being there, then he was practically naked and became completely naked showing himself to be dickless, then you turned into some half changed something and passed out. Now don't you think through all of that, I would be curious?"

"What are you saying?" Her mind was racing a thousand miles a minute.

"I went through your purse. I saw your list. I saw my name as one of the people listed under Megan's Law. Now are you going to tell me what the deal is or not?" He asked still smiling.

Quickly getting her wits about her, Serena stood.

"I think I have out lived my welcome."

"I guess at this time I should stand as our very own State Supreme Court Judge exited into her deliberating chambers?" He asked sarcastically, stopping Serena in her tracks.

"What is it that you want Ratigan?"

"I don't know yet. I like you Serena, a lot. There have been all sorts of news reports about men ending up dead. There has been a string of bodies all across the state and all of them, not most, all of them were registered under Megan's Law and or have been previously convicted to a sex crime. Coincidence? I don't know. But it's cutting it awfully close, that you being who you are, ended up at my door, me being who I am. Don't you agree?"

"You are insane." She snickered walking to the front door.

"If you leave now Serena, if you leave this way, I will make sure the whole world knows who you are. I have nothing to loose, everyone already know who I am. However, we like each other. I have respected your choice as a woman because I want you to give yourself to me willingly. I could have taken you over and over and over again by now. If you stay with me, we can do great things together."

"Exactly what kind of great things?" She asked, suddenly feeling alive again, her feelings of betrayal saturated the lustful emotions that were clouding her judgment.

"Well, I don't exactly know what your kick is, but I was thinking you could help me out of a few rough spots I got myself into. I am a changed man; you can see that for yourself. And in return, I will help you out of your little problem." She stood slowly and walked over to her. He stood behind and caressed her arms. "You truly are and exquisitely beautiful woman." He admired. Serena's skin crawled and she wanted to just rip his throat out.

"And just so you know, if you try anything, you will not leave here alive. Finding out what you are has forced me to take some precautions." He smiled stepping away from her.

In that instant, she felt Elizabeth calling to her. She locked into her mind and felt every emotion, every worry every pain. She learned about Dyania.

"Oh no"

"It's not that of a bad deal. After all you are already a murderer, just like me." Vincent took offence to her reaction.

"No, no, no, no…" She began to cry as she fell to the floor. "I need to go home. I cannot talk to you about this now. There is an emergency and I need to go home." She told him. He walked towards her and took her hand trying not to alarm her unnecessarily.

"You cannot go now Serena, we are in the middle of something." He advised her.

"You don't understand Vincent. I am not asking your permission. You don't know me, whatever you think you know, you don't know me, and right now there are things I need to attend to. Her mind had begun to open up and she was kicked off her feet when she felt the collision, the taste of blood, heard the screams. She fell to the ground and put her hands to hear ears. Her eardrums began to bleed as she spun around on the floor and began to morph in and out of semi-human state. She couldn't control the flood of sensation that came at her.

He jumped out of her reach and grabbed for his gun. He was so frightened that he wasn't sure what was going on.

He didn't want to take any chances.

"Call me a taxi." She demanded. He thought she said it out loud, but when she asked again, he realized that the words were in his head. She was telepathic. The thought almost made him jump out of his skin. "I have to go home now. My sisters are in trouble. Hospital. I have to go." She panted; her voice was of no threat to him, her thoughts of no danger. She just wanted to go.

Reaching into his pocket he grabbed his car keys and slid them on the floor to her. She looked down and picked them up.

"Thank you. We can finish this later." She forced herself up from the floor and willed her legs, one before the other to the door. Vincent's Maxima was parked in front of the house. He had been out early getting food from the supermarket and he had not had time to put it in the garage. Dragging herself to the driver's side, she got in and turned the ignition. She had a violent attack of pains to her arms and chest. The spider venom had turned on her and the tattoo of the insect reared its head and starred at her. Ignoring it she pressed on the gas and took off. She understood and got the point. She had been negligent, caught up. How dare her dare to dream for herself.

She had decided to head home and change, but somewhere in the middle of her journey, she felt a snap. She swerved recklessly to the side of the road and stopped suddenly. The snap was so loud, she thought she had punctured a tire, but she knew it was not a tire. She felt the life of her friend drain from her body. She closed her eyes and focused in; sensing her anger and pain the way Cathalina had taught her in the beginning. Channeling her hatred and the unjustness of this world, and in it, as she looked with her conscience and her mind's eyes, she saw it, she saw Cleo taking the life of her friend.

Her mouth dropped in shock and skepticism. It couldn't be true, Cleo loves Cathalina, she must be seeing wrong, sensing wrong. She grabbed her belly and doubled over in excruciating agony. She couldn't find tears; her mind sought some sort of answer, justification for what she saw. Her hands shook violently and she couldn't hold on to the steering wheel.

"Please, oh please, oh please, oh please let this not be true." Serena looked at her hands and willed it still, put her indicator on that she was merging back into traffic and took off. There was no need for her to go to the hospital anymore; now, she needs to take care of Cleo.

\*\*\*\*\*\*\*\*\*\*

Cleo ran from the hospital as fast as she could before the doctors and nurses begin swarming around Cathalina's lifeless body. She couldn't risk getting caught, especially if those detectives were on their trail. She hopped into Natalia's Honda Accord and thanked her lucky star that she didn't drive her own car which would have stood out like a sour thumb. She put the car in gear and headed towards Biscayne Bay which led to Cathalina's upscale practice. She looked around cautiously and parked towards the back of the building and then waited until she saw no prying eyes to enter. She reached into her purse and prayed that she still kept the copy of Cathalina's keys in her purse, she hadn't needed to use in since the others came on board.

She searched frantically amidst makeup, and small toys, brushing away a handcuff; she saw the spear set of keys lodged in the bottom of her purse. She breathed a sigh of relieve and fumbled with the locks until they opened.

Stepping onto the plush white carpeting that was heaven for any foot, she fell to the floor and began to cry. Everything was signature Cathalina. Her unique style and touch, her class and taste in expensive furnishings and electronic toys. Down to the very smell of her was lingering in the air.

Cleo's large frame jerked and throbbed with each shattering realization that she would never see her friend again. That in that moment she fulfilled a promise she also said good bye and would not be able to attend funeral services or explain to the others why she did what she did. For Cleo this was the only sin she had ever committed. She looked at the time and realized that she had to pull herself together. She jumped to her feet and walked over to Cathalina's desk and searched for the button to open the hidden wall areas for her wall safe. She found the button and set out to work. The day was ebbing away and there was too much to do.

\*\*\*\*\*\*\*\*\*\*

Dyania walked briskly next to Taylor closing the car door behind them in the parking lot and heading into the building where Dr. Cathalina Shehkar held her private office location. They walked into the building and down the corridor to her suite.

"Nice place. It must cost quite a pretty penny to have an office at this location." Dyania observed, turning to look about her. "Its breath taking." Taylor smiled as they stopped briefly to check the exact location they were trying to find.

"It is quite a place. She must do very well as a doctor. But I still don't know why you wanted to come here; she committed a crime of self defense against rape in a sleazy club bathroom. Why are we investigating her?" His tone had gotten more somber as his thoughts raced.

"I don't know Jamie; I just know that there is more to this. Worst case scenario we find a next of kin to inform about her accident. So far we have only found Elizabeth who we already know of, and a few others we have yet to look into that were noted in her palm pilot. But something just doesn't add up with her."

Outside in the hallway Cleo could hear voices. She rushed through shredding the last of what she found in the safe and scurried to put things back in order so it wouldn't be noticeable. She stuffed the shredded materials into a black paper bag and wiped the glistening tears from her blushing cheeks. She stopped momentarily to listen to the voices. She had an eerie feeling in the pit of her belly, then panic pushed her to move faster. She estimated they were right around the corridor and soon they would be approaching Cathalina's office. She wasn't sure who they were but at the mention of her friends' name she dread consumed her and began she moving as quickly as she could. She needed to get out of there. Do they realize that Cath is dead? Are they coming after her? The thoughts were swimming in her head like a thousand ocean ripples against the shore.

"Let's stop talking and see what the good doctor can prescribe for us." Dyania encouraged Taylor to keep walking. She didn't want to be out in the hallway much longer. She was anxious to see if her hunches were on target. She just really needed to know and she tugged lightly on his sleeves to nudge him along. They were right at the bend in the hallway and Cleo could hear them as if they were right in front of her.

"Dyania." She turned to look at his face and closed her eyes as he pressed his lips against hers. She opened her mouth and allowed his tongue to explore hers and moaned slightly at the exquisite gentleness of his kiss.

Cleo grabbed her bag and the plastic bag she stuffed the shredded stuff into and cracked open the door. She peeked at the corner and saw a man and a woman in a passionate embrace.

The thought brought her back to so many moments she had loved and made love to Cathalina. The way her soft small hands felt running down her spine. Fresh tears sprang to her eyes and fell to her shoulders. She gathered her things and quietly exited the suite. The door squeaked and she looked up, terrified that they had heard as they can now see her. But they were still locked into their kiss.

Slowly, Taylor pulled away from Dyania and her eyes opened to glow at him.

"That was nice."

"Thank you. I just wasn't sure if….I mean, I really wanted to…" Dyania placed a long graceful finger to his lips.

"That was nice." She said again with a sexy half smile that hinted to more than what she said in those three words. Taylor was pleasantly surprised at her receptiveness. She had been so locked into work, thinking about work, figuring out work, that he didn't even think she had noticed him. But she had. She had been staying at his place for the past week. Though she had her own bedroom and private bathroom, she had a roommate for the first time in her life and this man, behaved as if he didn't even know who she was. She was tired of the way the others fall at her feet and grovel as though she was beyond special. This man made her feel ordinary, she had been special all her life, with him, she felt normal and it felt good.

"Now, can we go so we can get to bigger and better things?" She winked at him and caused his heart to speed up to the rhythm of drum beats. He smiled shyly and allowed her to lead him. They turned the corner and looked at the door that read: DR. CATHALINA SHAHKER., Ph.D Psychologist.

"Wow! Now that is nice." He reached to touch the exquisite engravings on the door and looked at Dyania. "Is that engraved on platinum?" His awe was obvious. "And no one stole it?" He laughed as Dyania nudged him in the side with her elbow.

"You know you just crazy. Look around you. The people in this building do not need to steal. Can't you see that just about every sweet has their information engraved in gold."

"Yeah, but this is Platinum. Not white gold."

"Well, the lady has got taste and she wants to be different. What can I say?" She smiled. She knew there was something about Cathalina that she liked. She liked her even more as she ventured deeper into her life. The woman stood up and said NO. It was gruesome and it was disgusting but some times the message needs to be said in a way that's heard. She couldn't stop thinking about what kind of passion it would take to pull off that kind of job.

"Did you bring her keys from her purse?" Taylor asked as he fumbled around in his pockets and only came up with his own keys.

"I got you." Dyania dangled the keys to tease him playfully and then put it into the lock. "Wait, this is strange." Dyania wrinkled her nose in concern.

"What is it?" Taylor asked reaching to assist her with the door.

"It's already opened Jamie. Do you think she would leave her office opened?"

"Somehow that does not seem possible to me. I mean, yeah the place is upscale, but inside an office are client information and private documentation." He reasoned. Suddenly Dyania's intuition picked up something, she wasn't sure why but she began to run. Unknowingly she followed

Cleo's trail down the hallway and out the back entrance of the building. She got outside just in time to see a car take off. It was speeding so fast that there were tire tracks left behind. She wasn't sure why, but she just felt that person in the car had beaten them to something. She walked back in to find Taylor behind her.

"What happened? You took off like a bat out of hell."

"The minute you noticed the lock something was triggered in me. It was like an image, a thought, and idea, I'm not sure. But I followed it. Sometimes these impressions are so real; it's as if I can see an infrared outline of what's happening or people who are no longer there." She paused. "Once I tap into it." She looked at Taylor who eyed her peculiarly. She shook her head and walked away. Damn I cannot believe I said all that out loud. What's wrong with me? Shit, now he is going to think there something wrong with me. She thought as she shook her head disdainfully.

"Are you saying you are psychic?" He asked playfully, but Dyania didn't see the mirth in his comment and it annoyed her.

"Did I say that?" She sneered. "Forget it!" She fanned her hand at him and walked back toward the suite. Taylor followed behind her trying to figure out what he said to piss her off, when his pager went off.

"Oh crap!"

"What?" Dyania turned abruptly.

"Come on lets go. That's a code blue."

"What does that mean?" Dyania asked on his heels as they exited the building and headed back towards the car.

"Gotta call and find out. But it's urgent and with this code it's never good news." He told her as they got into the car and picked up the radio and called into the station.

## MAN KILLER 21

Elizabeth was awakened suddenly by the jerk on her shoulders. She groggily comes to her senses to see Serena only inches away from her face.

"Serena," she called her name and then an emotional tidal wave took her, "oh Serena, where have you been?" She cried into Serena's shoulders as Serena tried to understand herself exactly what happened to her. How could she explain to Elizabeth that she was caught up in rapture, that her dreams and fantasy for love and a normal life took her into another dysfunction that disappointed her?

"I…I don't know Elizabeth. Something happened to me."

"Oh, oh are you okay? I couldn't sense you, I couldn't feel you." Elizabeth confessed, "I couldn't feel anyone. "Then the message; They are following me Serena?"

Serena sat next to the disoriented and bantering Liz and tried to decipher through what she had to say, while still trying to sort out the flood of emotions that have decommissioned her.

"It's Francesca, she sent them after me and now they are coming for me, oh God." She broke down in tears and shook as she reclined back beneath he covers.

"Who's Francesca?" Serena's bewilderment eluded her. "Don't you know, can't you feel it, her?" Elizabeth lashed out. "Why don't you understand? Cleo was right, you are not good enough. You have abandoned us. Me." Serena looked at the woman who was slowly loosing her mind and felt a piece of herself whither away mentally.

"Cleo, what do you mean Cleo? That bitch killed Cathalina and she is going to pay." At the moment that the words escaped Serena's lips, Elizabeth's hands made contact so hard that Serena's lips bled.

"You are such a fucking liar. You don't know what you are talking about. Cleo is in love with Cath you blind fool, has been since forever. She would never hurt Cathalina. You are the one who fucked up. You are the one who Cathalina wanted, loved and trusted. You are the one who disappeared. And now, the police, they found her. She is in the hospital and I cannot even go see her. Now she is in the hospital and..." She fell into a new wave of wailing and howling as Serena waved her hand to hit her back. Then she dropped it, she realized that Elizabeth was really shaken up, she couldn't handle anything right now. She was more messed up than she was.

"I am sorry Liz, I am going to fix this, I promise. Everything is going to be okay, wait and see." She told her as she rose to leave. Elizabeth calmed for a moment and shook her head yes that she understood. As Serena walked from her bedroom she was suddenly stopped by a huge object that came wailing at her, Elizabeth had grabbed her phone from the night stand next to her and hurled it at Serena as she was about to exit.

"It's all your fault Serena. It's all your fault." She accused and fell into another fit of bawling. Serena stopped for a moment and wondered what happened to her, her life, her dreams. Instead of accomplishing anything she had fallen deeper into a depth of dysfunction and unhealthy behavior.

"Just look at what's going on around me." She said out

loud to the no one in particular. "I have failed." She chuckled as sad realization as she turned away from Elizabeth and walked toward the door. There was nothing more she could do there right now. She needed to find Cleo and Kill her.

\*\*\*\*\*\*\*\*\*

Dyania and Taylor were shocked to arrive at the hospital to learn about Cathalina's death.

"Damn, what the hell is going on here?" Jamie asked as she punched a fist into the hallway outside of Cathalina's hospital room door. "There must be something we are missing, something bigger than just this." He turned to Dyania and the physician who just explained to them that Elizabeth's neck was broken.

"There were no signs of a struggle; the only scenario is that the perp is a friend." Taylor analyzed through the information.

"I would seem so, I guess." The doctor told them, tears glistening on his cheek as he attempted to conceal his deep sadness for the loss of Cathalina. He had met her though the ranks as she excelled. He was great friends with one of her undergrad professor. He remembered his friend's constant marvel at this one particular student who seemed to understood the plight of human flaw and grasped medical science with such ease that he couldn't even fail her, even though he knew she had not even attempted to study. She found thoughts and loopholes in the very theory that man have lived with since Darwin. He remembered they had watched her career slowly and as she finished her doctorate and opened her own private practice, single handedly drawing clients to her just from the name she made for herself as a student, during her internship and eventually took clients away from her very own mentors and professors. She was a shrewd business woman, but she could not be faulted. She knew her stuff.

As a black doctor, getting on in age, she was a joy to watch, even though they were in different fields. He remembered his old friend, tried to convince her to go to medical school. But she was purpose driven. They were not sure what the desire was or where the passion lie, but this is what she wanted, to understand the mind.

"Who would do this to someone so wonderful, so young?" His old voice cracked under the pressure of his thoughts. Accomplished in his own right, he knew that if it was a friend, it could be a couple things, but he kept those thoughts to himself, including the thought that maybe, Cathalina didn't want to live. Maybe this was a form or Euthanasia.

"Well, friend or foe this person is a murderer and some of these cameras must have caught something. There must be something to help use." He rambled on, fury fueling his rage. He felt like punching something or someone. His muscles flexed with anger and Dyania watched him, fascinated by his intense emotions. She was glad he was as passionate about the cause as she was, but this is just another death, another casualty in the daily work of an officer.
Her thoughts were drawn back to the doctor, who signaled that the hospital security was approaching. He coughed, gathered himself together and forced a smirk to his face.

"Thanks you gentlemen." He nodded as he took the package from them and watch as they walk out of ear shot.

"What's that?" Dyania reached for the large envelope.

"I had already requested the tapes that detailed all coming and going in this area within the past eight hours. We could narrow it down to a closer time, but I think you might rather do that." He offered somberly.

"Thank you." Dyania told him, realizing that the loss to this graying sophisticated doctor was more than he was saying. She watched his aging profile walk as briskly and steadily down the hallway as a man in his mid twenties. He seemed to be in his late to early sixties, but from his strides, you could never tell.

"Let's get out of here." Jamie told her without taking her hand or reaching for the package. He just turned and expected her to follow. Dyania didn't like that, but she realized there were extenuating circumstances she didn't understand, and she was very interested in finding out more about this Cathalina Shekhar who have stirred this up here in Florida.

Outside, Jamie took a few deep breaths to quell his anger and Dyania watched him, observing the intensity of his emotions.

"What now?" She asked, wondering where his next thoughts were leading.

"Now, we go and watch every second of those tapes until we find something to go on. I am not letting this one go." He told her and walked toward the hospital parking lot and his car. Again, Dyania followed. She felt that she was on autopilot and this would lead her to exactly what she came her for. They got in the car and drove quietly back to the Sunny Isles Police Precinct in North Miami Beach Florida. She followed him into the station and watched as the officers from her previous contact scattered from her presence with fear, while others, having learned about her since she first arrived, watched on curiously intrigued. She nodded at them politely and followed Jamie who seemed oblivious to the rest of his precinct's reaction to her.

*********

Cleo couldn't contain her grief and her anger when she returned to Sex Cell. She paced and pounded on everything in sight. She went to her special place where he kept her alligators and sat in the missing Limousine the police was searching for in the connection with the dead man's body that was thrown from it on the major Miami highway. She held on to the steering wheel and banged her head until it was sour, then she rested it there and cried. She must have fallen asleep because she didn't feel or sense that there was anyone else there with her.

She was startled when she felt the gentle touch on her shoulder. She looked up to see Natalia and was not surprised. "What are you doing here? This is my private place."
"Yes, I know. This is why I am here. You need me." She smiled trying not to swallow as she held her breath. She couldn't understand how Cleo seemed so comfortable there. The place stunk.

"Get out of here Natalia, not only don't I need you, I don't even like your skinny little ugly KKK ass." She lashed out at her and the words stung Natalia. She had always thought of Cleo as more than a Madam, and felt that the woman felt some exceptions to her. She didn't understand why she was saying this, but she held her ground and swallowed her pride. Cleo was all she had right now and she was going to hold on to that hope.

"Yes you do need me, and I need you. We have an agreement remember?" Natalia reminded her. She was pushing the envelope with Cleo and didn't want to focus on or be concerned about the moment that Cleo was emotionally distraught. She wanted her bastard sister dead and didn't realize she was teetering on the edge of Cleo's impatience.

"You don't seem to understand me, I DON'T need you. I don't need anybody now that Cathalina is dead." She emphasized, "but not to worry, Serena has hers coming and she will be getting it very soon." She told her, somberly returning her head to the car's steering wheel.

"What do you mean dead? How?" Natalia was alarmed. It wasn't possible. Cathalina was the love of Cleo's life; she would have done anything for her. She reached back to Cleo and touched her hair and saw her shoulders shake with grief.

"She's gone. What am I going to do? And now the police those bastards." She went from vulnerable to angry in a breath and Natalia was left with a thousand questions running through her mind.

"Come on Cleo, we have a lot of work to do. We can talk about this but we have to keep moving." Natalia wanted Cleo to stay on track. She was on a mission and Cleo breaking down would not help either of them.

"Natalia, just go and leave me alone. I already told you that things would be taken care of, so just leave me the fuck alone for a minute." Cleo flared, stomping Natalia for a moment and then enraging her.

"Cleo, you have to get up, you are wasting time and I need my car." Natalia frustration reaching a boiling point and she reached to pull on Cleo's arm to nudge her away and out of her transportation. "I need to get out of here for some fresh air." In that instant Cleo's arm went flying and connected with Natalia's nose. The power of her anger was so strong that with the immediate contact Natalia flew backwards falling on her posterior with her mouth wide open in shock.

She squeezed her eyes shut as she felt the crackling of human bones beneath her and knew that she could be among them if she does not thread lightly. She touched her nose for evidence of the blood she felt slowly staining her face.

"You have crossed the line one too many fucking time

Natalia. You have been given too many leeway and your disrespect is about to cost you your life if you don't watch your fucking step." Cleo glared at her so hard that goose bumps invaded the woman's flesh. Looking at her sitting on the floor where she crashed with a bleeding nose put a smile to Cleo's face, she looked to her right where her animal pets were and looked back at Natalia as the thought crossed her mind to feed her to them. She felt her anger bubbled over and her smile became sickeningly creepy as she rose to get out of the car.

Suddenly Natalia had become apart of her problem, her annoying nagging have irked her for the last time. She needed to remember who she was playing with and who was in charge. She walked over to her and kicked her hard in her stomach with her spiked leather strapped books and watched as Natalia doubled over again in pain, gasping for air.

"Go get my whip Natalia, and return here with it immediately." She paced around her like a vulture on the attack of a wounded animal and looked down, she was so blinded by her fury and the very sight of Natalia only began to fuel it with what she now know, and knowing who Natalia really was, a descendant of people who once enslaved hers and thought her worthless, a carrier of the bloodline of hooded cowards who thought her people inferior.

"Get up." Cleo demanded once again, watching Natalia's struggle.

Natalia obeyed, rising tentatively to her feet knowing full well that Cleo rage could flare again and send her back down. She scurried to the spiral stair as best she could, nursing her wounded ribs and aching belly. She made her way to Cleo's office retrieving the cat of nine tails with the biting snake heads. As she walked back her anger flared. She was better than Cleo, above her. Why should she do what she told her to? She looked at the weapon in her hands and dropped it to the floor and ran to the private room Cleo had set up for her friends. As the steel doors shut behind her she turned and looked around the conference room where not so long ago she watched Serena turned into a monster and dropped Cleo like a bag of lard.

She admired Cleo's taste and appreciation for seclusion and privacy, the woman was ingenious at coming up with secret hiding places. If she didn't know this was there, she would never have thought to look. There was no way she would allow Cleo to continue to boss her around. She was going to get Serena with or without Cleo's help and she would make Cleo pay for touching her if it's the last thing she did. She had to get out. Sneaking out the back entrance of the conference hideaway she was free. But where would she go now?

Cleo waited and waited for Natalia to get back so she could take out some of her anger on her back, but she never returned, making Cleo's anger bubble and fester. She ran up the spiral stairs and found there on the ground her whip that Natalia had dropped upon deciding she would not allow herself to be punished anymore. Fury surged through Cleo as she raced back down the stairs and into Natalia's car. She's had enough. Natalia was right, she did have a lot of work to do and she was going to do it. It was her friend's dying wish and she will take care of Natalia later. She smiled as she thought back about the young girl. She had no where to go.

## MAN KILLER 22

"Listen Taylor, I have to go. There has to be a way for me to check on the one and only other contact we knew that Cathalina had before she was murdered." Dyania became restless looking at the videos in Taylor's precinct. She hated the feeling of everyone watching her and she was uneasy. There were so many people coming and going on that video, it was hard to tell who went into the woman's room and killed her.

"Wait Dyania, I think you are moving too quickly. Check this out." He pulled her closer to him and shivered as she leaned in, closing the space between them. Pulling himself together to regain his focus, he pointed to the video screen.

"See what time its registering on the monitor?" He turned slightly to look at her. "What time did the coroner record the time of death?" He was wondering if she saw what he did, but she didn't seem to get it.

"Just tell me what you see Jamie, I want to go pay Elizabeth a visit. I came here for her and right now she is the only connection to your dead bodies." Dyania voiced absentmindedly.

"Look, the coroner recorded her time of death at 3 pm correct?" He made eye contact with Dyania and she shook her head. "The monitor is showing this woman. Look, pause the tape." He told her as he pointed at the video. "There, this woman, fair skin toned, short hair, over weight." They had the video stilled as Cleo looked through Cathalina's hospital room door with tear streaked face.

"She seemed distraught. Is that tears." Dyania's interest now peaked.

"Look at the time that was recorded, 2:50pm. She was the last person to go into the good psychiatrist hospital room between 2:50 and 3pm when her death was recorded." He pointed out. "Now start the video again. See there." He said excitedly stopping it again, "at 3:10pm she left the room. No one else was seen coming or going." With his eyes wide with enthusiasm he looked at Dyania who finally got it.

"We've got her. Now we can go see if she signed in to get a visitor's pass. We might get lucky with a name we can track." Dyania hugged him eagerly.

They both jumped up and ran out of the precinct and back to his car. As they drove, there was another code blue over Taylor's radio, but this time he didn't have to go far and was already headed in that direction, an attempted murder to investigate at Larkin Community Hospital.

"When it rains it pours." Dyania said as she shook her head, annoyed at yet another detour, as she watched Taylor call in as the closed reporting homicide detective in the area.

"Well, she is not dead," he commented humorously,

"probably a case of domestic violence. We just need to show up so the abused feel better, she will refuse to press charges and we will be on our way." He tried to comfort Dyania who only starred out the window and fondled with her necklace. It helped her to think when she felt uneasy. "You okay?" He asked pulling her out of her thoughts.

"Yes, I heard you." She turned to him and smiled reassuringly at him as he sped to the hospital. They walked to where the hospital staff directed them and saw a slender woman sitting shivering outside the triage area watching as the two male doctors whispered among themselves. When the doctors saw them coming they stopped and greeted them as the flashed their badges for identification.

"This woman claims that she was beaten by Serena Kowtow." Dr. Media whispered only for the two detectives to hear. Taylor chuckled as she was jolted by the news.

"Come again?" He asked not believing his ears.

"This woman, claimed that our esteemed State Supreme Court Justice Serena Kowtow have assaulted her for having an affair with her man servant." Dr. Hernandez clarified. "We don't know what to believe. She is beaten pretty badly and she described the Justice and her home with such detail, it's hard to believe she is making it up. Yet..." He paused.

"Yet, it seems so unbelievable Dr. Media finished.

"She claimed she tried to kill her, that she escaped. Dyania listened to the interchange while carefully eyeing Natalia. She seemed genuinely distraught.
She walked over and carefully sat next to her.

"Hey," Dyania smiled, "are you cold?" She asked observing Natalia's ripped shorts and smeared T-Shirt and the goose bumps rise on the woman's arm under the blazing air conditioning pressure.

"A little." Natalia answered suspiciously.
Dyania stood up and walked up to the Triage window and whispered to the nurse.

"May I have a blanket for this patient please?" She asked pointing at Natalia. But Natalia was not shaking because she was cold; she was shaking with fear, wondering if she got herself too far over her head and if she could pull this off. She had no idea that Cleo had such powerful friends. Until the doctor asked her if she meant the State Justice Serena Kowtow, she didn't know that's who she was. Now she had to follow through with the plan.

Dyania returned and gently placed the blanket over Natalia's shoulder.

"That's better." She smiled again.

"Are you going to arrest me?" Natalia asked.

"Why would we do that? You are the victim here. If someone tried to kill you, it does not matter who they are, they have to be held accountable according to the law." Dyania told her confidently, but had a strange feeling that her words were not comforting to the woman. "Are you afraid of her?"

"Yes." Natalia dropped her eyes, afraid to make eye contact where this woman with the gently piercing eyes might see right through her.

"You don't have to be afraid. We will just ask that you come and direct us to her home where you last left her, we will take it from there." Dyania looked up to see that Taylor was wrapping up his conversation with the two male doctors.

"Hi, I am Detective Taylor. I am sorry about what happened to you." He stooped causally before her.

"Ready?" Dyania asked and he nodded.

"We are going to need to come along with us okay?" Natalia looked at Dyania before looking back in Taylor's direction, dropped her eyes to the floor and nodded yes. Dyania helped her to her feet and released her arm so she didn't feel like a prisoner while walking opposite her with Taylor sandwiching her on the other side.

\*\*\*\*\*\*\*\*\*

Serena fought to control her urges to transform as anger and resentment filled her as she drove back to her Coral

Gables home. The ride there was not as tranquil as it once was, the vehicle not the luxury transport she had become used to, and her life was falling apart. She drove slowly absorbing Elizabeth's words, how torn apart she looked. She felt horrible as though apart of her had left her, she felt lost.

    As she neared her premises she knew something was wrong and was not able to identify the emotion. She slowed down as she neared the premises. The usual safety and serenity she felt when driving up the scaling moss and ivy covered walls was no longer there. Punching in the codes to the entrance of her home tears came to her eyes. She felt overwhelm and she didn't notice the Honda Accord parked a little way down the block from her home. As the gates pulled open, she drove in and slowly came to a stop at the end of her long driveway leading to her front door.

    Something was different and she knew it. It just was not the same. She sat still and looked at her home that now seemed strange to her and empty to her, the void so overpowering she felt as though she was being filled to explosion. Her emotions and psyche became gorged and swelled. She felt totally off balance and the hot and cold flashes she felt, the surges of anger, empathy and fear were eating at her. She felt paralyzed where she sat and was not sure whether she should go in or stay in the car. She thought back to Cathalina, the moment she felt Cleo break her neck, Elizabeth's words and could stop the sounds of anger and pain that gushed through her brain. The voices were crushing her brain and the tremendous loudness and demands of them were irresistible. She placed her hands to her ear to stop the chilling sounds from violating her mind but she couldn't. The dam on her tears loosened as they rolled down her face as she envisioned her body recklessly and without purpose ripped into her for control. The spiders poison and her hormones chaotically blending as she became psychologically disheveled.

Cleo got out of the car and walked to the gate and stood there watching wondering if Serena would get out from where she sat in that strange car. She already knew the code, a perk of going through Cathalina's things. She would get her if it was the last thing she did.

Cleo looked up from her obsession as a car neared the semi private and secluded premises and watched as it slowed down. She began to move around to seem inconspicuous, looking to the ground as if she had dropped something and wondered why the vehicle was driving so slowly. She looked up inadvertently and made eye contact with Natalia as car pulled over and parked directly across the street from Serena's residence.

Sensing the unusual vibration of energy Dyania perked up her antennae and paid closer attention to the woman who she rode beside in the back seat and looked curiously at the woman across the street attempting to find something in the grassed area of the front sidewalk of the premises. "Is that the Court Justice?" Dyania asked her and looked to Taylor for confirmation. Natalia swallowed hard and nodded no. She was so choked up with fear.

Cleo stood up and began making her way back to the car parked behind the strange vehicle with Natalia in it. Her heart raced and she wondered why Natalia had followed her and brought cops. She feared that the woman had reported her and blown the cover off of Sex Cell after mysteriously disappearing when she ordered her to go her whip so she could receive a lashing. Even though Natalia shook her head no, Dyania's instinct told her there was something more to this story. She got out of the back seat and walked slowly toward Cleo whose palms had begun to sweat. He hadn't had a run in with the cops in years. She despised them and this one had cop written all over her. This whole situation stinks. If she got her hands on Natalia she is a dead woman, was all she could think.

"Hello," Dyania greeted flashing her badge. "Do you know the resident of that home?" She asked nonchalantly.

"No, I don't." Cleo answered her, trying to keep the harshness of her tone under wraps.

"So why were you loitering in the area?" Dyania asked again, not looking up, as she reached for a pen and grabbed her notepad from her jacket vest pocket.

"When has it been a crime to walk on the sidewalk?" Her annoyance got the better of her.

"License and registration please?" Cleo moved to get into the car, "you can get it from the passenger side. Its okay, I won't bite." Dyania's instinct went into overdrive. She could smell the fear on the woman, she sensed something was wrong and tried to keep her excitement down as she teased, slowly filling in the gaps as she looked over the tan Honda Accord. It seemed strangely familiar but she couldn't quite place where she had seen it before.

"Please stay here." Dyania walked back to Taylor's vehicle and asked him to run the registration license and license plate number which she wrote down since there is no front plate requirement in the state of Florida. As she began walking back to Cleo she heard Taylor's urgent request for her to return. Cleo flinched, she knew was caught.
Dyania rushed back to Taylor as he began cuffing Natalia in the back of the vehicle.

"This plate and vehicle is registered to our guest here. Natalia Kowtow. Isn't that right?" He asked rhetorically, sarcasm dripping with every word.

"But that's the name of the Justice she alleged attempted to murder her? I don't get it?" Dyania said, the magnitude of the situation all clumping together. "That car seems so familiar to me, and now it's being driven by a friend of Natalia here who just accused a notable Justice of attempted murder who just happened to bear the same last name?" Dyania ran the scenario off out loud to make sense of it, and watched as Cleo made an attempt to make her way around to the driver's side of the car for a quick getaway.

"I don't know what's going here, but it's going to get figured out mighty fast." Taylor insisted, but Dyania had already taken off to catch Cleo. She was banging at the door for Cleo to open but Cleo had other intentions. She placed the key in the ignition and started the vehicle. Taylor jumped out of his car to try and assist Dyania but Cleo pressed on the accelerator and almost knocked him over.

Dyania dropped her gun and began running. Her speed gradually accelerated as if her feet had grown wings and she grabbed onto the rear view drivers side mirror. With all her might she used her elbow and banged into the drivers side window splattering the glass and causing Cleo to lower her head behind the dashboard to protect her eyes from the shattering glass. Not being able to see the car swerved, sending Dyania's legs flying as she held on to the mirror for dear life. The brief moment of loss of direction for Cleo gave Dyania a leeway and she reached in and grabbed Cleo by the neck. She felt the scales on Cleo's neck rise and her fingers began to slip. Dyania grabbed for the hemmed neckline of her top and tried to pull herself into the car causing Cleo to turn sharply, spin and made a wide circle turning the car back in the other direction to face where Taylor was parked and was back in the car with Natalia calling for back up.
The car moved fast swinging Dyania from side to side uncontrollably. As soon as the vehicle slowed, Cleo tried to throw herself on the passenger's side to get out of the door, but

Dyania grabbed onto her arm from where she was hanging through the driver's side door. Cleo kicked at her accidentally putting the car back into drive, they both looked at each other alarmed, but Cleo figured that she had nothing to loose at that moment. Natalia had blown the cover of her operation and she had just killed her lover. She was not going back to jail.

  Dyania sensed what Cleo was going to do and tried to stop her. Simultaneously, the necklace she wore, the gift from her dead parents, its brass and silver clung to Dyania's neck and where the pendant rest between her breast it stuck in between her cleavage and began to burn the mark of the three interwoven spiders into her flesh. Still half hanging out the window Dyania's body sent the smell of burnt flesh from her chest, Cleo's eyes flung wide open. At first she thought the car was on fire, but then realized that it was only the woman who was hanging on to her.

  Cleo took the agonizing moment of the detective's hesitation and pressed her foot to the gas causing the car to go skidding off the streets causing some random drivers to veer out of the way of danger. Cleo braced herself as she couldn't see sprawled from the driver to the passenger side when the car rotated and skid on the side walk and crashed with a bang into the wall of Serena's private premises.

Hearing the commotion, Serena got out of the car and started to walk back down her long driveway to see what was going on, but then something stopped her. She looked back toward her house where there was no commotion.

  Why hadn't Jason come out to see what was going on? She had been sitting at her front door for awhile now, why wasn't he there ready to open the door at her beck and call, ready to perform his services? Then she remembered the dispute when Vincent came by and how ugly that was. She turned back and began walking toward her door. Then she heard the screaming and a loud crash.

    Again she started to go and look what was happening, this quiet residential upscale neighborhood does not see or hear much commotion, but Serena was distracted and distraught. She had her own issues to deal with and she needed to figure out who she was going to make Cleo pay for what she did to Cath. Jason would help her. He was always great to talk to, had some wonderful ideas. Why didn't she think of that before?

    Her spirits lifting she turned back toward her large front door and stood there as she collected herself. She was a mess, but Jason would take care of her. He would clean her up, make her a hot bath and a cup of hot cocoa and make her feel all better. Convincing herself, she turned the knob and put a smile on her face, she will be happy to see Jason's deep dimples and long neat dreadlocks when she opened the door. His rich deep cocoa colored skin will glow at the sight of her, his eyes will shine with love and adoration; his pecks will flex to show her his excitement. Yes, she will be okay as soon as she was on the other side of the door.

Man Killer

## MAN KILLER 23

    The ambulance and police cursers rushed to the scene where no one in the crashed vehicle moved. Taylor rushed over to Dyania but was held back just incase. He was working closely with her, and though he is used to seeing gruesome scenes, it's different when it involves a partner or loved ones. Natalia couldn't stop screaming, they had to administer tranquilizers. She was psychologically traumatized seeing her car crash with the only person who helped her.
    When the paramedics cleared the scenes of the debris from the car that seemed to have be totaled in the front end and pulled Dyania and Cleo from the rubble, they were shock to find that they were not badly hurt, or worse, dead.
Cleo had broken both her legs, had a few crushed ribs and had passed out when her head hit the dashboard. They took her out and rushed her to the nearest hospital. Dyania's condition was inexplicable. She was wrapped almost in a webbed cocoon that protested her from the impact of the crash. She didn't have any injuries other than the ones she sustained when she broke the window and stretched her body into the car. She was a little daze when they touched her as the almost marshmallow like substance liquefied and began evaporating.
    Everyone turned to look at each other; if they hadn't seen it with their own eyes they would have said it was not true. She brushed herself off and walked over to Taylor or starred at her jaw hanging and totally flabbergasted.

She reached for his face with her left hand and shook his head back and forth.

"Hey, anybody there?" she joked. He closed his month and swallowed hard. "Why are you looking at me like you've just seen a ghost?" She asked almost oblivious to the fact that she walked away from a car wreck that should have broken her body in half. Taylor continued to stare at her dumbfounded. He couldn't find his voice.

"We have a lot of work to do, let's go check out what's going on inside of the Honorable Judges house. This is all too strange that these two were connected. Maybe she knows something about what's going on here." She spoke nonchalantly to Taylor with her back turned to him, and then began walking towards the vast premises gate. As she approached the alarm, she began to press numbers to corresponding letters onto the intercom. The gate buzzed softly and began to retract. "You coming?" She asked him, as if what she did was as natural as opening her eyes.
Still taken by the mysteries of the day, Taylor could not find words to speak, so he just followed her, leaving the cops and paramedics to clean up the mess they left behind.

"Dyania!" He finally called finding his voice, "are you okay?" He caressed her arm and moved his hands around her face and neck to feel for himself that she was okay.

"Stop it Jamie. You're embarrassing me and we are not in private." She teased.

"I am sorry, I didn't mean..." He began to blush and realized she was poking fun at his curiosity. "Its okay, seems like someone is home and I have a few questions I would like answered."

"How do you know someone is home."

"This car is not cold, and the tire tracks are fresh." She signaled showing him on the graveled driveway the tracks leading to the car tires. Taylor scratched his head amazed and followed her to the door.

Pushing the door open that was already ajar they were shocked to be met with the scene of Jason's decaying body that had been hanging from the chains for days. Taylor couldn't take it. He had seen many a grisly scene, but the events of the day weakened his stomach and he began to regurgitate. Dyania moved like a pro as though she was expecting his sudden reaction and grabbed a hold of him then lead him to a wall where he could find support and recover.

"Come when you are ready." She told him and walked away. She surveyed the entrance, the female clothing on the floor down to white lace panties, bra and shoes. She whistled as she looked at the large extravagant interior and then turned to Taylor. "Beautiful isn't it?" He looked at her astonished, as if she had lost her mind. She was behaving as though she was having a walk in the park.

Taking out his handkerchief he wiped his mouth and forced himself not to vomit again. Suddenly, she looked up and her eyes focused on an opening that seemed to be a hidden stone door in a wall. From where she stood it was dark. With determined steps and purposeful strides she walked up to the opening that was an entrance way leading down into darkness. She felt for the stairs as her eyes adjusted to the darkness and Taylor ran to catch up with her. She seemed to navigate through the darkness with ease as though she had climbed up and down those very stairs a million times before, while he had to feel for the wall since there was no banister to prevent an ugly trip and fall.

The stair ended at a clearing of what seemed nothing more than a domesticated cave like something out of the Flintstones. Her sudden alt caused Taylor to bump into her back as they starred into the opening of the cave. He was once again met with one of the most horrific death scenes he had ever seen; A woman, naked with olive skin and beautiful bountiful curly auburn hair, lay on a stoned bed, one of two in the middle of the room. Class cages inserted into the walls on four corners, and coming from everywhere, crawling in every which direction, there were spiders. Three distinct different species and black scorpions situated the body and covered her so completely that not one inch of her face could be seen.

Her body shone white beyond the dark blanket the insets made over her. There were so much of them; it would seem as if the woman had walked into a nest. They crawled all over the walls, the floor the ceiling and fell like rain as they tried to fight each other or a morsel of their dinner.

Dyania began to walk in there and Taylor reached for her arm to try and stop her. She turned to him and smiled warmly, but the chilling cold in her eyes would be something he wouldn't soon forget. They were like marble, glassed over as though she was blind. With every step she took, the path became clear as though she was Moses parting the red sea, and slowly they closed the opening behind her. Nothing fell on her. As the path behind her closed, the spiders became drawn to the Taylor's presence and began a beehive attack towards him.

He started to run, but was afraid to leave Dyania. In that instant he heard the command from her lips as authoritative as though she was speaking to a child.

"NO!" She didn't turn around, but her right hand was behind her in a definitive gesture. The spiders turned obediently and went about their way, ignoring him.
Again, Taylor's mouth fell open, and he rubbed his eyes as tears began to obscure his vision.

"Oh God, Oh God, please protect her. Please let her know what she is doing." He prayed, not knowing at what point he fell to his knees. He had never been a religious man, but at that moment he found faith.

He wiped his tear streaked face and watched, as Dyania reached for the woman's face.

"It's her." She said almost in a trancelike voice. The spiders cleared away from her face where Dyania reach out to touch. "It's your State Supreme Court Justice. She had been poisoned by the foreign spiders. The Brazilian Wandering Spider couldn't protect her. She turned to walk back toward Taylor and again the room cleared where her feet landed. Taylor looked up at her and in the center of her chest the pendant fell and slightly above it; a red outline like a glowing flame burned in her chest and seared her flesh. She reached to the door and in one motion; she pulled Taylor to his feet with ease and led him back up the stairs.

"I don't think there is anything else we can do for them. Lets get to the precinct and find out what we can from Natalia, and then I would like to go and visit Ms. Chung in North Miami Beach. She is not too far from the precinct." Taylor didn't have to say a word and couldn't. She made sense and her direction was focused. As they arrived at the car, Natalia began coming to.

"What hap..." before she completed her questions, Dyania reached behind her and slapped her so hard she passed out again.

"Nothing more from you for now." She stated and nodded that Taylor continued his call for paramedics and a coroner to return to the address for the two bodies they left behind

## Epilogue

Cleo was verbally abusive and brazen in the hospital as they healed her scars. She refused to talk to the cops, and behaved insane every time they threatened to arrest her. Running into the wall they considered attempted suicide and second degree murder but she was determined she would not go to jail again.

When Dyania and Taylor showed up and told her that Liz was dead, that's when she really lost it. They didn't want to tell her, but she insisted on knowing how her friend died. The last time she saw her she was okay.

"But she was not okay Cleo. You said it yourself. She was upset about not being able to contact Cathalina, and her conscience was eating away at her about what happened back in Georgia with Francesca."

"I don't give a shit about any Fran bitch." Cleo spat.

"You killed her!" She accused.

She became so violent that they had to tranquilize her daily, eventually placing her on Prozac and Zoloft intermittently. She was monitored under 24 hour surveillance and her hands strapped to her bed to protect her from herself and visitors from the police and medical teams.

Dyania walked out and sat defeated next to Taylor.

"Did you tell her she slashed her own wrists in the bathtub and bled to death?" She felt a profound lost and couldn't express it to anyone.

"No, I only told her of her death when she spa zed out on me." Dyania hung her head. "Something is still missing. I just don't know what else to do now. It's almost time to return to Atlanta. I need to draw up my reports and put this case to rest.

Taylor was not sure what he could say to help, so he gently placed his arm around her shoulder and she gratefully rested her head on his strong shoulders. They sat there in silence for what seemed like forever before a group of doctors, psychologist and psychotherapist approached them.

"Let's go." Dr. Mariano smiled understandingly at them. Her old wrinkled face filled with wisdom and her light hazel eyes glowed with truth. Her hair which was now completely white from age was pinned elegantly in a bun neatly on top of her head, and was an amazing contrast next to her deep ebony skin. She stood strong and tall and walked away exuding pride and elegance.

Dyania and Taylor stood and followed the esteemed group of physicians to the conference room where the police chief, a representative from the mayor's office and a few other well-regarded attendees waited anxiously to understand how and why they never found or knew of these women who had been the cause of so many unsolved deaths and missing persons for more than a decade. Everyone wanted Cleo's head on a platter with Natalia as their star witness, helping the police to uncover all the dirt behind the prestigious Sex Cell. The gators in the hidden dungeon were taken by animal protection and the bodies being checked by forensics for identification. Having searched the home of Honorable Serena Kowtow and come across the gruesome horrific findings they had left in the wake and after math of her death, everyone was still spell bound that all this happened and no one knew.

"Dr. Mariano, can Cleopatra stand trial?" The police

chief asked silencing the pandemonium of discussion between individual groups of people.

"We don't know yet. We still need to keep her under observation." She answered the sadness of it all visible on her experienced face.

"How could people like this function, have normal lives, accomplished, successful and once beautiful women, pull off one of the most ghastly and horrific serial killings and no one knew about it?" The rep from the Mayor's office asked.

"That's simple," one of the world's most noted psychoanalysis jumped in, nodding permission from Dr. Mariano who led the team. "These women are functional psychopaths."

"What the hell does that mean?" A member from the Miami Police Investigations asked annoyed at what seemed to be the runaround.

"That just means that, the same way we have functional alcoholics who can be drunk and go about their normal lives, and functional drug addicts doing the same, there are functional psychopaths. Functional alcoholics and drug addicts are still alcoholics and drug addicts. They still crave that fix and that high; they still will beg, rob, steal and kill for that one fix when they are feinting." The analyst explained.

"Think about it this way," Dr. Mariano interjected, "abuse victims make some of the best actors. They have to live all those years of pain and shame believing no one cares or wants to know. For them, the pain is constant, like breathing. Like air, you cannot see it but you know its there." She paused and looked around the room at the unsympathetic angry faces ready to send Cleopatra to the grind. "For years after their abuse, they can feel it on their skin, relive it in their minds. Unless they receive the right treatment and learn to live as healthy productive members of society, this pain never goes away."

"These women," added another of the therapist among the group, "are actually some of the most brilliant women mentally to be able to pull this off. Look at their profile." He suggested as he shifted through some papers and everyone in attendance followed suit, trying to find what this man made reference to. "Ah," he said finding it. "Turn to the second to last page of your folder, our honorable judge, beat the odds and became a Florida State Supreme Court Judge at such a young age. Had she continued on that path she would have made history." Flipping through the pages excitedly, "Now turn to the other page. Cathalina Shakher a well accomplished psychologist in her own right. Elizabeth Chung, a noted Broadway star and the youngest of them, born with what would be considered a deformity yet she excelled and was one of the most beautiful women alive. Even the patient we have here, Cleopatra, who we have yet to find any relatives or loved ones. Look at the empire she created, with Swiss bank accounts and monies we have yet to count. Don't you find it fascinating that you and I who are standing here in judgment of them, accusing them and we could not begin to even fathom the inner workings and greatness of their minds?"

The group of more than twenty people became quiet ad the realization of the hurts and pains of these women overwhelmed them. Some tear up and others didn't bother to wipe the drops of sadness that dampened their face and smeared their make-up. The chief was appalled and showed no sympathy. His anger boiled at the way every one seemed to be eating up every word these doctors said.

"Bullshit!" Yelled the Police Chief, "they are not great anything. They are the scum of the earth, and Cleopatra or whoever the hell she is, will pay. She is stupid; all her friends abandoned her leaving her to take the blame." He snickered causing a wave of chaotic discussion amongst the group.

"Listen to me." Dr. Mariano said softly, training her eyes on Dyania whose eyes were filled with remorse and sadness and Taylor who sat strong, the pillar of strength she needed to lean on.

"I have had enough Doctor." The chief said reaching for his had and gathering his papers.

"You need to understand this from the victim's point of view, from the medical point of view. These women are sick, just like many other ill people out there, walking around without getting the proper treatment. I am sure, as we investigate this further and in the years to come, we will learn that these women were hurt badly. Statistics show that 87.5% of victims become victimizers. We are in a state of distress and need to break the silence and deal with this. This is the extreme of such travesty, but how many more men, women and children, are being raped, abused and told to keep their mouths shut? How many are still afraid because of shame they think they will bring to themselves and their families." She shook her head as her voice cracked. She looked at Dyania again and swallowed hard, fighting to regain her composure.

"This is true." Another medical professional jumped to her aid. He quietly walked over to her and stood tall.

"There have been studies to prove that it's a terrible cycle of abuse. Just like domestic violence and spousal abuse. We already know for a fact that children will grow up to be abusive parents, and women become abusive mothers. Though this is the most extreme case of perpetual cycle of abuse we have ever seen, it is still what it is." He said calmly, forcing the group to listen more intently.

"I don't care what you say. This does not excuse their responsibility for what have happened." The chief balked.

"No one said it did." Dr. Mariano responded.

"Well somebody is going to have to pay, and answer for the all this mayhem I will now have to deal with." He retaliated angrily.

"I understand Chief. I understand." She reached for her papers and pulled a chair from the head of the conference table. Her legs were tired and had given way. "I understand." She said again to his retreating back, then reclining into the chair, focused once again on Dyania who only sat their quietly. The youthfulness of her face cutting through the hard edge and façade she displayed earlier. Dr. Mariano nodded her head.

She would need to talk to that woman soon, before it all starts all over again.

## The End

# A TESTIMONY OF SEXUAL ABUSE

Author Kim Robinson's Story
www.Kim-Robinson.com

I was five years old when I visited a holiness church with a relative. In my fragile young mind, the preacher had tremendous power. He would touch a person on the head and they would pass out, men would come with stretchers and take these people away. Later that evening after church, my relative preparing dinner and the door bell rang. It was the preacher from church that morning. At some point she needed to get something at the store. I ran to the door to go with her, but she told me to stay with our company, it would be rude to leave him alone.

As soon as the car went down the driveway, the Preacher told me to come and sit next to him. When I walked over he pulled me in front of him and reached under my dress and pulled my panties down. He picked me up and lay me on the couch while he explained to me that if I ever told anyone that God would make sure that everyone I knew and loved would die and go to hell. I could not even scream. The pain was excruciating as he plunged into my small body. I was petrified. When it was over he reminded me of the warning several times as he pulled my underwear back up over my mary jane's and up my leg smearing the blood that ran down my leg when I stood. I sat through dinner scared and in pain and did not say a word. I listened to the radio and when they spoke to me, I looked down at my plate and answered.

When my parents returned I attempted to tell my father but the preachers warnings stopped me. A few weeks later I was told that my father was dying. I thought it was my fault. I spent my childhood panicking every morning if I did not hear my father's snores fearing that he was dead because maybe I had spoken in my sleep and revealed something I should not have.

I did not like myself much growing up; my awkward frame did not develop as fast as my friends and I was a tomboy, not because I wanted to be, but as a way of not having to talk to boys other than friends. When I finally did start talking to boys I picked the gangsters, car jackers, drug dealers, bank forgers and abusive men, who cared no more for me than I did for myself. I ditched school and hung out with men who were much older than I were. I continued to make bad choices in men and always landed in an abusive relationship.

I gave up on being happy emotionally, so I was going to make up for it financially. Men would have to pay me for sex. I became numb to life and I did not care for my health or safety. I made bad life choices as a result of my sexual abuse. I used and sold drugs, worked as an escort selling sex under the façade of a date and later ran my own escort service.

I did not care for myself or for my three year old son. My self hatred and disgust for what I had become made me an unfit mother. I traveled the states working. It was seven years before I saw my child again. Even once out of the business, the hurt was too big and I had no idea how to fix it. I was a functioning addict, medicating away too many bad memories that threatened to come forward. He and I struggle to have a relationship today It took me hundred of thousands of dollars in therapy and clinics to survive the hardest fight I had ever experienced. That surpassed having gang fights and guns held to my head, shooting and watching others die in my presence because I was used to fighting, torture, guns and death. The hardest thing was beginning to feel again. My disassociation with church and the memories that made me an atheist were too painful and I spent thirty years trying to keep the memories away. As apart of my therapy I had to attend church again. I began to understand that God did not send that preacher to rape me, he was a sick man who I prayed and hoped had gotten caught before he could hurt too many more children. I survived every thing in my life, the penitentiary, abuse and drugs so I can fight God's war as I gladly do today.

Now that I have come to have a relationship with God, I realize that everyday of my life was to prepare me for where I stand today. A mother, a wife, a person who donates time to tutor and counsel troubled at risk children, and last an author who knows that telling her story will help someone else who may be in the same situation.

*Disclaimer:*

*Kim Robinson have given permission to print her story publicly. There is no pay now or in the future. Her story is a humanitarian gift.*

# GLOSSARY:

1. Cathalina Shekhar- Psychiatrist (Man Killer Recruiter). Black and Indian (Hindu Indian) Mix. Her real name is Chinmayi Shekhar. She wears the traditional mark of the red dot on her forehead and a mole on the left side of her lips. Footnote: Indian Baby Names. Http://www.indianexpress.com.

2. Malignant Eroticized Countertransferance- Richard D. Chessick, M.D., PhD. Professor of psychiatry and behavioral sciences. North Western University, Senior Attending Psychiatrist, Evanston Hospital. (Journal of the American Academy of Psychoanalysis copyright 1997). The American Journal of Psychoanalysis Vol: 25 Number 2, summer 1997: Pages 219 and 226. This is occurs in the situation where the doctor and patient are involved in an affair where the doctor looks to the patient for meeting of an emotional need.

3. Pavlov Dog-Reference to dogs who would drool upon hearing a bell because they had been conditioned to associate the bell with food through the close proximity in time of the ringing of the bell and the serving of meals to them.

4. The Sistine Chapel painting- A painting done by Michelangelo Buonarroti in 1512 in Rome to show the creation of Man and his history up to Noah. This painting done on the ceiling of the chapel was painted only by Michelangelo and its beauty is awe inspiring.

5. <u>Childism</u> - A reference to the hatred of children which is shown from the abuse they suffer from adults.

6. <u>Labia majora</u>- the large outer lips of the external sexual organ of the female (vulva). The labia minora are the small inner lips which come together to form a hood over the clitoris.

7. <u>Gonorrhea</u>- Gonorrhea is a sexually transmitted disease (STD). It may grow and multiply easily in the warm, moist areas of the reproductive tract, including the cervix (opening to the womb), uterus (womb), and fallopian tubes (egg canals) in women, and in the urethra (urine canal) in women and men. The bacterium can also grow in the mouth, throat, eyes, and anus. If not treated this disease may cause serious and permanent health problems in men and women. http://www.cdc.gov/std/Gonorrhea/STDFact-gonorrhea.htm

8. <u>Genital herpes</u>- This is a sexually transmitted disease (STD) caused by the herpes simplex viruses type 1 (HSV-1) and type 2 (HSV-2). Most genital herpes is caused by HSV-2. Most individuals have no or only minimal signs or symptoms from HSV-1 or HSV-2 infection. When signs do occur, they typically appear as one or more blisters on or around the genitals or rectum. The blisters break, leaving tender ulcers (sores) that may take two to four weeks to heal the first time they occur. Typically, another outbreak can appear weeks or months after the first, but it almost always is less severe and shorter than the first outbreak. Although the infection can stay in the body

indefinitely, the number of outbreaks tends to decrease over a period of years.
http://www.cdc.gov/std/Herpes/STDFact-Herpes.htm

9. Syphilis - A sexually transmitted disease (STD) caused by the bacterium Treponema pallidum. It has often been called "the great imitator" because so many of the signs and symptoms are indistinguishable from those of other diseases.
http://www.cdc.gov/std/Syphilis/STDFact-Syphilis.htm

10. Anti-serum - an animal or human blood serum containing one or more specific ready-made antibodies and used to provide immunity against a disease or to counteract venom.

11. Passive Aggressive Behavior - behavior which is characterized by negativity. A person with this condition will at times fluctuate between going along with a     plan and actively resisting it by voicing complaints or doing some other act     which more or less is a display of unreasonable reluctance.
http://www.straightdope.com/columns/030530.html

12. Pedophiles an adult who has sexual desire for children or who has committed the crime of performing sexual acts with a child.

13. Megan's Law - Megan's Law is named after seven-year-old Megan Kanka, a New Jersey girl who was raped and killed by a known child molester who

had moved across the street from the family without their knowledge. In the wake of the tragedy, the Kanka's sought to have local communities warned about sex offenders in the area. All states now have a form of Megan's Law.

14. Testosterone - a male steroid hormone produced in the testicles and responsible for the development of secondary sex characteristics.

15. BDSM - Bondage, dominance and sado-masochism. A sadist is someone who derives sexual or psychological pleasure by inflicting harm and/or pain on another individual. The masochist on the other hand achieves sexual gratification by experiencing pain either psychologically or physically.

16. The Black Widow http://www.desertusa.com/july97/du_bwindow.html. The black widow spider has a potent neurotoxic venom and is considered the most venomous spider in North America

17. Crocodiles- http://www.fpl.com/environment/endangered/contents/american_crocodiles.shtml#TopOfPage

18. Hermaphrodite- A Person born with both a vagina and a penis. Normally, only one of these sex organs is fully functional. Unlike Elizabeth Chung in the novel who has both her vagina and her penis operating equally healthy.

19. Nymphomaniac-A person who is considered

uninhibited, who desires sex frequently or sex with multiple partners, usually participates in deviant sexual behaviors typically categorized as fetishes or freaky.

20. Eunuch- A man, born as a man who has no penis due to castration. Dictionary definition is male without testicles and/or penis.
http://www.rotten.com/library/sex/castration/eunuch/

21. True Spider- One who bares the mark of one of the three deadly spiders.

22. Brazilian Wondering Spider- http://www.petbugs.com/caresheets/P-fera.html. The Brazilian Wandering Spider is not for the "pet keeper". Brazilian Wandering Spiders are extremely fast, extremely venomous, and extremely aggressive. These large and dangerous true spiders are ranked among the most venomous spiders known to man. In fact, the Brazilian Wandering Spider is the most venomous spider in the New World!

23. The Brown Recluse- http://ohioline.osu.edu/hyg-fact/2000/2061.html. Beware of the bite of the Brown Recluse Record Courier Staff Reports February 6, 2005.
The Brown Recluse is so-named because they are very secretive. They are seldom seen as they hide under rocks and in crevices outdoors and in attics, boxes or dark closets indoors. They are nocturnal spiders that attack prey and subdue it with venom. And that venom is made up of many proteins and enzymes which destroy body tissue. The bite looks like "like

three pin pricks."

24. <u>Victim</u>- Someone attacked or have malicious actions taken towards them. Someone who has been acted on and usually adversely affected by a force or circumstance. Someone who has been injured, destroyed, or sacrificed under any of various conditions. A person that is tricked or duped.

25. <u>Pavlov Dog</u>- Scientific experiment where Whilst Ivan Pavlov was involved with physiological researches with dogs in or around 1889 that his famous dog research experiments with reflex conditioning or classical conditioning. He began to feed his dogs in association with the ringing of a bell. After a certain time the dogs were shown to salivate profusely in association with the ringing bell where the actual sight or smell of food was not also present. Pavlov regarded this salivation as being a conditioned reflex and designated the process by which the dogs had picked up this reflex classical conditioning.

26. <u>Euthanasia</u>- Suicide mercy-killing. A belief in the right to die and assisted death. This site list numerous accounts of Euthanasia where death have been administer by physicians and loved ones and various causes, dates and circumstances.
www.Euthanasia.com

27. <u>Prozac and Zoloft</u>- Anti-Depressant drugs used and administered to adults who tend to harbor homicidal and suicidal thoughts.

28. Psychopath- (According to the Webster's Collegiate Dictionary) A mentally ill or unstable person. Without Conscience: The Disturbing World of Psychopaths Among Us Robert Hare, in his 1993 book says: "Psychopaths are social predators who charm, manipulate, and ruthlessly plow their way through life, leaving a broad trail of broken hearts, shattered expectations, and empty wallets." "Completely lacking in conscience and feelings for others, they selfishly take what they want and do as they please, violating social norms and expectations without the slightest sense of guilt or regret."